D1617374

JODY FLEURY

The Beautician

Copyright © 2013 Jody Fleury
All rights reserved.

ISBN: 1484100794
ISBN 13: 9781484100790

All rights reserved under International and Pan-American Copyright Conventions. Published in the United States by CreateSpace.

This novel is a work of fiction. Any references to real people, locales, establishments, organizations, or events are intended only to give the fiction a sense of verisimilitude. All other names, places, characters and incidents portrayed in this book are the product of the author's imagination.

No part of this book may be used or reproduced in any manner whatsoever without written permission from the Author Jody Fleury
P.O. Box 1541 White Salmon, WA 98672

ACKNOWLEDGMENTS

Thanks to my husband, Cliff Fleury for being so supportive in my first attempts at writing, along with your valuable contribution to the editing.

Thank you Jolee Lamatrice, my daughter for attending the workshop with me that started this process, and your encouragement and contribution to the editing and marketing process.

Todd Borg, author of the Owen McKenna mysteries, how can I ever thank you for so generously sharing your expertise with me and other writers. The personal encouragement meant so much. Your workshop tips were invaluable, and a must for anyone who wants to attempt writing for the first time.

Janet Morison, thank you for being such a good big sister to me then, and now. Your work on keeping a family history filled in the gaps and provided the original idea for this book. Mom would be glad you put your English major to work for me in the editing process.

Thank you to my dad who had hand typed seventeen pages of his own idea for a book about building the house that are incorporated in this book.

Thank you to my friends Mary Beth Michaelis, and Charlene Fort, for pointing me in a different direction in the first weeks.

Thank you Amazon CreateSpace for providing a platform to self-publish or I would never have seen this in print.

chapter 1

VIEWING HER IMAGE in the mirror, Marian wondered if her make-up needed any final touches. No, her Lana Turner look was nearly perfect. She and Lana could be sisters except for her very pregnant condition.

She had thirty minutes to get her daughter, Janie, off to school and still arrive at the beauty shop well in advance of her first appointment with Marge. She would stop at the front desk to see if there were any messages.

Yes, someone named Captain Frank, at Fort Benning, would like you to call. It's about something happening to Andy. Get Janie to school, she thought, and then call Captain Frank. Fifteen minutes later, she was calling the operator asking for the base at Fort Benning, Georgia.

There wasn't much privacy in the small beauty shop located on the ground floor of the Ralston Hotel, in Columbus Georgia. Therefore, when a voice came through the phone saying, that Marian's husband Andy was seriously injured but he is alive, Marian began to cry. The other patrons in the shop all stopped what they were doing. In wartime, this scene was playing out in someone's life every day.

Just as Marian hung up the phone, Marge pushed her way through the front door of the beauty shop.

"What's going on in here? This place is as quiet as a mausoleum," she exclaimed.

Marian's boss pulled Marge aside and whispered the news about Marian's husband.

Not being the type to shrink back from anything, Marge approached Marian and took hold of her with both hands. "Come on, honey, let's go into the bar where we can talk."

Marian followed, half in a daze with tears running down her cheeks. Marge motioned to the bartender to bring her a shot of bourbon. "Here honey, drink this down," Marge said as she pushed the drink across the table and into Marian's hands. "Now tell me girl, what has happened to Andy?"

Between sobs and sips of the bourbon, Marian told Marge about what had happened this morning.

"He was in a plane crash in a place called Oujda, Africa. The propeller of the plane broke off in the crash and came through the plane. Captain Frank said Andy helped save his men by getting them out of the plane before it caught fire! Oh Marge, I'm so worried, Marian sobbed. Captain Frank said Andy's wounds were serious enough to ship him back to the United States. The Army will contact me as soon as Andy is assigned to a hospital stateside. Captain Frank also said they try to send injured soldiers to a hospital as close to their home as possible. I need to get reservations on a train for Janie and me to get back to California right away."

"It's okay honey. Fred and I will help you with everything. You just go on back to your room and I'll bring Janie home after school."

When Janie came home from school, she was quiet. Marian noticed Janie's skin felt hot. Marian told her daddy was coming home, but not about the injury.

"We are going to take a train back to grandma's house in California, won't that be fun?"

"I guess," Janie said halfheartedly.

On Monday, Janie came down with measles. She and Marian had to be in quarantine in the hotel room for two weeks.

Marian was nearly four months pregnant, she had very little money, and she was facing a trip from Georgia to California with a seven-year-old. During wartime, train tickets were very hard to get. How could this be happening she thought to herself? She poured a glass of wine, unaware this was the third glass today. Suddenly she heard the phone ring. It was Marge.

"Hi honey, how are you doing? I thought I had better check on you two to see how things are going today. Is Janie's rash gone yet?"

"Marge, I'm so glad you called, being cooped up in this room for two weeks has been awful. I don't think I can play another game of Go Fish, or read Ferdinand the Bull one more time. Janie's rash is gone, thank God, and the doctor will release us in two days, but I can't get train reservations for California for at least three weeks. I don't know what I'm going to do."

"Don't worry honey, while you have been playing Go Fish, Fred and I have been working on getting you two back to California. I'm driving you in my new car. I have never been out west and I decided it's about time to see this country. We can even do a little sightseeing along the way. Fred was able to get enough gas rations to get us there. We can leave as soon as you two are ready."

By June 10, 1943, the unlikely trio was on their way to California, just two young women in their twenties and a seven-year-old girl, packed in a new Buick Convertible.

On the way to California, the girls bought a postcard in Tallulah, Louisiana, dated it June 15, 1943, and wrote, "On our way, see you soon," and mailed it to Marian's mother Lillian, in Stockton, California.

A few days after leaving Louisiana, they had a flat tire. The map said they were just one hundred twenty miles from Holbrook, Arizona, but it was getting late and they needed to find a place to stay the night. As they sat in the car alongside the road, Marge and Marian talked about what they should do.

"The map doesn't show any town between here and Holbrook," Marge said.

"I saw a farm house a while back, but I don't remember exactly where it was. I don't think it was more than a mile or two, but I can't be sure," Marian replied.

"Well, we have to get help before dark, so you stay here with Janie, and I'll start walking back to the farm house to get someone to help." Marge stated with her usual confidence.

Worried, Marian said, "But Marge, what if I was wrong and it was a lot farther than I thought, you could be walking for hours."

Marge looked at Marian and said, "Well if you have a better idea, I'm listening." Marian said nothing.

"I didn't think so," Marge said. As she began walking, she looked back over her shoulder and yelled, I'll bring back help."

Marian and Janie stayed with the car. It was over an hour, no one had come by, and Marian was beginning to worry about Marge.

"Mommy, when is Marge coming? I'm hungry and I don't like it here all alone, I'm scared. This is a stupid trip anyway," Janie whined. "You said we were going to take a train to grandmas, not ride in this dumb old car."

Just then, an old beat up truck pulled up behind the car and a big man with dirty clothes got out. He was unshaven, and his black eyes leered out from under his filthy hat.

"Mighty fancy rig you got here lady. What y'all doin' all alone? Where's yer man?"

Marian froze not wanting to let him know there was no man.

Just then Janie blurted out, "We have a flat tire. Marge went to get some help at the farmhouse, but she hasn't come back, she has been gone a long time, and my daddy is coming home from the war, and we are going to my grandma's house in California. Have you ever been to California?"

"Shush Janie," Marian scolded. "The man doesn't care about all that, and Marge will be here any minute now."

"Well let's see if'en I can fix that flat," the dirty man said.

"Uh... well I guess... that would be okay," replied Marian with some hesitation.

"You got a key fer this trunk?"

Feeling a bit safer now that the stranger meant no harm, Marian opened the trunk, and the man began to work on changing the tire. Janie continued to babble on asking questions of the man in the dirty clothes. She told him about school and how she liked to paint and read books. In a few minutes, he dusted his hands on his pants and said, "Okie dokie, Mrs. Y'er good as new."

Grateful but guilty about judging the man by his appearance, Marian said sincerely, "thank you so much, would you take this? She held out a dollar bill. "I wish I had more but..."

The man interrupted, "No need Mrs. you just take care of that young'un, she's as perrty as a picture," and he smiled showing a few missing teeth.

Just then, Marge arrived with a man named Tom, the farmer from down the road. It was late afternoon by now and the farmer insisted the girls have dinner with his family and stay the night. They could get an early start in the morning. He knew the man in the dirty clothes and told him to follow him back to the farmhouse. When they arrived at the farmhouse Bessie, the farmer's wife was on the porch waiting to greet them. Tom took the man in the dirty cloths out to the barn.

"George that was a fine thing you did helping those ladies. I have some corn, potatoes, and green beans over here. More than we can eat. Here, take this home to Sally and the kids. What do you have now, five youngsters?" Tom said.

"Yep, and Sally's gonna have another next month I reckon."

"Well doesn't that beat all?" Tom said, as he patted George on the back.

"If you pull that truck over here, we can fill her up with gas before you go."

Tom and Bessie had only one child, a boy named Willard, Will for short, and he was one year younger than Janie was.

Will took Janie out and showed her his pet goose, and he had a dog too. They played until it was time for dinner. Janie was so excited. She had never been on a farm before. After being in the car for several days, it felt so good just to run and play. Marge and Marian helped Bessie with dinner while Tom checked out the car's tires, water, and oil.

Marian explained why they were heading to California. Meanwhile Bessie prepared a wonderful dinner of fried chicken, fresh corn on the cob, mashed potatoes, with gravy, and homemade apple pie.

"That dinner was so wonderful, what a stroke of luck having a flat tire here." Marge joked.

"Yes Bessie, thank you so much, and you too Tom. You folks have been so wonderful." Marian added.

"It's our pleasure to help the family of one of our boys overseas. We just hope you'll be together again soon," Tom said.

After dinner, the dishes done, the children in bed, the adults sat out on the porch of the old farmhouse and talked about the war. The night was clear and the stars were bright above them. It was so peaceful here, yet somewhere there was a terrible war going on with men dying.

The next morning they were all up early, Bessie had prepared breakfast, she packed them a nice lunch, hugs all around, and the girls were once again on their way.

Marian sent her last postcard from Holbrook, Arizona on June 21, 1943. She said, "Dear Mom...had some tire trouble, expect to hit California by early next week sometime," Love, Marian.

The rest of the trip was uneventful, and several days after arriving in California, Marian finally got word as to where

Andy had been transferred. He was in Bushnell Hospital in Brigham City, Utah. If this is close to home, I had better get the Army a map of the United States, she thought to herself.

Now that Marian knew where she would be going, Marge decided it would be time for her to head back to Georgia, as she had been gone over a month.

"Marge, I'm so worried about you going back alone," Marian said.

"I'll be fine Marian. I plan to stop and see Bessie, Tom, and little Will on the way back. I wrote to them and they invited me to stay for a few days. That should break up the trip nicely. I'm going to miss you girl. Don't forget me. And as soon as you get settled, let me know how Andy is doing, you hear?"

"Of course I will," Marian said. "And I could never forget you!"

Later in the month, Marian and Janie arrived in Utah. Again, the task of finding a place for Janie and her to live was the first thing on Marian's list. She eventually settled on the attic owned by a Mormon family close to the hospital, and Marian's work, and the school where she enrolled Janie.

One afternoon after work, Marian sat down and wrote to Marge.

Dear Marge and Fred,

Andy's injuries are worse than I had expected. Three of the toes on his right foot had to be amputated which is requiring several surgeries, and extensive rehabilitation. He wants to stay in the Army, if they will let him. He will probably walk with a limp, but they think other than that he should make a full recovery.

I'm only a couple of weeks from delivery, and I'm so big, I don't know if I will ever get back to normal. The Roberson's are hoping for a boy, and I think my dad would like that too, but Andy and I don't care. We just want to have a healthy child. Janie is doing fine in school here, the children are nice, and she has made a few new friends.

How was your trip back to Georgia? Did you stay with Bessie, Tom, and Will, as you had planned? I still think of that fried chicken dinner Bessie made for us, and how peaceful it was on that farm. I was so relieved to be safe, warm, and welcome. Janie keeps asking if she can have a pet goose like Will's. There's not much chance of that when you are in the Army, right?

If Andy is allowed to remain in the Army, he would probably have a desk job at Fort Benning, so keep your fingers crossed we might be together again in Georgia.

Tell all the girls at the Ralston Hotel beauty shop I said Hi, and how much I miss all of them.

Mother and Frank were sorry to see all of us go. They had such a good time with Janie while we were there. I haven't mentioned to them we might be going back to Georgia, no use worrying them about something that might not happen.

How is Fred doing? I'm sure he is glad to have you home again. Tell him how grateful I am to him for arranging our trip west.

Time to get ready for work, I'll write again soon.

Love,
Marian

While the family was still in Utah, Marian gave birth to their baby, another girl. They named her Joad.. The following year Andy returned to active duty at Fort Benning, Georgia.

Marian and the children would again follow Andy to Georgia, where Janie started the fourth grade, her fifth school in four years. Marian returned to work at the Ralston Hotel beauty shop, but this time they would be living on the base at Fort Benning. She and Marge reunited at the beauty shop and life again seemed to be normal.

Marian had been through a lot in the last year. The trip with Marge and Janie across the country by car, the shock of the serious nature of Andy's injuries to his foot and leg, and the birth of her second child was more than she could have anticipated in her young life. Marian worked in the day and partied at night. She and Andy played cards, danced, smoked, and did a lot of drinking. Marian was beginning to like the taste of alcohol.

Davy, one of Andy's brothers visited them in Georgia, and he fit right in. He was just twenty-three at the time. He had followed his older brothers Andy, and Johnny, to University of California, Berkley, but he quit school in nineteen forty-two to join the Navy. At the time of his visit, he had just graduated from the Navy's flight school with Marian's younger brother Bob. Everyone loved Davy because he was full of life, good looking, and best of all he had a great sense of humor. He played Go Fish with Janie, by now her favorite game, and he tossed Joad in the air catching her as she hollered with delight. He was Marian's favorite of the Roberson boys, and they spent much of their time together just talking.

"Marian, how did you get stuck with that brother of mine, because he is so boring? You and I could have really partied." Davy said jokingly.

Marian blushed, and said, "Davy, you are such a tease, no wonder all the girls are after you. You'll definitely be one of those Navy guys with a girl in every port."

"No, Marian, those ships are too slow for me, that's why I'm going to be a pilot, that way I can get to all the girls a lot faster." He quipped.

Just then, Andy came in, and as he grabbed Davy's hand shaking it he said, "So good to see you man. You're looking great!"

"See what I mean Marian?" Davy said, grinning at her with his little boy smile.

"Oh I see what's going on here, Andy said, laughing slightly, your trying to steal my girl. Marian, hide the children, this guy's dangerous."

"He's on to me, Marian, what can I say?" Davy said, faking humility.

"Marian, I arranged for a sitter for the girls tonight, so the three of us can go out. Go put on your dancing shoes because we are going to show this sailor how we Army men party!" Andy said.

The three of them hit two different clubs, and Davy did his best to attract every uncommitted girl in Georgia. He stayed for a few more days, before he had to return to Alameda, California, for duty.

A few months later, Andy was home before Marian that day. He knew she and Davy had become close when he visited them last fall. Andy had arranged for Marge to take the girls for the night and when Marian came home he had a glass of wine waiting for her.

"Marian, the girls are with Marge. Come over here and sit down. I'm afraid I have some bad news, Andy, began. Dad called me today to tell me Davy was killed. He didn't die in combat, he was on a training mission over San Francisco Bay, and his plane crashed. They have not recovered his body.

"Oh that can't be Andy, not Davy, Marian cried. It must be a mistake. If they can't find him, maybe he survived the crash as you did. Maybe, they are wrong about him." She said hopefully.

"No baby, it's no mistake, they have thoroughly searched the area of the crash, and there were no survivors. I'm sorry," Andy said with tears in his eyes.

Marian continued crying as she drank the wine, and they tried to console each other as the night wore on.

Davy's death was devastating to Marian, especially after Andy's narrow escape. This can't be happening she thought to herself. Adding to her grief she needed to support Andy, after all Davy was his brother, and she needed to be strong now, she could cry alone later.

During the next several months, they got through their grief, life settled into the old routine. Gossip at the beauty shop was more about who was coming home and focused on what was happening in the war.

In the spring of 1945, things were heating up in the area around Okinawa, and on May 24, 1945, just one year after Davy's death, Andy's brother Johnny was killed. The news of Johnny's death arrived by a letter sent from Andy's father. Over the next year the awful process of grieving began again, the shock, the disbelief, the anger, and eventually the acceptance.

This time however, Marian would begin to question the decisions Andy and his brothers had made. Was it all worth it? Davy's life had only just begun, there was no wife, no children, nothing but the memories of a young man as a star of his high school baseball team. Johnny, left a wife and baby girl, the same age as Joad, who would only know her father by photos and the stories the family provided to her over the coming years. With the injuries Andy had sustained and two of his three brothers now dead, Marian had enough of war, and the Army. She convinced Andy to retire.

In 1946, Marian and Andy started the journey back to California, this time in a 1939 Ford. Janie was almost eleven-years-old and Joad was not yet three. They packed the car with everything they owned, which was the way most people moved from place to place during the war.

By 1947 people began to resume the lives they had before the awful news of the bombing of Pearl Harbor.

chapter 2

It was the era of the "Glamour Girl." Women of Marian's generation who had gone to work in the factories, aspired to be models, airline hostesses, and of course movie stars. Marian's personality and her natural beauty were real assets for a beautician. Maybe now the war was over she would be able to follow her dreams. The strength she had gained during the war years made her an accomplished businesswoman, however, one with a problem.

After a short time in California, Marian and Andy began to look to the future. They were going to own their own home, battle their own cockroaches instead of rented ones, trap their own mice, and have their own mortgage to worry them.

Nearly five years in the Army had taught them everything. They knew it all. They had rented every known kind of contraption loosely called a human habitation from California to Georgia. It was going to be easy. All they had to do was find a home with none of the objectionable features they had enjoyed from coast to coast, get a G.I. Loan, and live happily ever after. There was nothing to it.

There was no problem in picking the place, that is, if you brought it down to a matter of states. At the time there were forty-eight stars on the flag, but well, you know how it is if you live in California. From there on it got a little bit tougher. The state is about two hundred miles wide by seven hundred miles long. Moreover, they would want to live and raise their two girls in a small town in the mountains and with trees of course. It needed to be safe, and in addition, they wanted a real sense of community. Marian settled all the difficulties by stating flatly, "We are going to live at Lake Tahoe."

They decided the south shore of Lake Tahoe had all this and more. After several months of looking at cabins, houses and vacant land, they entered a new subdivision. A black and yellow sign proclaimed the name *Lodi Pines*. Logs cut from the roadway were piled in rows along the black top road, which was divided in the center by a row of trees left standing,

As they drove slowly up the road, the salesman said, "This is such a lovely parkway."

Andy and Marian were favorably impressed. They found out later of course, that the trees would all be removed before the County would repave the road. They also noted all the streets were named for the children of the subdivider, who was apparently fed up with the streets named, Sierra, Pine, and Tamarack. They commented later they were glad he didn't have any children named Omar or Abner.

There it was Lot #5 on Herbert Avenue, Bijou, California. With the sun, pouring in through the trees the white stakes designated the boundaries. There was a huge clearing behind the lot and there was an abundance of large pine trees along both sides. A few pines were scattered closer to the center of the one hundred by one hundred foot lot. This was to be the place and nothing, according to Andy, remained but the obnoxious and perhaps gory monetary details.

"How much down and how much a month and at what interest rate," Marian asked.

"Three hundred dollars down," the salesman began, and after some scratching with figures in a little notebook, "about twenty-two dollars a month for five years, payments decreasing monthly over the five year period to sixteen dollars, with six percent interest included in the payment, "the salesman proudly proclaimed.

"Everything here is too much, but we'll take a sixty day option on that arrangement for twenty-five dollars, to be applied toward the down payment if we accept," Marian stated firmly.

The salesman countered with one hundred dollars, but he was beat before he started, not knowing the full extent of Andy and Marian's bank balance was twenty-five dollars.

They signed the necessary papers not knowing where they would secure the additional money to complete the terms of the agreement. Andy would later council others, "never try to build a house when the full extent of your capital is twenty-five dollars."

There were no beauty shops at Tahoe at that time, so they lived in Gardnerville, Nevada, where Marian's mother and stepfather were currently living. Janie could go to school there, and Marian could work in the only beauty shop in town. Andy would make the sixteen mile drive over a dirt road known as Kingsbury Grade each day with Joad, and start building their future home on the lot in Bijou.

They would manage to scrape together the necessary funds to complete the contract with the help of one of Marian's Uncles, and yes, the G.I. Loan. Andy started clearing the lot. Marian's mother, Lillian and her husband Frank, moved to Tahoe so Frank could help Andy with building the house.

Frank was a tall thin man, whose only claim to fame was he was a cowboy. Somehow, in his youth, he had an accident costing him his left eye, that, and his love of wine made him almost unemployable. He was very kind, and he had a wonderful sense of humor. He loved Marian's mother, who he called Doll. He was an Irishman, and like many, he loved to sing. He taught Joad Irish songs, a few of them came from pubs were he occasionally worked as a bartender when he was a young man. Some of those songs Marian and Andy would wish Joad didn't know. Although he was not an ambitious man, he was a good man, honest, and not without talent. Lillian, was a quiet reserved woman, Frank's opposite, and she was a hard worker, frugal, but not cheap. She worked as a hotel maid all of her life. She and Frank were products of the Great Depression, which taught them the most important thing in life is to own your own home, and have food in your stomach.

Andy and Frank had only six or seven months of good weather to get the house started and closed in enough before the winter snow would stop any work outside from taking place.

Andy and Joad would leave Gardnerville early each morning in the old Ford and head up the Kingsbury Grade, and each day Joad would get car sick, and the old Ford would overheat requiring at least one stop next to the road where water was available for cars.

"Daddy, are we to the water place yet? I don't feel good." Joad said weakly.

"Just two more turns Joad, can you make it?" Andy said hopefully.

"I'll try, Daddy," Joad said bravely.

Andy pulled the old Ford over and got Joad out of the car and said, "Just walk around a little, but stay off the road, and you'll feel better pretty soon."

He proceeded to lift the hood where the steam was already escaping the radiator, and took the water bag over to the pipe that protruded from the makeshift rock fountain that held a sign saying, NOT FOR DRINKING. He filled the bag, returned to the car, carefully loosened the radiator cap, and began to fill the radiator, a routine that was an everyday occurrence.

"Okay Joad, are you ready to saddle up?" Andy said jokingly.

"Daddy, this isn't a horse, it's a car, and we don't have any saddles anyway," Joad scolded.

"Oh I'm sorry. I thought it was a bucking bronco, because steam was coming out of its nose!" Andy teased.

"Daddy, you are so silly. We have to go to work now," Joad ordered.

By late May Andy, Frank, and Joad had finished laying out the foundation and Sunday morning found the entire family plus Frank's bachelor crony all gathered around with Andy waiting to hear the praise. Charley, the crony, brushed the few remaining hairs on his head, spit, walked the entire perimeter of the one hundred by one hundred foot lot, scanned the neat double lines of tape laying out the boundaries of their future castle, spit again, and said, "Mr. Jesus! Twelve hundred iron men for this sand pile! I'd have sold you half a mountain with a hot springs for that kind of dough."

Charley's disapproval was all that was required to place the seal of complete satisfaction on the work to date. Therefore, Andy and Marian began the task of raising enough money for lumber to build the forms.

By the end of June, nineteen forty seven, Marian was able to rent a small building in Bijou, to start her own beauty shop. It was to be the first beauty shop on the South Shore.

She and Andy rented a little nine hundred square foot cottage not far from where they were building the house. They lived there until the house was completed. Janie was enrolled in the sixth grade for the fall term. Her seventh school since the war had started.

When Lillian and Frank had moved to Tahoe, Lillian took a job as a maid at Lakeland Village Motel. Once there, They rented a small cottage where they lived.

Many family members would help Andy with building the house when they had a chance, although Andy, and Frank, did most of the building. Joad was with them every day. She might not have been that much help, however she was a good gofer.

The south shore of Tahoe in those days had less than three hundred year- around residents, so it was a very close-knit community. People owned their own businesses for the most part, and many of them were dependent on tourism in the summer months to make a living. Everyone knew everyone, and of course, everyone knew everyone else's business. What better place to share all of that great gossip than at Marian's Beauty Shop.

The shop at Bijou was small and was located next to Nel's Varity Store, and across Highway 50 from the Conolley's Bijou Inn. Inside the beauty shop was a reception desk that held Marian's appointment book. It was furnished with a light tan leather love seat with a small round coffee table in front. The table held a copy of the latest Life Magazine and two books of the newest hairstyles of the movie stars. The colors were earth tones with a classic western cowboy motif. On the right was one comb-out station with a large five-foot square mirror proudly displaying Marian's Cosmetologist license. Across from the mirror was the shampoo bowl and an upright hair dryer. Two louvered doors separated the back room from the rest of the shop. The back room consisted of a counter for holding a sterilizer, and underneath the counter was a bin for the used towels, and a covered waste can. On the left was a cabinet that held clean towels and new unused supplies.

The regular patrons of Marian's were a varied lot. Daffy owned the dress shop, and was the cousin of the fire chief's wife. There was Bell, who was the wife of one of the casino owners. Bell was a tall buxom woman in her mid-thirties. Mattie, was a local contractor's wife and she was a polished, well-educated woman and very beautiful. Mrs. Rich was a petite lady in her early-seventies and was as funny as a stand-up comedian. There were the spinster school teachers, identical twins in their late sixties, appropriately named Iris and Elsie.

Of course, nearly every woman came into Marian's at one time or another but these ladies were the regulars.

Tuesday, June 14th, 1949, Marian's day was a busy one. The morning was booked from nine o'clock when the door opened, until two-forty-five that afternoon. Daffy was Marian's first appointment of the day.

"Hi Marian, did you hear the news about Bell?"Daffy asked.

"Good morning Daffy, no is Bell okay? Nothing bad has happened I hope," Marian replied

"Oh hell no, she got drunk Saturday night at the club, and beat the snot out of Pete Burkhart. They said he was playing black jack at one of the tables and giving that cute little dealer a bad time. I don't remember her name, Sally, I think. Anyway, he was giving her a rough time, and Bell came over to see what was going on. Of course Bell was three sheets to the wind, and told him to knock it off or she would throw his ass out of the joint."

"Pete came back at Bell with, who the hell she thought she was talking to. Bell never said a word just proceeded to take a punch, and knocked him clean off the stool. Pete picked himself up off the floor, and everyone was yelling, good for you Bell! He took a swing at Bell and she just let him have it with three or four good punches. He was out cold. She had security clean him up, and they eighty-sixed him for the rest of the month."

Marian proceeded to put the drape around Daffy and they walked over to the shampoo bowl, Marian started talking as she began shampooing.

"Oh my God Daffy, that's getting to be a habit for Bell, she is never like that unless she is drinking too much. I really like Bell, I've gotten to know her a little because she comes in to get her hair done, and a manicure a couple of times a month and she's so much fun. She always has everyone in stitches when she's here. She has a million stories. I wish I could be more like her, not the drinking of course. She just seems to be a really fun, happy person under that gruff exterior."

After rinsing, Marian wrapped the towel around Daffy's head and walked with her to the comb-out station. As she sat down Daffy continued to talk about Bell. "Yeah, well I don't think she's all that happy, she seems to have a real dark side. No one really knows her very well, and we don't know anything about where she came from. She doesn't seem to have anyone but Bud, and that damn casino."

"Maybe some of us could try to befriend her. We could include her in some of our activities away from the casino atmosphere. I think she has an appointment with me later this week and I'll try to think of something by then," Marian said enthusiastically.

Just then, Mrs. Rich came through the door.

"Good morning girls! When you're my age, all of you are girls."

"Good morning Mrs. Rich," Marian replied, "we really appreciate being called girls, don't we Daffy? I won't be long with Daffy, she is almost ready for the dryer."

"I don't mind waiting, after she gets under the dryer I can gossip about her," quipped Mrs. Rich.

"Be careful what you say about me, Mrs. Rich, because even under the dryer I can read your lips," Daffy replied.

"Okay, I'll try to remember that, Daffy. By the way, do you have anything new in the dress shop in my size? I'm going to my granddaughter's wedding September twenty-sixth in Sacramento, and I want to look chic, or is it chipy? Oh lord, no. You know what I mean. I just don't want to look like an old lady," Mrs. Rich said.

"I have a couple of dresses you might like in your size, and they would be perfect for a wedding. You would look chic and definitely not old. I was just telling Marian about Bell before you came in," Daffy continued.

"Oh my, I heard about that business with Pete Burkhart. You know she has had a real tough life going clear back to her childhood. Bud told my Jack her mother killed herself when Bell was only twelve years old. Bell was the one who found her. I guess her mother shot herself with a shotgun. Can you imagine a poor little girl having to see such a thing? My stars, there are some things I can't understand for the life of me. Bud told Jack that Bell looks just like her mother at the same age, and sometimes he finds her just staring at her mother's picture and looking at herself in the mirror. Bud is worried about what she might do someday when she is like that," Mrs. Rich continued saying. "My, my my" shaking her head as if she were trying to understand.

Everyone was quiet for a minute and then Marian said, "I was just telling Daffy maybe some of us girls could befriend her a little more, ask her to join us in some activity away from the casino. Maybe we could all go shopping in Reno, something like that?"

"Oh, that would be nice dear, let me know when, and maybe I could tag along too. That's if you girls wouldn't mind having an old lady come along?"

Daffy spoke out, "Old lady, what old lady, when it comes to shopping, I know you can run circles around the bunch of us."

Marian walked Daffy to a dryer and adjusted the heat, while Mrs. Rich made herself comfortable in front of the big mirror.

Daffy was now under the dryer, and Marian had begun shampooing Mrs. Rich's hair, when a woman no one knew came through the door. Marian asked, "May I help you?"
The woman introduced herself as the inspector from the California State Board of Cosmetology, flashed her credentials, and told Marian, "No I will just look around myself. Where is your sterilizer located?"

Marian pointed to the small back room and said, "Right back there on the right, my towels are in the cupboard on the left."

As Marian finished shampooing, she walked Mrs. Rich to her station, and she said, "I know you said you wanted to try a new style for the wedding. Do you want me to style this a bit now, or do you want to wait for your next appointment just before the wedding? If we do it now it will grow out some, so it is up to you."

"Oh, let's do it now, if you have time, my hair doesn't grow very fast anymore, so I'm sure it will be fine." Mrs. Rich replied.

As Marian began to cut, Mrs. Rich noticed Marian's hands were shaking, not a lot, but enough that she noticed.

Just then, the inspector came out from the back room and walked up to Marian and said demandingly, "How long have you been a licensed cosmetologist?"

Marian, a bit surprised at the question, answered, "It will be five years in June."

"Then I'm sure you know you don't store the towels next to the permanent wave supplies," the inspector snapped.

Stunned, Marian looked at the inspector and said, "No, I didn't know that. Everywhere else I have worked we stored the towels and supplies in the same cabinet."

The inspector looked at Marian with disbelief and said, "Well, I don't know where else you've worked, but this is California, and we have very strict regulations here.You better learn them if you want to keep this shop open. I'm going to write you up with a warning this time, but if it happens again, well, you could lose your license!" She wrote up her notice and handed it to Marian, and stormed out the door.

Daffy popped her head out of the dryer and said, "Well, just who the hell does that woman think she is? She sure got up on the wrong side of the bed."

Mrs. Rich said to Marian, "Are you alright dear?"

Composing herself, "Oh yes, Mrs. Rich, I'm just stunned a little. The state board does impromptu inspections. I was told when I worked in Gardnerville, California inspectors were real sticklers for the rules, so I have been extra careful to do everything by the book. You know they can close up your business if you don't do everything right. It's important though because you don't want to spread any germs to your patrons," Marian said.

"Germs," Daffy scoffed. "You can eat off the floor in this place. No germ could live once it set foot in here," as she pointed to the door.

The women continued to talk and Marian took Daffy out from under the dryer, and said, "Okay, Mrs. Rich, your turn to cook."

Daffy lit up a cigarette as she sat down in the chair for her comb out.

Marian said, "Daffy, do you mind if I join you before I comb you out? I think I could use a cigarette right now."

"Sure Marian, I've got plenty of time. No one comes into the dress shop on Tuesdays. Maybe because they know I get my hair done on Tuesday."

Marian looked out the window and said, "I don't know why things like this get me so upset, it's not like I haven't been through a lot worse. I guess it's because this beauty shop means so much to me. Andy and I finally are getting a home of our own, even if it is only half finished, we are just so happy. I don't want anything to ruin that."

Just then, Mattie entered the shop and Marian put out her cigarette and started Daffy's comb out.

"Hi Mattie, "Marian said cheerfully," we've had an interesting morning, and I'm just about finished with Daffy, so if you don't mind waiting for just a bit I'll be with you real soon. We are doing a perm for you today, aren't we?"

"That's right," Mattie replied," you are the only one who gives me a perm that doesn't make me look like a wooly sheep. It's always so soft and it lasts me nearly two months, I just don't know how you do it."

"Thank you Mattie, that's so kind of you to say."

Ten minutes later, Daffy paid Marian and was on her way. Marian was rapping the permanent wave rods in Mattie's hair when Mattie said, "Chester and I are going to the casino tonight for dinner and drinks and we thought you and Andy might like to join us if you don't have other plans."

"I'd love to Mattie, I'll ask Andy when he brings my"... Just then, Andy came in the door of the shop with Joad toddling along behind him.

"We brought the hard working woman a little lunch. I hope we aren't interrupting any important gossip?"

"Andy, Mattie was just telling me that she, and Chester are going to the casino tonight and they asked us to join them. Are you free tonight? Do you think we could go?" Marian asked.

"I don't see why not, but you are the one who has to get up for work tomorrow. All I have to do is hammer a few nails and try to keep this one out of trouble," Andy said as he pointed to Joad.

"It's settled then. We will meet you at the Gateway Club in the bar, about seven if that will work for you two," Mattie said.

"It's a date," Andy said as he took Joad by the hand and left the shop.

Mrs. Rich's hair was now dry and Mattie's permanent was processing. Marian finished combing out Mrs. Rich, took her check, and scheduled her next month's appointment one day before the wedding. Marian rinsed the permanent wave solution out of Mattie's hair and applied the neutralizer to set the curls. Ten minutes later, she removed the curling rods and rinsed repeatedly.

"We are all set Mattie," Marian said. "Do you want me to cut a little of this around the neckline for you?"

"Whatever you think Marian, you are the expert and I trust you completely, "Mattie replied.

Marian continued with Mattie, and neither of the women said anything for a while as Marian worked with the hairstyle.

"That should do it Mattie, and as you know it will be a little tight for the first few days. Don't wash it for three days, and then treat it normally. It should last for a couple of months or longer. Use this conditioner for the first week when you wash it, that will keep it soft. If you have any concerns, make sure you come in so I can take care of you right away," Marian reminded her.

Mattie paid, thanked Marian, and as she was leaving she turned and said to Marian, "I'll see you tonight at the club, okay?"

"Right, Thank you Mattie, we will see you at seven, "Marian said smiling.

After Mattie left, Marian sat down on a little stool in the back room and lit up a cigarette, taking a long drag she sighed and said out loud, "My God, what a morning."

She put out the cigarette, took a few bites of the sandwich Andy had brought, and drank her cold coffee left over from the morning. Then she locked up the beauty shop and began the short walk to the new house. She was anxious to see what progress Andy had made today.

chapter 3

EARLIER THAT MORNING, Andy was just finishing the wall framing and had begun on the ceiling joists, when fate stepped in in the form of a wizened retired contractor from San Diego.

It was the habit of people passing by to stop and chew the fat while going about their nonexistent business. This always gave Andy the excuse to stop work and have a beer, which both Frank and he enjoyed. The conversation occurred about as follows.

"Big house you got here," the contractor said.

"Yeah, pretty big. Have a beer?" Andy replied.

"Sure thing. Thanks. Which rooms the kitchen?" the contractor asked.

"It isn't built yet, there's going to be another wing over there." Andy replied pointing to the south.

"What you building a hotel? Where's the staircase going in?" the contractor asked.

"No staircase, this is a single story, "Andy stated.

"What you going to do with all that room under the steep roof, with no staircase?" the contractor questioned.

"Roof's going to be quarter pitch. There won't be any room under it." Andy answered.

"That's bad up here. Danger of heavy snow scares suckers off a flat roof job. No body won't buy it, "the contractor continued.

"We don't plan on selling it." Andy said smiling.

"If nobody will buy it, bankers won't mortgage it, "the contractor said.
"You sure?" Andy asked.

"Sure I'm sure. Benn in the business forty years and here is how you stud a corner. Better than the way your're doing. Saves you eight feet of two by fours, and gives you an inside nailing corner, and makes your support narrower for those funny looking corners all you young fellers are using now. Beats the hell out of me why anybody wants two winders in a corner," the contractor said.

"Want another beer?" Andy asked.

"Nope. Gotta go. Nice day aint it?" the contractor said as he left.

"It was," Andy mumbled as the contractor ambled off down the road.

Andy and Frank looked at each other, then looked at the house, which had somehow lost a lot of glamor in a very few minutes. Then they headed for the beer.

"What do you think?" Andy asked Frank.

"I don't know, he was right about the corner studs," Frank replied.

Andy thought about that for a while trying to counter with something good. "That's purely mechanical. Roofs are functional. He was wrong about the winders," Andy said.

They both laughed.

"We better ask Marian tonight," Frank said.

When Marian arrived at the house, Frank and Andy were preoccupied with the best approach to the problem of how to convince Marian that they should have a two-story house with a steep roof when she wanted a one-story house with a relatively flat pitched roof. Both were aware from long experience that they faced a battle. Nothing was said until after supper, and the kids were in bed.

She opened the subject.

"Well, get it off your chest. I can see that something is wrong with you two. Are the walls going to fall down? Do you need more nails? What is it?" Marian said.

They plunged into the story, explaining the visit, advancing theories, offering solutions. When they were run down, they fortified themselves with a stiff slug of brandy and waited for the firestorm.

Marian fooled them. She just sat there. She didn't look mad and she didn't look sad. She just sat there.

"Weren't you listening?" Andy asked gingerly.

"Why yes, we have to have a two story house, you said, in order to mortgage it. I was just sitting here planning my staircase. I have always wanted a staircase rising out of the living room, sort of like this," Marian made several swerves and some unlikely swivels with her right hand, but you will have to draw me a picture of how the outside of the house will look. I won't have my house looking like a cracker box," She said.

With the problem of the two story house now behind them, Andy and Frank were working on the upstairs, the new home was starting to really take shape, and Marian was excited to see it moving so fast. It looked huge compared to the little cabin they were currently renting. After looking at all the new work, and picking up the tools for the day, they all got in the Ford and headed down the street to drop Frank off at Lake Land Village. Marian and Andy left for dinner at the club, and Janie was given the babysitting task with Joad.

Over the next couple of months, this was their routine, and Marian and Andy became regulars on the social scene of the south shore and the casinos. Andy was getting a small disability check for his injuries sustained during the war, and he was selling life and homeowners insurance to the people at Tahoe. Marian's beauty shop income was allowing them to purchase the materials needed to build the house and still maintain an active social life, which included a good deal of drinking and gambling.

At the beauty shop, Marian's patrons would look forward to hearing about the progress on the new house, but most of all, the colorful stories that went along with it.

Today, Marian was doing a manicure for Bell, and Mrs. Rich had come in to get her hair done for her granddaughter's wedding in Sacramento. Daffy had also stopped in to deliver a dress to Mrs. Rich that she had picked out for the wedding.

Bell said, "Marian, you need to give us an update on the progress of the house. Are you going to be able to move in before Christmas?"

"I sure hope so Bell. The kids are climbing the walls in that little cabin, and we've had to depend on Janie to take care of Joad if we want to go out in the evening. Andy and Frank take care of Joad during the day, but Andy tells me he isn't sure who he has to watch the closest, Joad or Frank.

"To give you an idea of what he is up against, yesterday Andy was working downstairs on some plumbing for the kitchen when Frank called out to him. Frank was upstairs nailing down the sub-flooring. He called Andy's name several times and sounded a little frantic. Andy went upstairs to see what was wrong and found Frank was lying on the floor on his back. Of course, his first thought was Frank had a stroke or something, but as soon as Andy got there, Frank sat up."

"Frank was as white as a sheet. All he could say was," don't tell Doll his nickname for my mother, I'm paralyzed, I can't move my legs!"

"Andy tried to remain as calm as he could and told Frank to put his arm around him and he would lift him up to his feet and maybe if they walked around he would get the movement back in his legs. As Andy tried to lift Frank, he was like dead weight. He encouraged him by asking him to try to get his legs under himself to give Andy a little more leverage. Frank even more upset now, told Andy," I just can't. My legs are paralyzed." Andy decided to look at Frank's legs. That's when he saw the trouble. A nice straight line of nails followed along the seam of Frank's coveralls. Frank had nailed his coveralls to the sub-floor."

All three women roared with laughter, Bell had tears running down her cheeks because she was laughing so hard. "Marian, that is the funniest story yet," she said, unable to control her laughing. Mrs. Rich and Daffy were laughing too.

"I thought you were working here," Andy said, when he and Joad came in with Marian's lunch. "Sounds like you are having way too much fun. What's so funny? Or is it a joke for girls only?"

Marian said, still laughing a bit, "No, I just told the girls about Frank nailing his coveralls to the floor yesterday."

Then Andy joined them in the laughter adding, "Yeah, funny now, but yesterday for a while I didn't think it was so funny."

Joad said, "Daddy, why is everyone laughing?"

Andy quickly changed the subject by saying, "Joad, put your mother's lunch in the back room and hurry up because we are going to get an ice cream cone at Mr. Globin's store." She ran to the back room and then straight back to the front door and said, "Come on daddy, hurry before the ice cream is all gone."

Daffy had brought Mrs. Rich's dress for the wedding. It was pale yellow with a pattern of dainty little pink flowers, and although it was sleeveless, it had a matching jacket that came just to the waistline. The dress was straight, and ankle length. Mrs. Rich was petite, and had quite a nice figure even at seventy plus years of age. Marian and Bell thought the dress was beautiful and perfect for Mrs. Rich.

Marian said, "That dress is so perfect! I have just the thing to match that beautiful dress."

Marian went to the back room and brought out a decorative comb that had tiny pink and yellow flowers on it. She placed the comb toward the back of Mrs. Rich's head, just below the crown, and she arranged some curls on each side of the comb.

"Oh Marian, you are a genius!" Bell and Daffy gasped.

Marian handed the hand mirror to Mrs. Rich and turned her so she could see the back of her head in the big mirror.

Mrs. Rich exclaimed, "Oh my word, Marian that is perfect, my granddaughter will be so proud of her granny. Thank you girls for helping me, I feel like Cinderella all dressed for the ball."

Bell said, "Wait here and don't leave until I get back." She rushed out the door got in her car and took off.

Daffy said, "Well what's that all about?"

"I sure don't know," a puzzled Marian replied.

Mrs. Rich was still admiring herself in the mirror, and was unaware of Bell leaving. The women continued to talk and ask Mrs. Rich all about the wedding, where was the reception going to be, how many guest they were expecting and so on. Mrs. Rich gladly filled them in on all the details.

Marian said, "You know girls one of my secret ambitions has always been to own a wedding shop. Mrs. Rich did you tell me your granddaughter was having a garden wedding?"

"Yes. Betty, that's my granddaughter's name, is having the wedding in the back yard of her mother's home. It is a beautiful setting on the Garden Highway. The property has about four acres of grass area that goes right down to the river and boat dock, and the yard has beautiful landscaping. Since gardenias are Betty's favorite flower, she has arranged to have them all around the gazebo where they will take their vows. Her young man is very nice and good looking to boot. The reception will be there too. I think they did that for the grandparents so we won't have to drive any place else, but the house is quite large so there will be plenty of room for everyone. They are catering the food. Thank the lord for that or I might have been commandeered for the task. I'm sure it will be wonderful and they will be very happy."

Marian asked, "Will they live in Sacramento?"

"Oh yes dear, they both work in Sacramento."

Bell pulled up in front of the beauty shop and jumped out of her car. She was carrying a small box in her hand when she came in the front door.

Bell said to Mrs. Rich, "I have a gift for you, and I don't want to hear another word about it." She handed Mrs. Rich the small box.

Mrs. Rich carefully opened the box and inside was a pair of earrings that each had a little pink rose surrounded by tiny white and black pearls.

"Those were given to me by my grandmother, but they are too dainty for me, so I have never worn them. When I saw that dress, and the comb Marian had, I thought about them, and they would be perfect to complete your outfit. What do you think?" Bell asked.

Mrs. Rich put on the earrings, and she got tears in her eyes, they were perfect. She turned to the three friends she had made at the beauty shop and said, "As old as I am I have never had dearer friends than you three girls. Thank you all."

"We all love you too, Mrs. Rich," the three women said in unison.

After the women had gone, Marian sat down, lit up a cigarette, and reflected on the last several months since she had opened the salon at Bijou. They were good months. Not only was she profitable, she had made some good friends too. These women were not just patrons of the beauty shop. They had become like sisters sharing with each other their most intimate feelings.

She thought about the years during the war, and Marge, and wondered where Marge was. Life had been so busy she hadn't been able to find time to write. I must do that, she thought to herself, Marge doesn't even know where I am. She was such a good friend, how I could be so thoughtless. I will write to her tomorrow she said to herself.

The next morning Andy got up early to start on the house. October was almost here and the weather was already getting colder. He knew the snow could come anytime now. He had to get the house closed in before then, so he would be able to work inside all winter. He would have to tell Marian there was no chance of moving in by Christmas. He knew they would be spending the winter in the rented cottage. He did hope, with a little luck, they would be in the new house by June or July.

The house was a big under-taking. It was to have four bedrooms, and one full bath upstairs. The downstairs had a very large living room with a fireplace. Marian wanted the living room and the kitchen separated by a large bar in place of a dining room. She thought it would be great for entertaining. Then there was that stairway Marian had in her head. A small den/office, and one more bath downstairs. The kitchen was very large. Dutch-doors were both at the front entry and the rear leading to the back yard. Marian had sketched out what she wanted, and Andy had done his best to accommodate her wishes. The house was to be rustic design inside, with of course, Marian's favorite western motif. They would be using lots of natural rock from around the Tahoe area in the fireplace, bar, kitchen, and bathrooms.

Marian had little time to help as her business was growing every month. Andy kissed Marian as he dropped her off at the beauty shop, and he took a still sleeping Joad, to continue work on the house. Frank joined him later in the day.

Marian arrived nearly two hours before her first appointment, and she decided to sit down with her coffee and cigarette, to write the long overdue letter to Marge.

Friday, September 26th, 1947

"Dear Marge, I can't believe it has been over a year since I've written to you. So much has happened. I hope you and Fred are well, and your life is good. I'm so sorry I didn't let you know where I was. After Andy and I returned to California, we decided we needed to have a place we could call our own, and one a little distance from our families.

We both needed a fresh start after the war so we began to look around at where we could put down some roots for the girls, and ourselves. We were very fortunate to be able to purchase a lot in Bijou, on the south shore of Lake Tahoe. I took a job in a beauty shop in a little town called Gardnerville, Nevada, it's about twenty-five miles from where we are building the house. For about a year, Andy took Joad and drove from Gardnerville to Tahoe everyday as he started the construction. Following that, we rented a little cottage, where we are living while Andy completes the house enough for us to move in.

We were able to rent a small building at Tahoe to open my own beauty shop. My first visit from the California State Board Inspector didn't go so well, but I'm still in business, so I guess it wasn't as bad as I thought. I sure could have used a drink after that visit! Andy is selling insurance when he is not working on the house.

Tahoe is such a beautiful place. Do you remember how much we both liked Flagstaff, Arizona? Well this is very much like that, except with the added bonus of the most beautiful lake I have ever seen. The winters can get very cold with plenty of snow. I know how you hate the cold, but I hope you will be able to come visit us sometime. Better wait until the house is finished so you will have a place to sleep. The little cottage we are renting isn't much bigger than the room Janie and I had at the Ralston Hotel, in Columbus..

Mother and Frank moved up here too. Frank is helping Andy build the house and mother is working as a motel maid. They have rented out both of the houses in Stockton, until they decide what is next for them.

I have half a dozen regular patrons, and there are walk-ins a couple times a month. So far, I have the only beauty shop in Bijou. That isn't saying much because there is only about three hundred year-around residents on the South Shore. The North Shore of the lake has even fewer, and the east and west sides just a smattering of folks, mostly summer vacation cabins. It is 'the sticks' as you would say.

We are just a little over a mile from the Nevada state line. There are three casinos there, and each of them has a bar, dancing and entertainment, and of course live gambling. A patron of mine, Bell, is part owner of one of the casinos along with her husband Bud. They are great people and Bell reminds me of you a little. Andy and I go to the casino on Saturday nights a couple of times a month, if we are not too tired. Most of the people here go there occasionally, as there is hardly any other entertainment. There is a small movie theater in a Quonset-hut style building, like what we had in Georgia, on the base. Seagraves marina is at the end of Ski Run Boulevard. They have speedboats that take people on tours of the lake in the summer months. The ski hill is a small rope tow that starts just about a mile in the opposite direction from the marina. The main highway, US-50, separates the lakeside from most of the residential and business areas. My beauty shop is right beside that highway.

Daffy is another one of my regular patrons and she owns one of the dress shops located right on one of the corners of Ski Run Boulevard and US- 50. Yes, she is 'daffy', but she has a great selection of nice clothes for women. I really like her too, and we have become good friends. Across the highway is another clothing store called Tahoe Togs and she has clothes for children too. I haven't had a chance to meet her yet, but I intend to go in there soon and get acquainted.

Mrs. Rich, another patron, would like me to open a shop at Camp Richardson, that would be open in the summer months for her guests. Andy and I have discussed the idea, but we have way too much on our plates to think about that right now. Maybe, after we are settled in the house.

Janie is twelve years old now, and loves school here. I think she is finally able to feel a little stability. We depend on her a great deal for babysitting. Joad is four, going on twenty. She is with Andy all day, and between being the 'gofer' for Andy, and making mud pies she is pretty busy.

We are going to have some new neighbors, the Burnsides's, they have two children, their daughter is the same age as Janie, and they have a son who is four years older than Joad. They live in Davis, California where Al, Mr. Burnside is a math professor with UCLA, and Emily, his wife is the postmistress for Davis. They are also building a house. Theirs will be a summer cabin only. People here are very self-sufficient for the most part, and everyone is willing to help one another out when needed. This is the kind of community I could have only dreamed about being part of.

Oh, my first appointment just arrived. I will get this in the mail to you today, and give my love to all the gals at the Ralston Hotel beauty shop."

Love,
Marian

"Good morning, Mattie, how are you this morning, and how is Chester?" Marian said in her usual cheery manner.

"Everyone is just fine. Chester has been very busy cutting and delivering firewood, it's that time of year you know, and many people wait until the last minute." Mattie replied. "That reminds me, Chester asked me to check with you to see if you know of anyone who needs wood who may not be able to afford it. Chester tries to make sure everyone who needs wood gets it, even if they can't pay. He says no one should go cold or hungry just because they might be down on their luck. If they don't want to take it for free, they can work it off by helping with the Christmas trees in November."

"Mattie, you and Chester are such good people, I don't think folks in our little community have any idea how much you both do to make this a better place to live. Times can be real hard for a lot of people here, especially in the winter when there is very little work" Marian said.

"With all Chester and I have I don't think either one of us could sit down to a meal, or go to sleep in a warm bed, knowing someone in our community was cold or hungry. We are glad to have the opportunity to help," Mattie said. "Is there any new progress on the house?" Mattie asked.

"Things are coming along, but I'm pretty sure we won't be in this winter. Andy hasn't said anything, but there is still so much to do. We have been going as often as we can to get rocks to finish the fireplace, but they are hard to find."

"Oh, I have just the place, we own some land up by Fallen Leaf Lake, and that area is full of rock that would be perfect for a fireplace, in fact Chester used some of it when he built ours. Much of it is quartz and there are various colors of green black and gold. You and Andy are welcome to go get it anytime. You better hurry though because we get snow up there well before here in the valley."

"I'm closing the shop on Mondays, starting next week, because business is slower now school has started and people are getting ready for winter and the holidays. I'll tell Andy to stop by and see Chester to get directions for how to get there."

Marian finished washing and putting the pin curls in Mattie's hair and walked Mattie to the dryers. After Mattie sat down, Marian adjusted the heat on the dryer, and said, "Mattie would you like a magazine to look at while you're cooking, or perhaps a cup of coffee?"

"The coffee would be wonderful Marian. I was running a little late and didn't get a chance to finish mine this morning."

Marian went to the back room and poured a cup of coffee for Mattie, adding one cream, and one teaspoon of sugar she knew Mattie used. As she brought the coffee, she picked up the copy of Life Magazine, and handed both to Mattie who was under the dryer. Marian walked over to the small reception desk and looked at her appointment book. Her next patron was not scheduled until two o'clock, which would give her time to walk up to the house, and still be back in plenty of time.

Marian was finished with Mattie by ten o'clock, and thanking her she scheduled Mattie's next appointment. After Mattie left, Marian put the little round clock sign on the door that said she would return at two o'clock, and she started walking up the road to the new house.

When she arrived at the house, she saw Joad on the roof of the pump house. Before she could say anything, Joad saw her and yelled, "Look mommy, I'm a paratrooper just like daddy!" With that, Joad, jumped off the ten-foot roof, rolling on the ground.

Just then, Andy came around the house where Marian was standing in shock. "Hi Baby, what are you doing here so early?"

Joad jumped up and ran over to Andy saying, "Daddy I showed mommy how I jump like a paratrooper. I'll go show her again."

Seeing the shock on Marian's face, Andy said, "Not right now honey, Grandpa Frank needs you to help him pick-up the tools before we have lunch."

As Joad ran off, Andy told Marian, he had taught Joad how to jump without hurting herself by bending her knees and rolling as she hit the ground. "I can't watch her every second, and this is the best I can do to keep her safe. She knows she can only jump from the pump house on the side with the sand pile," He assured Marian. " Joad won't get hurt, and it will keep her off the second story of the house until we can get it enclosed. She is playing in the sand pile and making mud pies most of the time," Andy said.

"You mean when she isn't jumping off the roof!" Marian said sarcastically.

"Maybe you think she would be safer at the beauty shop?" Andy said. "Look Marian, one thing we have learned in the last several years is life brings a lot of risk. The best thing we can do for our kids is teach them how to manage risk, and I don't think it is ever too early. What do you think?"

"Well, when you put it that way... I guess it makes sense, but jumping off a roof?" Marian questioned.

Andy put his arms around Marian, gave her a kiss, and said, "I'm hungry, what do you say we have some lunch before Frank starts drinking his."

They both laughed and headed for the house. Marian told Andy about her conversation with Mattie that morning, and about the rock at Fallen Leaf Lake. They agreed to go the next Monday, for the rock and get as much as they could to finish the fireplace. Then she told him about Chester wanting to know if anyone was in need of wood for the winter.

Andy said, "You know, Janie has been asking for an extra sandwich for lunch this last week, I don't think it's for her, because you know she eats like a bird. Maybe I'll see if I can find out where the mystery sandwich is going."

After lunch, Marian returned to the beauty shop and her next appointment was with Iris one of the twin schoolteachers.

Iris was about ten minutes early for her two o'clock appointment, but that was fine with Marian as she had arrived at the shop by one-thirty herself. Marian greeted Iris, and they talked about how short to cut Iris's hair. Marian proceeded to wash Iris's hair and started her haircut. As she cut, she asked, "How are classes going this year?"

Iris replied, "We have more children this year. I'm teaching the second and third grades. It's tough because that's when we start teaching the children to read. Some of the children come in prepared for reading but others hardly know their alphabet. It is quite a challenge to deal with the extremes, especially with two grades in one classroom. I love teaching and I try to find ways to engage each student. One of the most rewarding things is to see how the children help each other. Sometimes I think I learn more from them than I ever teach them."

"My step-mother is an elementary teacher and she helped Janie learn to read. It was so important, because after Andy joined the Army, we moved a lot and I'm sure if Janie hadn't known how to read she might never have learned. In Georgia they held her back in the fourth grade. They said she was too small, and the Army kids moved around too much. Her grades were fine and she was reading above grade level. We were furious. We took her out of public school, and put her in a Catholic school for a year before we moved back to California. She's a very bright girl, but that really hurt her self-esteem. I hope being here in a small school will help her get her confidence back." Marian said.

"Oh, don't you worry about little Janie. She is doing just fine here. She has made some good friends, and they are all the good kids. You know we teachers talk, and we know if one of our little ones is going in the wrong direction," Iris assured.

"We appreciate that," Marian said, "Janie is a trooper. I'm afraid we depend on her too much watch Joad. With both of us working, and Janie being eight years older she has to watch Joad, a lot. She is very capable, but sometimes I'm sure she resents having to drag a little sister along. Not to mention Joad can be quite a handful."

"How is Elsie? I haven't seen her for a month or so." Marian asked.

"She is doing well, but she has been very busy getting ready for the new school year. She teaches sixth, seventh, and eighth grades. There is a lot more preparation to keep those pre-teen minds busy. That age is a little more rebellious than my little second and third graders. I just have to make sure they have plenty of physical activities at recess and lunchtime so they can sit still when it is time to learn. Elsie's students need to be challenged academically and believe me, it involves a lot of preparation to keep them engaged. How is Andy coming along on the house?" Iris asked.

"It's slow, but sure. We are going to go get rock for the fireplace next Monday. Mattie, was in the shop this morning, and she has kindly offered to let us take as much rock as we need from their property at Fallen Leaf Lake. With enough rock, Andy will be able to finish the fireplace because it will be our main source of heat for a time. Oh, by the way, Mattie asked me something when she was in, perhaps you could point me in the right direction. Chester wants to know if there are any families who might need some fire wood for the winter, you know, someone who might not be able to afford to buy it. I know you can't divulge anything about the children's personal lives, but perhaps you could tell us who to ask." Marian said.

"Actually Marian, the school board does know of such families. There aren't more than a couple, thank heaven, but they would be able to contact the families and let them know about it. Just tell Chester to give Mr. Johnson a call." Iris said.

"Great, I'll do that. Chester is also willing to let them work it off by helping him with Christmas trees if they would feel better about it than taking it for free." Marian added. "

"That's good, Iris said, because one family I know the man of the house is very proud, and might not take it if he thought it was charity. "

Marian thanked Iris, as she always did with each of her patrons, and scheduled her next appointment. She closed the shop and headed to the house.

chapter 4

THE FOLLOWING MONDAY after Andy and Marian got Janie off to school. They packed a picnic lunch, and got Joad ready for the ride to Fallen Leaf Lake to gather rocks for the fireplace. After the usual number of stops for Joad's carsickness, they arrived at the place Chester had described to Andy to get the rock. They were surprised at how much was available. Surely, they would be able to gather enough to get the fireplace finished.

Andy told Joad, "Stay where you can see your mommy and me and look for really special rocks."

"Okay, Daddy, I'll find real pretty ones, you'll see." Joad said.

By lunchtime, the trunk was nearly full, and the floor of the back seat had quite a few rocks too. Marian spread out a blanket and the three of them sat down to enjoy their lunch. Joad was finished first of course, and ran off to find some more rocks. Just as Andy and Marian were picking up the blanket, they heard a scream.

Marian looked up to see Joad about fifty yards away lying on the ground still screaming. As she and Andy ran to see what had happened, they saw Joad's hands and clothes covered in blood. Andy reached down, and as he picked her up, he saw the blood spurting from her leg.

Trying not to alarm Marian, Andy said calmly, "Marian get to the car, I'll bring Joad."

As he reached the car, covered in blood himself, He placed Joad, on Marian's lap and told her, "Hold this part of her leg together, and don't let up, hold it as tight as you can!"

He started the car and began driving as fast as possible down the winding road. Marian was terrified but did exactly what Andy had said. She talked to Joad, quietly saying, "Your all right honey, everything is going to be fine."

About twenty minutes later Marian said softly, "Andy, she isn't responding to me, she's getting cold."

"She's going to be okay, we are almost to Dr. Sawyer, just a few more minutes." Andy said calmly to Marian.

They reached the doctor's office and ran in the door carrying Joad, Dr. Sawyer, took Joad out of Marian's arms, and he and his nurse began to work quickly. After about ten minutes, Joad was still not responding. Just as Marian started to panic Joad came around.

Dr. Sawyers said, "You got her here just in time, she lost a lot of blood, and we had to put sixteen stitches in that leg, but she is going to recover just fine."

Andy held a sobbing Marian with both arms, and said, "You did great baby."

"You two can go in here and wash off some of that blood," Dr. Sawyer said, pointing to the bathroom in the small office.

Neither of them had realized how much blood they had on them. Their only concern at the time was to get Joad to the doctor as fast as they could.

Dr. Sawyer told them, "Go on home, you can come back for her in a couple of hours, she is going to sleep that long, and I want to keep an eye on her for a little while. You might want to bring her some clean clothes too. I had to cut her little coveralls off to get at that leg."

Marian said, "Are you sure? I don't want her to wake up and be afraid because we aren't here."

"I'm sure." Dr. Sawyer said emphatically.

After they cleaned up they returned to the new house. Andy unloaded the rocks they had gathered at Fallen Leaf Lake, and Marian went inside the still incomplete house.

Frank was inside and seeing Marian he said, "Where is tootsie?"

Frank had a nickname for everyone. With that, Marian broke down in tears, unable to respond to Frank for a few minutes. Then she started to tell Frank what had happened. Frank pulled a small flask from his jeans and handed it to Marian.

"Here, you take a little nip, it will help." He said.

"Thanks Frank, I think I do feel a little better," Marian said.

Later that day Andy and Marian returned to Dr. Sawyer's office to find Joad eating an ice cream cone and proudly showing off the bandage that covered her little leg from her ankle to her knee.

"Dr. Sawyer has ice cream for you if you get stitches," Joad said. "But we had to throw away my coveralls because they were all messy."

"Well that's okay, honey, we brought you some clean ones anyway." Marian answered.

Dr. Sawyer said, "Bring her back next week and we will take those stitches out."

"Do I get more ice cream when you take stitches out?" Joad asked.

"Yes, ice cream is for taking stitches out too." Dr. Sawyer smiled.

A couple of weeks had past when the mystery of the extra sandwich was solved. One of the children in Janie's class was coming to school without any lunch. Janie was supplying a sandwich, while one of her other friends was bringing some fruit, or a cookie. Andy was able to give a name to Chester about who needed some wood for the winter. Once again, the community had come together to help one of their neighbors in need. Tahoe was special in that way.

The next several months were routine. The building was slow due to days lost because of bad weather. By May, the snow was gone and progress on the house resumed at a much faster pace. Several friends and other family members came and helped from time to time and by the first week in August, the family moved into the new house. There was still a lot to do, but the plumbing all worked, the power was connected, and the fireplace was complete.

The Burnsides's cabin was coming along nicely, the framing was completed, and the roof was on, and the Cedar siding was nearly finished. They too would be able to occupy by the end of August.

Janie, and Milinda, the Burnside's daughter, had become friends, and Johnny, their son, and Joad were becoming pals too. Johnny was four years older than Joad, so he would have preferred the Roberson's had a son his age. However, Joad would have to do. It was her or no one. The kids played Monopoly, read comic books, and spent most of their time at the beach. The parents spent all the daylight hours working on the houses, sharing tools and only stopping briefly for a bite to eat.

Marian, was very busy now with appointments every day, all day long. She took Sundays and Mondays off to recover, wash clothes, and prepare some meals. Andy did most of the cooking, but on her days off, Marian liked to cook too.

One morning in September while Andy was working on the house, Joad was playing in the sand pile when suddenly she started screaming and crying.

"Daddy, daddy, it hurts!" as she ran to the house.

Andy dropped his tools and ran to see what was wrong. "What is it Joad? Tell me what is wrong."

Joad couldn't say anything she just kept screaming and holding her leg saying, "here, Daddy, here."

Andy pulled off her coveralls to discover a dead scorpion, and four large sting marks on her leg. Because of his service in Africa, Andy's training regarding poisonous scorpions had him very worried because he knew they could be deadly to a child.

Trying not to panic, Andy scooped the scorpion into a jar, and took Joad and the scorpion to the doctor's office. The doctor immediately called the poison control center and described the scorpion to them. To everyone's relief the variety at Tahoe that had stung Joad was not deadly, and although very painful, was not much worse than having several bee stings.

By early November, the house was complete enough to occupy. The Roberson family would be spending the holidays in the new house.

In early December, the house was completed, and it was a showplace. The fireplace filled one-half of one side of the large great-room. Most of the rock came from the area around Fallen Leaf Lake. The mantel was a large rustic beam, and the hearth was large enough to allow people to sit on it comfortably. On each side of the fireplace were large windows framed by knotty pine walls. Opposite the fireplace was a wall with windows looking out into the back yard, and forest beyond. A giant Christmas tree stood in the corner of the great-room. A bar separated the great-room from the kitchen. It was a twenty-foot arching structure made from the same rock as the fireplace. The bar top was laminated natural wood with a four-inch wide copper edge. The ceiling had six large beams crossing it with cowboy brands burned into each one. The floors were natural hardwood with only Navaho rugs covering them. Behind the bar were Marian's famous cowboy brand china, glasses, and copper placemats with the initials MLR embossed on each one. Windows surrounded the kitchen and the counters were a copy of the bar with the rock and copper edging. The den held an upright player piano that had belonged to Lillian, and the downstairs bathroom was off the den. Andy made all the furniture from lodge pole pines, and the cushions were custom-made leather. It was very rustic and a perfect home for Tahoe at that time. The stairway led from the foyer to the bedrooms that were all located upstairs, with the bedroom furnishings more traditional. The dressers in the master bedroom were on either side of the large room, and were built-in. Each of the girls had their own room, but on many occasions, Joad would sleep with Janie in her room because Joad was afraid of the dark. The fourth bedroom was Uncle Frank's room as they called it. The bathroom was very large with Marian's special bathtub. It had a five-foot square mirror enclosed in rock that came down to the tub edge. The same rock and copper edging was in each of the bathrooms. Marian couldn't wait to show off the house and with the holidays fast approaching it was the perfect time to invite everyone.

That first Christmas was a wonderful celebration with family and friends gathering in the new home. The regulars from the beauty shop and their families, business owners and their families, Lillian and Frank, Marian's father and stepmother, and of course Andy's parents. All came to see the house for the first time. That Christmas was the happiest Marian could remember. Everything seemed to be perfect. People she cared about surrounded her, the house decorations were beautiful, and of course, there was snow!

Everyone drew names for exchanging gifts, and the girls each received presents from the grandparents, and Santa, of course. At night, all the adults played canasta, and pinochle late into the evening. After the New Year, everyone left before any bad weather, and life was back to normal for Marian, Andy and the girls.

Andy's insurance business had grown too, and after the holidays were over many people at South Shore were encouraging Andy to run for supervisor. South Lake Tahoe had never had their own supervisor, and political decisions were made in Placerville, most of the tax revenue went there as well. In November of nineteen-fifty Andy won the election as the fifth districts first county supervisor. Marian's life was forever changed.

Marian had a black and white view of right and wrong, no room for gray area in her mind. Politics is a mostly gray area. Anything can be right or wrong with the proper justification, depending on one's point of view. Unable to deal with the pressures of being in the public eye, Marian's drinking became more frequent.

At first, it was exciting, having dinner with the Governor, the Attorney General, and their wives, and other dignitaries of the time. However, the constant parade of constituents wanting favors, and the calls at all times of the day and night, were turning Marian's sanctuary into nightmare.

Some of the people Marian genuinely liked. They didn't want anything they just enjoyed each other's company.

One such couple was Mimi and Nat. They had a summer cabin near the marina, and a Chris Craft speed-boat they kept in a slip there. Marian loved the lake, and boating even though she was not a strong swimmer. One Sunday, Nat called Andy, and invited him and Marian to go for a boat ride. Marian offered to bring a picnic lunch for the four of them.

"Hello Nat and Mimi," Marian said giving Mimi a hug.

"We are so happy you and Andy could come with us. It is so much more fun when someone else goes with us, and I feel so much safer if another man is along to help Nat with the boat." Mimi said.

Nat was a CPA in the bay area. He was a small man with a round face, and very small round glasses that he looked over the top of most of the time. He was not the athletic type by any means, and of course, he was not much of a drinker. The four of them climbed into the boat, and headed off to Emerald Bay to enjoy their picnic. They had fried chicken, homemade potato salad, deviled eggs, and Marian's favorite drink, Martinis. As the day was ending, the four of them loaded up the boat and headed back across the lake to the marina. Part way across the lake, Mimi's new hat blew off and into the water.

"Don't worry Mimi I'll get it!" Nat exclaimed, and he immediately turned the boat around to go pick up the hat. Of course, the wake of the boat sunk the hat, and Nat jumped in to retrieve it. Trouble was that Nat had on all his cloths and he couldn't swim.

Mimi didn't know what he was doing and she screamed, "Oh no Nat. Andy, Nat can't swim, please help him."

Andy couldn't see Nat in the water, and just as he was beginning to worry, up popped Nat to the surface. With the hat in one hand and his glasses still perched on the end of his nose.

Andy reached out to Nat and yelled to him, "Grab my hand Nat, as he extended his arm as far as he could toward Nat."

Nat thrashed about, and eventually got close enough for Andy to grab him by his cloths, and pull him into the boat. When everyone calmed down Mimi said to Nat, "What on earth were you thinking Nat? You know you could have drowned!"

"I don't know Mimi. I just thought I could save your hat." Nat said sheepishly.

"Well, Andy chuckled. You did save the hat."

Another one of Marian's favorites was Phil, who managed the county campground. He was down to earth and had a dry sense of humor.

Andy's mother was a social climber. She enjoyed putting on airs. When she was visiting that summer she answered the phone in the daytime when Marian was working, and it would go like this.

"Hellooooooo this is the Andrew Roberson residence."

Phil didn't know Andy's mother was visiting, and when he called, he thought Marian was joking with him, so he responded, "Well, Helloooooooo right back to you!"

Andy's mother, in quit a huffy tone said, "To whoooom am I speaking?"

Phil realized it wasn't Marian, and he quickly hung up the phone. He told Marian the story later, and they both laughed hysterically.

Telephone service in those days at Tahoe was the kind you would turn a crank on the telephone and an operator would come on the line and ask you for the number you wished to call. Marian and Andy's number was Kimball 47Y14, and it was a party line. That meant the line was shared with someone else who could pick up his or her phone and hear what you were saying. Everyone knew the telephone operator by name, Daisy. Therefore, a call would go something like this. "Operator, may I help you?"

"Hi Daisy, I would like to speak to Daffy," Marian would say.

Daffy's phone would ring and if she answered, you could talk to each other. This all took place by a switchboard. It was an upright large board with holes where wires were plugged in. A key allowed the operator to listen into the call. Therefore, you had to be careful about your conversation as whatever you said might be repeated all over town. Marian had a couple of missteps with the telephone.

One snowy day after several calls from Andy's constituents, Marian had just had enough of being nice. She answered the phone saying, "What the hell do you want?" The reply was, "Marian, this is Father O'Neal, I just called to ask if the girls were ready for their First Holy Communion service on Sunday?"

Humiliated for her remark, Marian replied, "Oh, Father, I'm so sorry. The telephone has been ringing none stop from people complaining about all the snow. Yes, the girls are looking forward to Sunday."

Father O'Neal, said with a slight chuckle, "Marian, I will say a little prayer for you and perhaps the lord will slow-up on this snow for a while. I'm happy Janie and Joad are coming on Sunday."

On Sunday, morning Janie and Joad were to bathe and dress for the big event. Joad was in the bathtub when the now familiar scream came. Marian rushed into the bathroom to see Joad examining her face in the big mirror.

"What are you yelling about?" Marian said.

Joad responded, by showing Marian the safety razor in her hand and pointing to her eyebrows. "I shaved my hair like you and Janie," she said, "and my hairs are all gone."

"Oh my God, Joad, you aren't supposed to shave your eyebrows."

"But that is the only hair I have," Joad said. "And now it is all gone too!"

With just the small tufts of hair that remained where her eyebrows once were, Joad looked more like a devil, than an innocent child ready for her First Holy Communion.

"It's a good thing I'm a beautician because I can fix it so you have eyebrows." Marian told Joad.

She dried Joad off, got her dressed for her First Holy Communion, and took an eyebrow pencil to what little was left of Joad's eyebrows.

The winter of nineteen-fifty-one and fifty-two, was the worst snow Tahoe had ever had. The push type plows could not clear the roads fast enough to keep them open. Both ends of US-50 were choked with snow too deep to plow with the equipment available at the time. The residents had to fend for themselves as the snow kept coming with no end in sight. Tahoe was ill prepared for anything like this, but everyone pitched in and helped those who needed help. Food was airlifted to the residents until the highway was reopened. Harrowing stories persist to this day about the winter of fifty-one and fifty-two.

The new house had snow above the doorways and Andy had to dig out so the family could get out of the house. Lillian and Frank came to stay when the storm started, but now it was time for them to attempt to return to Lakeland Village where they lived. Frank had been drinking a good part of the day and Lillian was very upset with him. Off she went in the snow headed for Lakeland. Andy concerned about Lillian trying to walk home in the deep snow, got Frank on his feet, and told him they were going home.

Frank said, "Okay son, let's go." Frank was in no condition to walk across the room let alone go a half mile in deep snow.

Andy managed to get Frank to hold onto Andy's shoulders as he walked ahead, but Frank kept stepping on the back of Andy's boots and nearly tripping him. Andy's bad leg caused him to walk with a limp in normal conditions, but with snow this deep, and Frank hanging onto him he needed a different plan. He thought about his army days and decided to try to get Frank to walk in step with him.

Andy said to Frank, "Okay Frank, we are going to walk in step. Hold on to me and march; right leg, left leg, right leg, left leg."

Frank just replied, "Gee fuzz boy, we ain't in the Army now."

Andy laughed and just kept saying, "left, right, left, right." Finally, they reached Lakeland Village. With Frank safely home, Andy returned to the house to tell Marian the story.

When spring came Andy and others made a plea to the Board of Supervisors for a rotary plow for the South

Shore. It was a first of its kind, and was quite a sight to see that huge plow throwing snow in the air and clearing the roads.

By now, Marian's drinking had become problematic. She was able to hide it to some degree, but on occasion, when she and Andy were in public she embarrassed him, and others. They began to argue and on occasion, those arguments escalated to violence. Andy had little patience for her problem and left her treatment to her personal physician, Dr. Branford. He prescribed barbiturates. Marian soon discovered she could take pills with no smell of alcohol on her breath. This made it easier to hide her addiction.

She opened the beauty shop at Camp Richardson that summer, and now had the pressures of operating both shops. She hired a beautician for the shop in Bijou, and she ran the one at Camp Richardson herself.

In early June, she received a phone call from her stepmother in Angles Camp.

"Marian," she said, your father is in the hospital, they say he has gone into a coma because of his diabetes. I think you should come, if you can."

"Is he going to be alright?" Marian asked.

"The doctors don't know, Marian, we just have to wait and see. Please come as soon as you can."

"I will leave here in an hour, but it will take me about three hours to get there," Marian replied.

By the time she arrived at the hospital it was dark. She ran down the hall to the room her stepmother had told her on the phone, but she was too late. The bed was empty, only her father's suit jacket lay in a chair next to the empty bed.

Just then a nurse came into the room and Marian said, "My father, where is he?"

The nurse stepped closer to Marian and said, "I'm sorry dear, didn't anyone tell you? Mr. Romaggi passed away about an hour ago I'm very sorry for your loss."

In total shock Marian sank into the chair clutching her father's coat to her chest and saying, "No, no, no daddy no, not you."

Marian stayed with her stepmother, and they consoled one another during this awful time. Marian's brother, Bob, lived close by, so he took charge, and helped arranged for their father's funeral. The following week she returned to Tahoe, and went back to work. Once again, she had no time to grieve.

She had not done any drinking, nor did she have any pills while she was in Angels. Her hands shook but no one thought much about it. No one there knew of her problem with alcohol and pills. Just like with Davy's death, Marian was ill prepared for the death of her father, and she never really got past it.

Summertime brought some interesting characters to Lake Tahoe. There was also the annual wagon train, which was a reenactment of the pioneer's trip over the passes to Placerville and in to the valley below the Sierras. It was like a parade for the residents of Tahoe. They would take up spots along US-50 to watch the many folks in costumes of the early pioneers. There were horses with fancy saddles, Indians rode bareback, and covered wagons with women and children riding inside. They all passed through Tahoe on the way to Placerville.

Jim Wall, the ice cream man had an old Greyhound bus that he had converted into his home. In the winter months, he lived in Florida. Summers were spent at Tahoe. He rented a small open building at the end of Herbert Avenue that he used as the ice cream stand. It was just big enough to hold one ice cream freezer with three flavors, Chocolate, Vanilla, and Neapolitan. He would cut the ice cream into two by four inch blocks, and insert a stick. He dipped the ice cream into melted chocolate, and rolled it in nuts. They were delicious! He parked his bus behind the building, and that is where he lived until it was time to move on to Florida for the winter.

Jim had a nose that was large. It was covered with a strawberry looking birthmark. That disfigured him making him hard to look at without staring. Frank had lost his left eye in an accident many years ago, and he knew about how people could stare or just avoid him. Frank and Jim became good friends and of course, Joad was often with Frank visiting Jim Wall. They were both wonderfully kind men. Jim became a good friend with the family and Frank kept in touch with him by letters long after they had both left Tahoe.

Jimboy's taco trailer was a very popular spot. Beachgoers would stop at the mobile trailer and buy a bag of tacos to take with them to the beach. These tacos became so popular the owner's, Jim and Margaret Knudson, eventually franchised the operation. They started out at Tahoe in the early fifties.

Boating and water skiing were a big part of everyone's lives and the Burnside's had a boat the kids all used. One Sunday Marian packed a picnic lunch and the Roberson family joined the Burnside's for a day at the beach. Johnny talked Marian into trying water skiing.

"It's easy Mrs. Roberson, you can do it, and I'll help you," Johnny said.

Wanting to be part of the fun Marian agreed and said, "Okay Johnny, I 'm counting on you to show me how."

Johnny proceeded to explain how to sit back in the water and keep the tips of the skis pointed up, bend your knees, and hold the rope with both hands.

"Oh, and Mrs. Roberson, if you fall make sure you let go of the rope," Johnny instructed.

"But what if I'm way out in the lake, I can't swim far," Marian said.

"The life belt will hold you up and we will come around with the boat to you up. It's easy," Johnny said confidently.

Marian now all prepared to take off, ski tips up, sitting back, and holding onto the rope she yelled, "READY!"

With that, the boat took off with Marian holding on for her life. She fell of course, but failed to let go of the rope! Looking like a porpoise popping up and down in the water behind the boat she finally let go. She was about forty yards off shore in water not much above her chest, but she began swimming for her life.

Everyone was yelling, "Marian, just stand up."

It was no use. She just kept swimming until she couldn't swim anymore without being on the beach. That was Marian's first and last attempt at water skiing. She did enjoy going to the beach to watch the kids swim and ski. However, her busy schedule at the beauty shops and with Andy's busy social schedule she rarely found the time. When she did go she always brought her brown wicker picnic basket with homemade fried chicken, potato salad, deviled eggs, and of course her martinis.

Johnny liked to play tricks on Joad. One of his favorites was what he called Joad traps. These traps were usually things he saw in comic books. Holes covered with pine needles, where he would call Joad to come find him causing her to fall into the hole. Amazingly, she was never hurt, and usually got out with little assistance, if any. Johnny was also a boy scout so every summer for a couple of weeks he would go off to scout camp. One such time when Joad was about seven, she decided to take some of her younger friends down to the meadow where Johnny had established a place they could smoke cigarettes. Joad and her three little friends went there attempting to smoke cigarettes, however, in the process, an old stump caught fire. Joad ran to the house to get water to put the fire out, after several trips to the house, and then back to the meadow, the fire was out. Only several hours later the fire trucks went flying past the Roberson's house and down to the meadow. Just then, the phone rang.

"Marian, is Joad home?" a voice said over the phone that Marian recognized as Peg's.

"Yes, she is drying the dishes." Marian replied, somewhat puzzled.

"Keep her there, I'm coming right over," Peg said, and hung up the phone.

When Peg arrived she explained her niece, whose father was on the volunteer fire department, had run to her Aunt Peg to tell her about the fire they had started, when she heard it was in the meadow. She told Peg how they had taken cigarettes from Marian and Peg and gone down to the meadow to smoke them. Fire was a serious problem then as it is now at Tahoe.

When Marian and Peg asked Joad about what they had done, Joad told them everything about putting the fire out with beer bottles of water.

"It was just an old stump, and there were no trees anywhere near there," Joad said crying.

Joad told them how Johnny had shown her how to smoke, and since his parents didn't smoke, he had her take Marian's cigarettes. Marian smoked a distinctive brand and she was probably the only person at Tahoe who smoked that brand.

The volunteers were able to put out the fire before it spread, and the following day Joad showed Andy and Marian where she had smoked and where the fire was. Fortunately, the fire she had started wasn't near the one that required the fire department. Apparently, Joad and Johnny were not the only kids who went to the meadow to smoke.

After Johnny returned from Boy Scout camp Andy, Marian, and Johnny's parents Al and Emily, all sat down at the Burnside's to talk to Johnny and Joad..

"Son you are a boy scout and you know how dangerous fires can be. A fire in these woods could burn all of our homes to the ground," Mr. Burnside scolded.

Johnny was glaring at Joad by now, and he knew what was coming.

"You not only did something you know we don't approve of, but you involved Joad. Because you are a Boy Scout you know better!" Al continued scolding.

"But…it is not my fault…sir, I wasn't even here," Johnny protested.

"It is your fault. You are the oldest, you are a boy scout, and you know better! Al continued. For your punishment, you will not be using the boat the rest of this summer. Now go to your room and think about what you have done."

Johnny was angry with Joad for a week or so, but he knew his father was right. It was his fault, he was the oldest, and he did know better.

Earning money for gas for the boat, ice cream from Jim Wall's ice cream stand, and tacos from Jimboy's taco trailer was an ongoing project every summer.. The kids would pick-up soda pop bottles. Then turn them into the stores for the deposit. Johnny and Joad also would find stray golf balls and turn them into the pro-shop for money. They would run errands for college kids who didn't want to leave the beach, to get them food from the snack shacks, or dive for beer cans they had hung from the piers on strings. The strings would mysteriously break causing the six-pack to break open, and the cans would fall to the bottom of the lake under the piers. The water was cold, so the college kids would pay Johnny and Joad to dive for the cans. Sometimes they paid as much as five cents a can.

There was a large swing set at Lake Land Village beach and Johnny and Joad spent a good deal of time there. They would swing as high as they could then jump out into the water, each one trying to outdo the other in distance, or with a flip in the air before landing in the water..

Johnny and Joad were both strong swimmers. One of Mr. Burnside's requirements for Joad and Johnny was that they had to be able to swim the length of Young's pier before he allowed them to take the boat out alone. They were all over the south shore of the lake on the water from Emerald Bay to Cave Rock. The boat was fourteen feet long, constructed of wood, and had a thirty-five horse Evinrude outboard motor. The best time to go out was early morning when the lake was smooth as glass, the water was a deep clear blue, and as the boat sped across the water, all you could hear was the sound of the motor. The Burnsides kept the boat in a slip at Seagraves harbor. Once the boat cleared the no wake area leaving the harbor the entire lake was their playground. One of their favorite spots was a short pier that had a tractor seat attached to the end of it, one could sit on the tractor seat, skis up, a couple of loops in the rope, and take off skiing without getting wet. Tahoe had so much shoreline with sandy beaches, that starting from the beach could be accomplished in the same manner. With so few people in those days, there weren't many rules governing the use of the lake or the beaches. Johnny and Joad hiked from Stateline to Meyers, played cowboys and Indians in the woods, climbed trees, fished and read comic books. Life was good for children growing up at Tahoe in those days.

Marian and Andy, and the Burnside's were able to allow the kids complete freedom with little concern for their safety.

In the winter, everyone snow skied or ice-skated. Marian decided she would try skiing, probably because she loved the ski cloths. She bought a pair of the tight fitting ski pants, and a ski sweater that had a big buck deer design on the front. She had a beautiful figure so she could wear the cloths nicely, and to her that was most important.

Peg was a patron of the beauty shop, she and Marian had become good friends too, so when Marian said she thought she wanted to learn how to ski, Peg was all for it.

"Marian that's a great idea. I would love to learn to ski. Why don't we take lessons together? There is a ski instructor at Ski Run, his name is Godey something, and he is one of those beautiful Nordic men. I'll schedule a lesson with him for the two of us," Peg said excitedly.

"Okay Peg, Marian said hesitantly, I'm off next Monday, so if you could make it for then, I can go."

"You plan on it. I will make it for Monday, would ten o'clock be okay?" Peg asked.

"Sure that would be fine," Marian replied, more excited now.

Snow skiing was not much different from water skiing for Marian. It was not that she was not athletic, she just always was more concerned about how she looked, and she didn't pay much attention to instructions.

Godey, was the ski instructor Peg had mentioned to Marian and he loved teaching women. He was very good looking, and knew it. He flirted with all the women and of course, the women loved his attention, Marian and Peg were no exceptions.

When Marian and Peg went for their first skiing lesson Peg said, "Marian what are we doing? We must be out of our minds, what if we break a leg or something?"

Marian laughed, "Peg, it can't be any worse than my first water skiing adventure when I forgot to let go of the rope after I fell. I looked like a submarine. I thought I was way out in the lake, and I started swimming for my life, trouble was I wasn't very far from the shore and I almost swam up on the beach."

"Oh Marian, that's so funny, but I guess you didn't think so?" Peg said still laughing.

Just then, Godey skied up to the two women who were precariously standing on their skis. "Good morning my beauties" Godey said, flashing his beautiful smile. "Are we ready for our first lesson?"

Peg just stared at him smiling. Marian laughed and said, "We are as ready as we are going to get. We were just saying maybe we weren't cut out to be skiers, what do you think?"

"Of course you are. I'm the best instructor, and you will be shushing the mountain like pros before long," Godey said confidently. "Okay, my beauties the first thing we will learn is how to walk up the mountain. Watch me, we call this the herringbone." Godey demonstrated using his skis by walking with the back of his skies in a vee shape to go up a small incline.

"Come, come along with me like little ducklings following their mommy," Godey instructed.

Marian and Peg struggled along stepping on the backs of their skies as they tried to imitate Godey's movements. As they started to get the hang of it, they started feeling more confident on their skis.

Peg laughed and said, "Looks like this is going to go a little better than your water skiing."

Just then, Marian got her skis crossed up and fell down on the snow.

"Maybe not, but I have no chance of drowning this time," She said.

Godey said, "This is good, Marian, lift this leg up, put your weight on the downhill ski, put your poles back here, and pull your po-po up like this."

"My po-po?" Marian said puzzled.

Godey pointed to his fanny and said, "Po-po."

They all laughed, and Godey said, "Okay, now your turn Peggy, fall down and then try to get up like Marian just did."

"That's good, very good. You see how easy this is?" Godey said, smiling at Peg. "Next, we will learn how to do a kick turn. We use this when we are on the mountain and want to turn around in the opposite direction."

After practicing several times, Peg and Marian were laughing and talking and Godey was flirting with them as he did with all his female students young and old. After the hour was up the women took off their skis and headed for the small building that served as a rental shop where they returned the skis and poles. Peg's house was not far from the ski hill, so the two of them walked back to Peg's for lunch laughing and talking about their ski lesson, Godey, and their po-po's.

All the elementary school kids at Tahoe skied, the school even made arrangements for the bus to take them to the ski run around three o'clock each day. This was physical education class and lasted one hour. Then the bus would pick them up and take them home.

Because of this, the Tahoe area produced a number of well-known junior skiers. Some of the kids joined a ski team called the Red Hornets. The ski hill where they practiced and raced was Edelweiss. It was located off US 50, and it had two rope tows and one T-bar. Their ski coach was Lutz Aynedter, a downhill champion from the 1940's who emigrated from Germany to California after the war. He was tough and disciplined, a no nonsense man. Joad joined the Red Hornets because her best friend already belonged to the team. She only lasted two winters with that team because she never liked Lutz, and that coupled with getting carsick on the drive to Edelweiss, she begged to quit the Red Hornets. The following ski season Heavenly Valley opened with a rope tow and one chairlift. It was less than a mile from the old ski run where Marian and Peg took ski lessons from Godey. Stein Erickson was the ski school director at Heavenly Valley, who started the Blue Angles ski team. The teams coach was a young skier, named Bill Johnson, who was well known on the ski circuit himself, prior to a serious leg injury ending his career as a U.S. Ski Team hopeful.

Joad was one of the first members of the Blue Angels team and skied with them until she left Tahoe. Many of the young people who excelled in the ski world belonged to one of these teams. Spider Savage and Jimmy Heuga were to become Olympic champions in later years. There were several other very accomplished skiers from Tahoe who perhaps didn't become as famous as these two, nonetheless each of them made quite an impact on Alpine skiing and racing at that time as junior racers.

Ice skating was another big pastime for the young people at Tahoe in the winter. Janie and her friends would go skating on Trout Creek winding around the bushes that lined the edges of the creek. This was not a safe place to skate, as the ice was thin in some places although Trout Creek was not deep. No one ever got hurt there, probably because kids knew the danger and were more responsible for their own wellbeing. One winter a couple of the contractors plowed a large area off Ski Run Blvd. for an ice skating rink. It became a great place for the teenagers to meet and skate. Around Christmas time, some of the parents would bring large thermoses of hot chocolate, and built a bon-fire to toast marshmallows. Tahoe was truly a paradise for young and old.

Near the end of Andy's first term as supervisor, the building that held the beauty shop at Bijou was torn down to make way for a new Shell Service Station. The beauty shop at Camp Richardson was seasonal so Marian took a part time job at a beauty shop near the State Line, which catered to the entertainers who headlined at the casinos. Marian only worked three days a week because she helped Andy with many of his projects. It was just a year before Andy's bid for re-election. He was very involved in other projects some of which were: *The Lake Tahoe Convention Bureau*, and *The Lake Tahoe Mirror*, which was the first weekly newspaper; and he was Chairman of a combined program of the County Supervisors Association's 43rd Annual Meeting, and the County Engineers Association's 38th Annual meeting for the State of California. Marian did her best as Chairwoman of the Ladies Entertainment Committee with the help of Mattie, Peg and Anita, three of her patrons from the beauty shop.

In November, Andy was defeated for re-election. Perhaps people speculated Andy had higher ambitions at the state level or that he was too involved in too many other projects. On the other hand, maybe it was because he and Marian had become too visible, thus exposing their personal problems to public scrutiny. Maybe people were just ready for a change. In any case, it was a devastating blow to Andy, because he had served South Lake Tahoe tirelessly to the best of his ability. Some of his accomplishments were he worked with the US forest service and local businessmen to secure a long-term lease for Heavenly Valley ski area. He also worked for the improvement of the old county road that went from Meyers to State Line. He was instrumental in securing funds to purchase a rotary snowplow after the winter of fifty-one and fifty-two. He was a conduit for local business people to work with the County and State governments.

Andy was resentful and felt unappreciated for the work he had done. So when in the spring of nineteen-fifty-five, Andy was offered a job as business manager of a mental hospital, located in Mendocino County, California, in a small town called Ukiah, and he was eager to take it.

When he and Marian visited the hospital where they would live, Marian said, "I don't want to live here, and I don't want the girls growing up on the grounds of a mental intuition."

To which Andy replied, "I'm going to take this job, there's nothing left for me at Tahoe, and there's nothing there for you either."

"But our beautiful home and the girls..." Marian protested.

"Janie will start college in the fall, and Joad is going into sixth grade she will make new friends here, she is a tough kid," Andy argued.

"But she is a skier, and Tahoe is the only home she has ever known, and all my friends are there too. I don't know anyone here. What will I do?" Marian pleaded.

On the seven-hour trip back to Tahoe, neither of them spoke. Marian refused to move from the home at Tahoe. Andy accepted the job, and one year later, Andy filed for a divorce.

Now, on her own, Marian rented a small space, and opened a beauty shop at the end of Herbert Avenue just a few blocks from their home. Janie had graduated from high school and was attending College of Pacific in Stockton, and spending vacations and summers at the Lake. Joad remained with Marian at Tahoe for the next three years.

Marian struggled with her addiction to prescription drugs and alcohol. Andy sent monthly alimony and child support payments that were quite adequate. Along with the beauty shop income, Joad and Marian could get by. However, Marian was a poor manager of money, and still lived well above her means. In Ukiah, Andy was making a new life for himself and remarried two years later.

Marian was still a very attractive woman at just forty-five years old. However, she still loved Andy. She didn't date, at least not openly. She did become involved with a married man, Robert, and for a short time, she was very happy. She even had stopped drinking for the most part. This affair was to be short lived.

One night late, she received a phone call from her friend Peg, "Marian, are you still up?" Peg said.

Marian replied, "Sure Peg, I was just reading a little, why?"

"Okay, I'll be right over," Peg said and hung up the phone.

When Peg arrived, Marian immediately knew something was wrong. "What is it Peg?" Marian asked concerned.

"Oh Marian, I don't know how to tell you this," Peg sobbed.

"Peg, what is it? Tell me what has you so upset?" Marian said.

"The sheriff called Sam tonight, Peg began, to tell him Robert was in a terrible car accident, and Marian, he didn't make it. I'm so sorry! Robert told Sam about you two, and that is why Sam asked me to come over tonight so you wouldn't hear it from someone else tomorrow," Peg continued.

At first Marian was too much in shock to even respond, but as the realization came that she had lost her lover, she began to cry softly. "No, this can't be happening again. What is wrong with me, everyone I love dies! NO, NO this isn't true, not this time. Peg please tell me this is all a bad dream. "

The next days and weeks were horrible for Marian, as each of her customers in the beauty shop asked if she had heard of the terrible accident, and how sad for Robert's family, and wasn't it awful. Of course, none of them knew of her affair with Robert, once again, she would grieve alone.

By nineteen fifty-eight, Marian was no longer able to keep the house, and she sold it for just enough to pay the debts she owed. She rented an apartment for Joad and herself at Al Tahoe above a service station, where they lived for just seven months.

Defeated, alone, addicted to prescription drugs and alcohol Marian had no choice but to leave her beloved Lake Tahoe and move into the small house Lillian and Frank owned in Stockton. The very place she and Andy had lived before buying the property at Tahoe.

chapter 5

IN STOCKTON WHILE sitting in the little house in the back, Marian was reflecting on the past and she decided to write to Marge once again. She had never received a response from her last letter and that was over seven years ago. Was it even possible Marge had received it? Oh, well what can it hurt, I'll try one more time, she thought, and she took out paper and pen to begin.

Dear Marge,

It's been such a long time since I last wrote to you and I don't even know if you received that letter. I hope you did, and that this letter finds you.

So much as happened it's hard to know where to start. I guess the most important things first would be the best place to begin.

Andy and I were divorced in nineteen-fifty-six. After moving away from Lake Tahoe, he remarried the following year. Janie was attending College of the Pacific, in Stockton, and I stayed on at Tahoe with Joad until last month, but I no longer had enough beauty work to keep the house and stay at Tahoe alone.

Joad and I have moved to here, and we are living in the back house of mother and Frank's, where you and I stayed for a time before you left to go back to Georgia. Maybe this will be a good thing in the long run, but it sure doesn't feel like that right now.

I have an interview with the manager of the beauty shop located in Smith and Lang Department store, on Monday. I'm keeping my fingers crossed that I will get the job. There are three other beauticians there and I would be the fourth if they hire me. I met one of the other beauticians when I turned in my application, his name was Darryl, and he was real nice and funny too. I was very nervous but he put me at ease right away. It has been a while since I had to apply somewhere they didn't already know me.

Janie was married last year, and Joad will start school in September as a sophomore. I can hardly believe that.

I hope you and Fred are doing well, and I would love to hear from you about what you have been doing all this time. You are the best friend I ever had and I don't know what I would have done without you during those war years. You are a rock and you always seemed to know just what to do no matter what. I wish I had your strength and confidence, I just seem to go along, and I never really have a plan to live by. When things don't work out, I just fall apart.

I still love Andy, but he has remarried, so I have lost him too. I have to make this work for Joad and me, but I really don't know where to start. Maybe if I get that job things will start to look a little brighter.

On the plus side, we do have a roof over our heads, thanks to mother and Frank. I have a new Plymouth Fury Convertible that is white with a red top. Joad will be getting her learners permit in November, and already she is driving me crazy about letting her drive. Janie was so much easier to handle. Joad challenges everything I say. She was very close to Andy, and I think she blames me for him leaving, or maybe it's just because she is a teenager.

Have you kept in touch with any of the gals from the Ralston Hotel beauty shop? I would love to know what has happened to them too.

Well I have gone on long enough so I will end for now. Please write to me if you have a chance. My new address is: 1864 Mt. Diablo Stockton, California.

Love,
Marian

Just then, Joad came in the house with two teenage girls.

"Mom I want you to meet my new friends," Joad said happily. "This is Sally, she lives right over there, pointing to the house across the fence, and this is MaryAnn, she lives across the street from Sally's. MaryAnn is my age and Sally is one year older than we are. This is my mom, Mrs. Roberson."

"It's very nice to meet you girls, and you may just call me Marian, you don't need to call me Mrs. Roberson." Marian said smiling at the girls.

"They are going to show me where we will be going to school. A new school is being built but it won't be finished this year so we will be going to school at the Jr. College campus. It's right next to College of the Pacific, where Janie went to college, isn't that great!" Joad said excitedly.

"Yes, that's nice, how are you girls going to get there?" Marian asked.

"Oh we can walk, Mrs. Roberson, It's not that far. We almost always walk to school, unless one of my brothers' drives us, but that isn't very often, so we walk most of the time," Sally said cheerfully.

"I told them you would take us in the convertible, mom. You aren't doing anything else right now are you? Please, please take us in the convertible, and then maybe we could go to the A&W drive in for lunch after we see the school?" Joad pleaded.

Marian said. "Well I guess I could do that, are you sure it's alright with your parents girls? I wouldn't want them to worry about you going with someone they don't know."

"Oh, it's fine with them," Sally said. "My mom and dad know you from a long time ago when you stayed here during the war."

"Okay, but did you ask your parents, MaryAnn?" Marian asked.

"No," MaryAnn said sheepishly. "I better go ask them."

"Let's all go together, that way your mother and father can meet me, and see who I am before they just let you go. Maybe your mother would like to go too?" Marian said.

After all the introductions, MaryAnn's mother, declined the invitation but said, it would be fine for MaryAnn to join them. The girls were so excited to go in the new Plymouth convertible, they we laughing and running to the car.

"Can I ride in the front seat?" Sally said.

"You girls work that out," Marian said. "I'm just the driver."

A few minutes later, the girls had decided Sally would get the front seat on the way over, and MaryAnn would get it on the way home. Off they all went to see the school and have lunch. The girl's friendship lasted until they all had graduated from high school.

On Monday, Marian arrived at her interview in her white starched uniform, polished white shoes, and her hair and make-up perfectly done. At forty-seven years old she was still a beautiful woman, in spite of the smoking and drinking she had done for nearly twenty years. She was very nervous because she knew everything was dependent on her getting this job.

Darryl came over to her as Marian was waiting to meet the manager, and he said, "it's okay, kid, you look great, and I've already told the boss she better not let you go somewhere else."

"Thank you Darryl, I'm so nervous, It's been a very long time since I was the one being interviewed. I'm so scared she won't like me." Marian whispered to Darryl.

The manager was a woman in her fifties, dressed very well, with short graying hair nicely done. She smiled at Marian as she approached.

"You must be Marian?" She said, reaching out to shake her hand. "My name is Leslie. Darryl, here, has told me I had better not miss out on hiring you, suppose we go in the office where we can have a little privacy and chat."

Marian smiled feeling more relaxed, and followed Leslie into the office where they both sat down next to each other.

"I'll get right to the point, Marian. I'm looking for a good stylist and more importantly one who is great with color. Do you do your own color?" Leslie asked.

"Yes, I do," Marian replied. "I have been doing color for over fifteen years now, and I have studied in San Francisco on a couple of occasions to learn more about the science associated with good, natural looking hair colors. So I would know what will work, and what you can do without damaging the hair."

"Good, Leslie said, that's what I'm looking for, someone who won't just slap a color on having no concern how that patron will look when they leave the salon. Our reputation is built on how our patrons look, otherwise why would anyone want to spend money here if they don't look fabulous when they leave."

"That's important to me too. When I first went to Tahoe, I didn't know anyone, and I worked very hard to please each woman who came into the salon. All of my patrons were with me for more than eight years, and they would bring me new business all the time." Marian answered.

"Okay, that brings me to my next question. Since you owned your own salon, are you going to be able to work for someone else? You know you will have to do things our way. We work six days a week here, and some nights and weekends will be required. You have a teenager, so is that schedule going to work for you?" Leslie inquired.

Marian replied, "Yes, Joad is fifteen now and she is very responsible. I have worked for other salons, and I don't have any trouble taking orders from someone else."

"Well then, let's go see what you can do. I would like you to do my hair." Leslie said, and she got up and motioned for Marian to follow her.

Darryl met them as they were coming out of the office and he said, "Leslie the general manager of the store wants to see you up stairs, as soon as possible."

Leslie sighed, and said, "See what I mean. Okay, Marian, you're hired. Can you start tomorrow morning at nine o'clock?

Relieved and excited Marian said, "Absolutely, I'll be here, and thank you very much!"

Leslie smiled, and headed for the elevator. Marian said to Darryl, "I'm so thankful you helped me get this job Darryl. I really need it, and I don't know how I will ever repay you."

"How about a home cooked meal?" Darryl said.

"Sure that's easy, how about tonight?" Marian laughed.

"Okay, it's a date. My last appointment is at five o'clock, would six-thirty work for you?" Darryl asked.

"That will be fine. Here's my address, see you then, and thank you again." Marian said as she turned to leave.

Marian stopped at the corner store on her way home and bought three T-bone steaks from the butcher. He was a single man about Marian's age, and her good looks had not gone unnoticed by him. He flirted with her as he cut and wrapped the steaks for her. Marian was so preoccupied she hardly noticed. She thanked him and continued her shopping, getting potatoes to bake, salad ingredients, French bread, and ice cream for dessert. When she got home, she took off her uniform, and put on her jeans and her favorite western shirt, lit up a cigarette, poured a drink, and sat down at the kitchen table. It was only eleven o'clock.

After taking a few sips of her drink, she started to straighten-up the house, and prepare for dinner. Joad ran in the house with Sally and MaryAnn right behind her.

"How did it go mom? Did you get the job?" Joad asked hesitatingly, noticing the drink on the table.

"Yes," Marian replied. "I did get the job, and I start tomorrow morning. I invited Darryl over for dinner tonight, as he put a good word for me. I don't think I would have got the job if it hadn't been for him. So I need you to be nice and help me with dinner, okay?"

"Sure mom, what time is dinner? Is Darryl your boss? Is he a beautician too? I didn't know men were beauticians," Joad said.

"Only the ones that are fairies," Sally said snickering a little.

Joad looked puzzled, but said nothing.

"Never mind, you just make sure you get home before five so you can help me," Marian said.

The girls left, but Joad was not gone for long because she remembered the drink on the table, and knew she better go home and make sure Marian didn't have another one, or there would be no dinner.

At six-thirty, Darryl arrived and they all sat down to dinner. Darryl said, "If I knew you could cook like this I might not have recommended you for that job. I would have hired you as a chef instead."

"Flattery will get you another dinner," Marian said a bit embarrassed, and she changed the subject. "Darryl, how did you decide to go into beauty work?" Marian asked.

"Well, my real dream is to open an interior design studio one day, but that takes a good deal of money to start. Being a cosmetologist was the fastest way to make enough money to live on and also put some away to someday make that dream come true," Darryl answered.

"That sounds interesting, interior decorating. My secret dream has always been to have a bridal store," Marian said.

They continued to talk and the three of them got along great. By the end of the evening, Darryl was calling Joad little sister. He and Marian were laughing about mistakes they had made. Marian told him about the time in Gardnerville when she had bleached her hair after having a perm, and her hair turned green and broke off at the scalp.

"I had to wear a turban for over two months until my hair grew out again," Marian laughed.

They continued telling stories while laughing and talking for a couple of hours when Darryl said, "Well we better call it a night, as you have a big day ahead of you tomorrow, and so do I for that matter."

"Thank you, Darryl, I'm so grateful, and we sure enjoyed your company. Maybe we can do this again soon," Marian said.

"Sure thing Marian, only next time we can go to my place, and I will cook for you and little sister. I'm a good cook too," Darryl said, as he walked out the door he waved. "See you tomorrow bright-eyed and bushy-tailed."

After Darryl left Joad said, "Mom, I really like Darryl, he is so nice. What did Sally mean when she said men beauticians were fairies?"

"It is complicated, Joad, I don't know how to really explain it except to tell you Darryl doesn't date women, he prefers the company of other men. He is a very nice person, and you could see for yourself how nice he is. He is our friend, right? And that's all that really matters," Marian stated flatly.

"Yea, your right mom, Sally just doesn't know him. I think he is real nice, and you're right, he is our friend," Joad said.

"Okay, off to bed now, I have a big day ahead, and I want you to take care of things here tomorrow while I'm at work. The lawn needs to be mowed, and clean up around both the houses please."

"I'm glad you got the job mom, I like it here. It's not bad that we aren't at Tahoe anymore, and you have a new friend too, Darryl," Joad said.

Things were good for the next couple of months. Marian was building her own clientele at the salon, Joad was adjusting to a new life quite different from the one at Tahoe, and Darryl had become a great friend to both of them.

In late September, Lillian called to say that Frank was in an accident and he was in the hospital in Reno. He was going to be fine but he was going to need to spend some time recovering, and it would be best if they came to Stockton for the winter, where it was not so cold. The people who were renting the front house were moving out October 1, so Lillian and Frank could live in the front house, and Marian and Joad could continue to stay in the house in the back.

Frank was not doing well when they arrived October 5th, and Marian called. Dr. Branford, and made an appointment for him to look at Frank.

"Mr. and Mrs. Reister," Dr. Branford began. "I'm not sure what Frank is suffering from, so I think we better admit him to the hospital so I can run some tests. I'll have the hospital call you as soon as we can admit him. Would tomorrow be alright if I can arrange it?"

Lillian was not expecting Frank would need to go to the hospital, so she asked, "Do you think it is something serious?"

"Well I don't know Mrs. Reister, that's what we want to find out, so we can take care of it and get Frank back on his feet. It won't take more than a day to run the tests," Dr. Branford said.

Frank said, "Okay doc, let's get to it. Doll, I'm not getting any better just staying at home so let's do as the doc says and find out why I feel so punk."

The next day Frank was in the hospital and several tests were completed. Dr. Branford called Marian, "Marian, can you stop by the office anytime today?"

"Sure Dr. Branford, my first appointment isn't until ten o'clock and my last one is at three, should I bring mother too?"

"No, I would like to talk to you alone. Can you stop by around three-thirty?" Dr. Branford replied.

The day drug on for Marian, as she knew something must be terribly wrong with Frank. Why would Dr. Branford want to talk to her alone? If it were just something minor, he would just tell her. As soon as she finished with her last appointment, she told Darryl, about the call from the doctor.

After listening to what Marian said, Darryl said, "Don't worry kid, he is going to be fine. Do you want me to go with you?"

"Oh thank you Darryl, as always you're there for us, but no, I better do this myself," Marian replied as she put on her coat to leave.

"Okay, I'll be home all night, so call me if you want too," Darryl said smiling as he gave Marian a hug.

When Marian arrived at the doctor's office, Thelma, Dr. Branford's nurse met her and said, "Marian come in to doctor's private office he'll be right in to see you."

"Thank you Thelma," Marian said. "How have you been? How is your family?"

"We're fine, Marian, thank you for asking. Doctor will be right with you," she said as she closed the door to the private office.

A few minutes later Dr. Branford came in and shut the door behind him. He didn't greet Marian with his usual jovial self. Instead, he pulled up a chair next to her taking her hand in his, he began," Marian, we have completed the entire test. I'm afraid I have some very bad news for you. Frank has cancer of the bone." He waited a moment before continuing, and then he said, "There isn't much we can do for him. He is going to be in a good deal of pain, and the only good news is he probably won't suffer too long. I've already talked to Lillian and Frank and explained the prognosis. It's a lot to take in at one time. Lillian is in disbelief, which is normal under the circumstances. That's why I wanted to talk to you. As I said, there is not much medicine can do for him except try to keep him comfortable. Hospital care in these cases is very expensive, and not all that effective. This is where you come in. I would like to have Thelma teach you how to give the injections. Frank will be on morphine until the end, and he will need injections every six to eight hours to help with the pain. Do you think you can do this?"

Marian was in total shock, what was Dr. Branford saying? Frank was dying and the doctor wanted her to give him shots! This must all be a bad dream she thought to herself.

"Dr. Branford asked, "Marian, are you alright? You don't have to decide now. I just want you to think about it. If you can do this, it will save your mother thousands of dollars, and probably more importantly, Frank will be more comfortable in his own home. We have known each other now for over twenty years, and I have watched you handle all kinds of very tough situations. I know you can do this. I wouldn't suggest it if I didn't think you could. Take a day or two, and then let me know what you decide. If you have any questions, call me at home, if I'm not in the office."

Tears were beginning to build up in Marian's eyes. She knew what she had to do. After all, she didn't have any choice. Her mother, and Frank, had always been there for her. When she and Andy were building the house at Tahoe, without Frank's help the house would have taken much longer and been much more expensive. When she had nowhere else to go they were giving her and Joad a place to live. Of course, she would do whatever it took, but could she? She wondered.

Dr. Branford said, "Just sit here for a bit until you are ready to drive home. I'm sorry Marian, I know what a shock this is."

"I'll be alright doctor, I just need a moment," Marian sniffled a bit. She composed herself, as she had many times before, and said, "I'll be fine now, just have Thelma call me when she has time to teach me how to give Frank the shots."

"That-a girl," Dr. Branford encouraged, patting Marian on the shoulder. "Go home now, and help your mother get through this. It won't be long, he doesn't have much time."

When Marian got home the house was empty, and so was her heart. She took off her uniform and shoes, put on her robe and slippers, and poured a drink.

The following couple of weeks were very hectic. She had to hold down her job, make sure there were groceries in the refrigerator, help her mother settle in, and all this in between trips back and forth to the hospital.

The front house was less than twelve-hundred square feet, it had two bedrooms, one bath, a living room, a kitchen, and a small breakfast nook, and the back porch had a washtub for washing clothes. Preparing the house for Frank's return home required, renting a hospital bed, and other equipment for his safety, when he was not in bed. Because the house was small, it would not be difficult for

Frank to get from the bedroom to the bath, or to a chair in the living room.

Thelma taught Marian how to give shots by practicing on an orange. She did all of this willingly, and of course, Darryl was always there to lend a hand, or take over one of Marian's appointments at the beauty salon, if she was not able to make it on time.

Finally, Frank could go home. Lillian was so happy to have him in their little house, away from the hustle-bustle of the hospital. For a time Frank seemed to improve. They all had Thanksgiving together and Marian began to be hopeful this was all just a mistake that Frank was going to be all right after all. However, by Christmas, Frank's pain began to be more severe, and more frequent, and he was losing weight. Marian began to give him the morphine shots as prescribed. At first, it was every eight hours, then every six hours, until by the end he was asking for them every hour. He had gone from a man of about one-hundred-sixty pounds before he got sick, to just over a hundred when he died sixteen weeks after coming home from the hospital.

Lillian was devastated. She and Frank had been married for over forty years, and he was the joy of her life, a life that didn't have much joy. Somehow, Frank always reassured her, and made her laugh, especially when things seemed the darkest. She had stayed strong until a week after the funeral, and then she totally fell apart.

"Marian, what am I going to do without Sweets? He did everything for me, and when things were bad, he always made me laugh. He took me to work, picked me up, packed my lunch, and fixed my breakfast and dinner. He took care of me when I was sick, he did everything for me. My Sweets is gone and now I don't know what to do anymore," Lillian sobbed.

Marian didn't know what to say, but she had some idea of what her mother must be feeling. She had felt that loss so many times herself. Davey, Johnny, Robert, and Andy, only with Andy there was always hope he would come back. Frank was not coming back, not ever. She hugged her mother and just said, "I know, I know how you hurt. I love you. We will get through this. You have Joad and me, Janie and her family, and Bob and his family, we all love you. We will help you through this just as you always have helped us."

Lillian sobbed more softly now. Marian stayed with her until Lillian was feeling somewhat better.

By the end of March, Lillian had decided to return to Reno, and go back to work as a maid at the Riverside Hotel. She returned to the little cabin she and Frank rented before he got sick. She wanted Joad and Marian to move into the front house so Joad would have her own bedroom. She could rent out the house in the back to pay the taxes and expenses to keep up the houses.

The last six months were more than Marian could handle, and she did what she had learned to rely on, she used pills and alcohol to get her through each day. She was drinking and taking pills all the time now. She would call her friends at all hours of the night crying or complaining about her life. She missed several days of work. Darryl covered for her as much as he could, but after a few months, she lost her job at the salon at Smith and Lang.

About a month after losing her job at Smith and Lang, Marian was able to find a new job, this time it was a smaller shop on Country Club Blvd. Just the owner, Remy, and Marian worked there. This might work well for her, less pressure, and a more intimate setting. She could give very personal service for a few select customers, and there were no quotas to make each month. Twenty-five percent of what she made went to the owner, and she was able to keep seventy-five percent for herself. This didn't include her tips.

Marian started dating Bill, the butcher at the corner store. She spent most Sundays with Bill in his boat on the river. They had a good time together and he enjoyed spending time with Marian. Bill was unaware of Marian's problems with drinking and taking pills. She was careful not to drink when she was with him. And Darryl still kept in touch, but they saw less of him now Marian was no longer working in the same salon.

Dr. Branford continued to prescribe barbiturates to Marian, even though he knew she was abusing them. She was calling him every month before her prescription was due to renew. This was a sure sign of the abuse, but still he gave into her. Perhaps because he knew she had been through a lot, and he genuinely thought he was helping. Whatever his reasons, it was not good, because Marian still resorted to alcohol, and used pills too, a deadly combination.

chapter 6

ONE AFTERNOON JOAD came home from school to find Marian on the floor. "Mom, what's wrong? " She cried. After trying to wake her and getting no response from Marian, she called Dr. Branford's office.

Thelma answered, and hearing how upset Joad was, Thelma said, "Joad, stay there I will call the ambulance right now, everything is going to be alright. I will call you right back after I get the ambulance on the way."

Thelma called an ambulance and then called Joad right back to try to calm her, "Dr. Branford is on his way to the hospital where the ambulance will take your mom. I'm coming to get you and we'll go to the hospital together. Everything is going to be alright, try not to worry, I'll be right there." Thelma reassured.

When Thelma hung up the phone, Joad heard the ambulance siren coming. In minutes, Marian was loaded in the ambulance and on her way to the hospital. Thelma had told the ambulance company she would bring Joad and not to take her with them.

While waiting alone for Thelma, Joad called Darryl. Sobbing, as she tried to tell Darryl what had happened. "I... I...think... mom's dead!" she wailed.

"What?" Darryl exclaimed. "What has happened? Talk to me Joad, what is going on?"

Continuing to cry, Joad tried to tell Darryl what had happened. "I came home from school, and she was just lying on the floor, she wouldn't wake up I tried to make her wake up, but she just wouldn't. She is dead, Darryl. I know she's dead!"

Just then, Thelma arrived, "Who's on the phone, Joad?" Thelma asked.

"It's Darryl, I called him," Joad said.

Thelma took the phone and said, "Darryl, I'm Dr. Branford's nurse, Marian is on her way to the hospital, by ambulance. I've come to get Joad and take her there. Dr. Branford is waiting at the hospital for Marian to arrive. We don't know what is wrong yet. But it could be an overdose, I'm not sure." Thelma said.

"What hospital? I'll meet you there. Joad is like a little sister to me, and she is going to need someone," Darryl said.

Thelma told him the name of the hospital and agreed it would be a good idea for him to come, just in case. A few minutes later Thelma and Joad were on their way to the hospital. Darryl immediately left work and met them in the emergency waiting room.

It was about a half an hour later when Dr. Branford came out to tell them Marian had a narrow escape, but she was going to recover.

"I'm going to keep her in the hospital for a day or two and keep an eye on her," Dr. Branford said. " Joad can you have someone stay with you until your mom gets home?"

Darryl, said, "I would like to stay with her, but I don't know..."

Thelma interrupted, "We only live a few blocks away from Marian's. Joad you can stay with us. I can take you to school on my way to work in the morning and that will probably work out fine."

"Can I go see mom now?" Joad said to Dr. Branford.

"She is sleeping now, but sure you can go in and see her," Dr. Branford replied.

"Can Darryl come too?" Joad asked.

"Sure if you would like him to go with you," the doctor answered.

While Joad and Darryl went in to see Marian, Thelma and Dr. Branford were discussing what to do next. The hospital had to pump Marian's stomach and she had alcohol and barbiturates in her system. She might not have survived had Joad not found her when she did. Marian's problem could no longer be ignored, and Dr. Branford would have to take action.

In the following days, Dr. Branford changed Marian's prescription. She was still drinking, so it was too dangerous to continue with barbiturates. Especially, since she had overdosed once already.

The next several months were very bad for Marian because she was trying to beat her addiction on her own. Bill stopped calling Marian after this episode. He had no idea she had a problem with alcohol and pills. He didn't want any part of that kind of problem. Marian was able to go a few weeks without drinking too much, which allowed her to work at the beauty shop on Country Club.

One of her regular patrons was a music teacher, who specialized in voice lessons. Her name was Rowena, and she had a studio behind her home off Country Club Blvd. She and Marian became fast friends.

Rowena made an appointment the week before Valentine's Day to get her hair colored, and arrived at the shop a few minutes early.

"Hi Rowena," Marian said cheerfully. "Come over to my station and we can get started."

"Okay Marian, I know I m a bit early," Rowena replied.

Marian put the drape around Rowena, and asked, "Do you have big plans for Valentine's Day?"

"As a matter of fact Marian, I wanted to invite you to be my guest at a music concert being held on Valentine's Day. I have two tickets, and I know how you love music, so I thought you might like to join me. That's if you don't have other plans." Rowena said.

"I don't have any other plans, and it has been so long since I have been anywhere, especially something musical." Marian said.

"Well good, then we have a date. It starts at eight o'clock, and did I mention it's a formal event?" Rowena continued.

"Great," Marian replied.

However, immediately she was concerned she didn't have any formal wear. It had been years since she had been anywhere that she would have to dress formally. She still had until next week, so she would go shopping for something to tonight.

That night after work, Marian went to several stores, but was unable to find anything she liked. She began to stress about the whole idea of going to the concert with Rowena, so she called Thelma, and asked her if she could help.

"Thelma I need your help, I have been invited to a formal event, a concert, and I don't have anything to wear. It has been years since I've had to dress for anything like this, and I don't even know where to begin. Could you help?" Marian pleaded.

"Of course, Marian, I would love to help you, and I know a few great places to find the perfect outfit. When do you want to go?" Thelma replied.

"Could you go Saturday? I don't have any appointments, and I know you don't work at doctors on Saturdays," Marian said.

"Saturday will work for me. I will pick you up about ten o'clock if that will be okay?" Thelma inquired.

"I'll be ready Thelma and thank you so much," Marian said.

On Saturday, Thelma picked Marian up as agreed, and they went downtown shopping. After trying a few stores, Marian was getting a little discouraged when Thelma said, "Marian, I know of one more store, but their clothes are very expensive, is that going to be a problem?"

"Well it depends on how expensive, I guess," Marian said.

The store was Levinson's, and it was very upscale, and so were the prices. They were out of Marian's budget, but that never stopped her. She found just the right thing. It was a Lilly Ann suit, beige in color with a fur collar. It was classic, and when Marian came out of the dressing room Thelma gasped, "Marian, you look beautiful in that suit!"

"I love this suit, and I think it will be perfect, but Thelma, it's three hundred dollars. Marian whispered. "Do you think they have charge accounts here?"

"I'm sure they do Marian," Thelma said hesitantly." But do you think you should spend that much? Maybe we can find something else a little less expensive?"

"Oh Thelma, I'm so tired of looking, and this is just perfect, if I charge it I can have it paid for in a couple of months from my tip money," Marian said.

Just then, the sales clerk came up to them, "That suit is absolutely stunning on you dear!" the clerk said.

"Yes, I like it very much," Marian stated flatly. "I have looked all over town, and this is the first store I found anything I like. I don't have an account here yet, but I would like to open one today if you could help me with that."

"Certainly Dear, we can have you fill out the appropriate forms now if you would like?" the clerk said walking toward the desk in the back of the store.

Marian winked at Thelma, followed the clerk to the back of the store, and sat down at the desk. The clerk handed Marian an application form to complete, and said, "I'll be back in a few minutes, if you need me."

Marian began to fill out the form, her hands were shaking, but this was something she was accustomed to by now. She completed the information just as the clerk returned.

As the clerk reviewed the application she said, "Would you like to take the suit today? Your friend mentioned that she thought you might want the hem altered on the skirt, is that correct?"

Marian, with some disbelief that the application didn't have to be pre-approved said, "Yes, I think I would like it a bit shorter."

"All right, if you would go back to the dressing room I will have my seamstress come to take the proper measurements," The clerk said.

Marian went back to the dressing room, put the suit back on, and waited for the seamstress to arrive. After the alterations had been pinned, Marian admired herself in the mirror. She did look beautiful. Clothes really do make the woman, she thought to herself.

"The suit will be ready for you to pick-up on Tuesday. Oh yes, don't be concerned if you don't receive a statement for a while, typically it takes forty-five days before you will receive the first one, following that you will receive statements monthly," The clerk explained.

"Fine," Marian said. "I will be back then." As she and Thelma were leaving Marian turned and said, "Oh, what are your business hours?"

"We are open from ten to six on Monday thru Friday, and Saturdays, from nine to seven. Of course we are closed on Sundays," The clerk responded.

As Marian and Thelma returned to the car, Marian began to giggle, "Thelma can you believe that? I just bought a three hundred dollar suit to go on a date with a woman! I must be out of my mind."

"Well, you just might be out of your mind," Thelma said laughing.

"I don't have to worry because the clerk said that my first payment won't be for forty-five days. That will give me plenty of time to save my tip money, and I should be able to pay for half of the suit by then," Marian said confidently.

Marian picked up the suit on Tuesday as agreed. Then she proceeded to charge a pair of heels, and a matching purse to go with her new Lilly Ann suit. She bleached her hair and applied the platinum toner, and by Valentine's Day, she looked like the movie star she had always dreamed of being. Rowena picked Marian up at seven o'clock, which gave them plenty of time to arrive before the start of the concert at eight.

"Marian, you look absolutely stunning. I don't think I've ever seen you dressed in anything but your uniform. Is that suit by Lilly Ann?" Rowena asked.

"Why yes it is, I found it a Levinson's, and I just could not resist it. I didn't know that store existed, and that's so funny because Smith and Lang is right across the street," Marian answered.

"Oh I love their clothes too, even though they are a bit on the expensive side, they're worth it," Rowena said.

Following the concert, Marian and Rowena stopped by at the Stockton Hotel Lounge, for a private reception for VIP's of the concert. Rowena, who was well known in the music community, was always invited to these events. Marian was careful not to drink at the event, she had club soda with a lime.

"Rowena, thank you so much for inviting me to go with you to the concert, I can't remember when I've had such a nice time, and met so many wonderful people," Marian told Rowena.

"It was my pleasure Marian. Maybe we can do it again sometime."

Starting in April Marian signed Joad up for voice lessons with Rowena. This was just one more thing she couldn't really afford, but that never stopped Marian.

In May, she decided to buy a new car from Thelma's husband Evert, who worked as a salesman for the Mercury dealer.

"Hi Marian, I hear you are looking for a new car?" Evert said.

"Well I have the Plymouth to trade in, and I'm not sure what I want yet. Except I want it to be a convertible of course," Marian replied.

"I've got one I think you will love over here. It's a new powder blue convertible, and it's loaded with all the latest gadgets," Evert said. "Here, sit down in it, and then we can take it for a test drive."

"It is beautiful, Evert, but I don't know if I can afford it. How much are the payments?" Marian asked.

"We can work something out with your trade in, come on let's take it for a spin and see if you even like it," Evert said as he opened the door for her. "Here, let me adjust the seat for you. See this is a power seat. You just push this button and the seat adjusts to where you want it. It has power brakes, windows, and power steering too. The radio is both AM/FM, and when you turn on the radio the antenna goes up automatically. The top goes up and down with this one button, then folds into the well behind the back seat, and it has a matching cover right here."

"Okay, let's take it for a ride, but Evert I don't really think I can afford a car like this," Marian replied.

After the test ride, of course Marian wanted the car and Evert told her, "With the trade in on the Plymouth your payments will be $57.29 a month for three years. The best part is you will have forty-five days before you have to make your first payment."

That was all he had to say, and Marian drove away in a new, 1960, powder blue, Mercury convertible, and no payment for forty-five days.

She and Joad went to Sacramento that weekend to show the new car to Janie and Bob. When Bob heard the story about no payment for forty-five days, he gave Marian the nickname, "Forty-five days Grace."

Not long after the trip to Sacramento, Marian began going to bars after work or on days when she didn't work. One such night she had the misfortune of meeting a man named Pete Connor. Pete was not a good man for Marian. He was insanely jealous, and when he drank, their arguments would escalate until he would resort to hitting her. He and Marian had an on and off relationship for the next few years.

Pete owned a fruit and vegetable stand located along highway 99 on the south side of Stockton. He was crude and ill mannered. Joad didn't like him, but she tried to get along for Marian's sake. When Pete and Marian were both sober, they got along okay, but if either of them was drinking, an argument was sure to erupt.

On Marian's birthday, Pete invited a few couples over to Marian's for a surprise bar-b-que party. Everyone was having a good time until the drinking got out of hand. Pete and Marian started yelling at each other and one of the men tried to step in to calm them down. Pete took a swing at him, missing, and hitting Marian in the face. Her nose started to bleed and Joad started screaming for Pete to leave. Sally's mother heard all the yelling and screaming and called the police. When the police arrived, they broke up the party and escorted Pete off the property. Pete was furious and said he would get even. After this, Marian had her telephone changed to an unlisted number and she didn't see Pete for several months.

By early in 1961, Marian no longer had a job as a beautician. Alcohol had finally taken control of her life. She was no longer a "functioning alcoholic," unable to control her shaking hands without a drink, she could no longer cut or style hair. Things had become so bad Joad left home as soon as she graduated from high school and moved to Sacramento not far from Janie and Bob where she took a job with the telephone company.

When Marian was not drinking, she worked for Pete at the fruit stand, and she managed to hold down a part time job at a donut shop about a block from the house.

One night after work Pete and Marian stopped into a local bar and after several drinks, a man sitting next to Marian at the bar began flirting with her. He asked her to dance and she accepted. As they were dancing, Pete was becoming more and more enraged. When Marian returned to the bar and sat down next to Pete, he cursed at her calling her very uncomplimentary names. She responded by telling him not to be so jealous, that she had only danced with the man. An argument ensued and they were asked to leave the bar. Outside they continued to argue and Pete started hitting Marian. She tried to protect herself, but it was no use he was much stronger than she was. The beating continued until someone called the police. The police took Marian to the emergency room for treatment. She had a broken arm and her face was badly bruised and cut. She refused to press charges against Pete. Unable to do anything else the police took her home.

Four months later, Joad received a collect call at work from Marian, "Joad," Marian sobbed into the phone. "Pete has left me and taken my car, and I'm in Gilroy, California, I need you to come get me."

"Where are you?" Joad asked.

"In Gilroy, he pushed me out of the car and took off without me. I don't have any way to get home, and I need you to come get me," Marian sobbed.

"Where is Gilroy?" Joad responded.

"It is near Santa Cruz, and you need to come now," Marian said again.

"Mom I don't have a car. Can't you call Pete and tell him to come back and get you?" Joad asked.

"Just never mind, I thought you would help me!" Marian said angrily and hung up the phone.

What could Joad do, she didn't own a car, and she had no way of getting her mother home. Somehow, Marian would just have to figure it out.

Marian reported her car stolen to the police in Gilroy, and Pete was arrested for car theft. He was tried and sentenced to four years in jail.

The same week of Pete's sentencing Marian received a letter from Marge's husband, Fred. It had taken him over three years. He wanted to call her, but decided that perhaps a letter would be best.

Dear Marian,

It has been some time since we received your last letter and Marge was very happy to hear from you. We were sorry to hear you and Andy were divorced. It was hard for us to believe little Janie is married, and Joad must have graduated from high school by now.

You must be wondering why I'm writing to you and not Marge. About six months before your letter arrived, Marge was diagnosed with breast cancer. She had two surgeries and treatments of chemo following that. She was a real fighter, but in the end, the cancer won and she passed away on February 14, 1960. I'm sorry I haven't written to you sooner, but I kept thinking I would be able to call. I looked for a phone number for you in Stockton, but I was unable to locate one. My hope is you will receive my letter, and you will know Marge always talked about how she wished you were closer. She too said you were her best friend, and she thought you were the strong one.

Truth is you are both strong women! Marge loved you and treasured your friendship. We will miss her.

Sincerely,
Fred

chapter 7

AFTER MARIAN RECEIVED the letter from Fred she went to one of the local bars and proceeded to get drunk. She got in her car and headed home. She just missed hitting another car, swerved, and ended up hitting a tree in the park near her home. She was dazed when the police arrived and they cited her for drunk driving. Amazingly, this was her first offense. She was required to pay a fine, and was on probation for six months.

Fred was right she was a strong woman. Now that Joad is grown, I only have myself to worry about, she thought. I need to try to make something good out of the rest of my life. First, I'll have to do something about the drinking problem. Maybe I should talk to Dr. Branford about this she thought.

She dialed the phone and listened to the ringing, not sure what she was going to say. Just then, Thelma answered, "Good morning, Dr. Branford's office, how may I help you?"

"Hello Thelma, this is Marian, I would like to make an appointment with the doctor."

"Okay Marian, what's the problem?" Thelma replied.

"I... well... it's about ... I think I might have a problem with my drinking and I've been thinking Dr. Branford might be able to help me," Marian said.

"Oh...," just a minute Marian," I'll see when the doctor can see you."

A few moments later, Thelma returned to the phone and said, "Can you come over to the office now? Doctor has had a cancelation and he can see you right away."

"Okay, I will be there in ten minutes," Marian replied.

On the way to the doctor's office Marian started to have second thoughts. When she arrived in the parking lot, she just sat in the car trying to decide if she should go in.

Thelma saw her drive up and she waited to see what Marian would do. After about five minutes, Marian got out of the car and proceeded to go into the office.

Doctor Branford instructed Thelma to cancel the rest of his appointments for the day, to call the treatment center to see if they could admit Marian. He knew he had to act fast as Marian would probably change her mind if given the chance.

When Marian sat down in Dr. Branford's private office she began, "I know I have done some pretty awful things over the years, and I also know most of the time it was when I was drinking. The pills aren't enough to keep me going," Marian began. "I can't hold a job because my hands shake too much to cut hair, or wrap a perm. Pete was not good for me either. I would never have been involved with a man like him if I hadn't been drinking. There will be another change in my life soon, as my mother needs to move back to Stockton. She is getting too old to do maid work anymore. She will be seventy-two in September. I have to take charge of my life, but I don't know where to start, please help me," She said, sobbing now.

"This is the first step Marian, recognizing your addiction to alcohol and pills, and then doing something about it. I would like you to go into a treatment center. Do you think you can do that?" Doctor Branford counseled.

"ADDICTION! Oh I don't think I'm that bad that I need to go into a treatment center doctor. Can't you just give me something so I can work this out myself?" Marian asked.

"All right then Marian, let's talk about what addiction is. I'm going to ask you some questions about how you live your life. I want you to answer them as truthfully as you can. Will you do that for me?" Doctor Branford said.

Marian didn't say anything, she just nodded.

"Have you lost a job because you were unable to go to work?"

Marian nodded, Yes.

"Have you spent money in an irresponsible way?"

"Yes."

"Have you had increasing arguments with the people you love?"

"Yes."

"Have you lost friendships or found people don't have time for you anymore?"

"Yes."

"Have you had an arrest for drunk driving?"

"Yes".

"Do you feel anxious or depressed?"

"Yes."

"Do you depend on alcohol or pills, and find you have an increased need for them?"

"Yes."

"Answering yes to most or all of these questions, is telling you that you have an addiction problem. If you are serious about getting help, you're the one who must make the decision for treatment. I can tell you if you continue to ignore your problem it will lead to jail or worse... death. There is an opening at the treatment center, and they can take you today. Thelma and I will take you home first to get a few things and then I can admit you. You will need to stay for a month to six weeks depending on how you are doing," the doctor said.

"Right now today! " Marian exclaimed. "I have things I have to take care of first."

"All you have to take care of Marian is yourself. You need to do this now, or I can't help you anymore. Thelma and I will take care of anything that has to be done," doctor Branford said.

With that, he got up, took Marian by the hand, and walked to his car. Thelma followed in Marian's car and they went back to Marian's house. After getting a few things, she agreed to be admitted to the treatment center just outside of Stockton. Doctor Branford and Thelma notified Janie, Joad and Marian's mother about where Marian would be for the next month or so.

The first days at the treatment center were very tough. The withdrawal from alcohol and pills was very rough on a Marian.

Later she said, "If I had known how bad this would be I probably would not have gone into treatment. First, the shaking hands. If I just had a drink that would stop, but then I felt sick to my stomach. The sweat was just pouring off me," she said. "I was hot, then I was cold, freezing, shivering, still the water poured from my body. The second day my heart was pounding against my chest and the panic started. The sweating, vomiting, and the trembling continued. That same night, I could see black spiders crawling up the walls and what seemed like flashes of light in my eyeballs. It felt like bugs were crawling all over my skin and I was delirious. I had lost all sense of time and I was sure I was going to die." Marian recounted.

Following the detoxifying process, she had three or four days of rest, good food, and exercise. She was weak but she was feeling better than she had in a long time. Then she began the real work of how to deal with her psychological needs, physical needs, and how to live free from addiction and regain her life. Forty-five days later, clean and sober for the first time in many years Marian was ready to begin a new life.

Janie, Bob, Joad, and Lillian were there to pick her up. She really looked great and laughing she said, "Well Bob, now you can really call me forty-five day Grace."

While Marian was in treatment, Dr. Branford had arranged for Marian to attend a 'high styling' school in San Francisco. Lillian had moved back into the front house and she had rented the house in the back to a nice older couple.

This school was designed to advance the skills of the most accomplished beauticians. There she would learn all the latest techniques in color and style. The classes were three weeks long. Charles the owner of the school would oversee the classes personally evaluating each student. Charles didn't believe in competition. He had found creativity was stifled by competition. When students encouraged one another, everyone did better.

At the end of the three weeks, there was a formal graduation ceremony with a sit down dinner. It was a fabulous night to remember and Marian had done very well all through the program never having a drink. In fact, she was so busy and thrilled to be a part of this program she never even thought about drinking. She did attend her AA classes while in San Francisco and continued to practice all she learned in treatment. There was plenty of alcohol served at the dinner, but Marian drank only club soda with a lime. She felt good about herself again. She had made more friends and Charles was impressed with her talent.

When Charles took the stage, the room quieted and he began, "I want to thank all of you for the dedication each of you have shown to this program and to the beauty profession. Each of you is a special person with your own unique talents. You are the ones who will carry the knowledge of what you have learned here into the everyday world. It doesn't matter whether your skills are used in a professional salon, or on a movie set, you will be the best in your profession, because of the dedication you have shown here. Please, all of you stand and take a bow." Applause, bows and laughter emanated throughout the room. "Now, "Charles continued, "without further ado, I have a surprise for all of you!" Lana Turner joined Charles on stage and applause burst out again." I think you all recognize our special guest, Miss Lana Turner! Lana is here to help me present a special gift to someone in the room whom I'm sure you will all agree has shown exceptional skill during this class. This person also has shown the ability to share her knowledge with each of you, as well as being able to learn new techniques that many of you brought to our class. Lana, would you please introduce our student."

"I would be delighted Charles, she said, Marian Roberson would you please join us on stage!"

Marian was dumbfounded, she just sat in her chair unable to move. The others in the class started clapping and cheering, "Marian. Marian." She finally got up from her chair and started to walk toward the stage with all of the other students congratulating her as she went. When she reached the stage, Charles took her hand and stood by her as Lana announced, "Marian it is my pleasure to tell you that you have been chosen for a position as a beautician with MGM studios in Hollywood, California!"

The room went wild with cheers and applause, and shouts of, "speech, speech." Marian couldn't believe this was happening, and as the room quieted, with shaking hands, this time not from drinking, she began to speak.

"I don't know what to say...Charles, I have learned so much here...and all of you, my friends, you have helped me so much...some of you know it has been some time since I have practiced cosmetology. Each of you has helped me to learn all of the new techniques, and you have been so patient...Thank you. Miss Turner, you have always been my idol. I never in my wildest dreams thought I would ever meet you in person!" Marian said, trying to hold back all of the emotion she was feeling.

"Well, Marian not only have you met me, but you will be my personal hair dresser for the first two months. Then you will join me on the set at MGM Studios," Lana said. Again, the room went wild with cheers and applause.

After the graduation ceremony ended, Charles invited Marian, to join him and Lana at his estate in San Francisco. There they talked about what was ahead and what arrangements had been made for Marian to start her new position. Charles knew all about Marian's struggles with alcoholism. He spoke frankly about the challenges she would face being part of the Hollywood scene. Lana, who herself had her share of difficulties, mainly with relationships, assured Marian there would be help should she need it. That was the reason for the first two months as her personal beautician.

"We can't throw you to the wolves without some defensive training," Charles said chuckling.

When she arrived in Hollywood Marian rented a small apartment where other people who worked on the movies stayed.

The first couple of weeks in were busy and exciting for Marian. She attended parties with the stars, and she was taken behind the scenes at the movie studios. Lana's mother also gave Marian lots of advice. She was a beautician herself for many years and supported herself and Lana by working eighty hours a week. Marian connected with AA where she had a new sponsor who helped her keep away from alcohol.

Her first official day was on the set of *Bachelor in Paradise*. During a break from shooting, Marian got a chance to meet Bob Hope, who starred in the film.

"I have to pinch myself all the time to make sure I'm not dreaming," Marian would tell people. "I'm so lucky to have had so many people who cared about me and never gave up on me, even when I had given up on myself."

Marian's days were long, and busy. The hair styling was demanding and challenging. It was exactly what she needed now. The movie was hilarious and upbeat, also good for Marian's wellbeing. After work she and some of the other beauticians would go out for dinner or go to watch filming on some of the other sets. All in all her first six months there were fabulous to say the least.

Then one afternoon Lana's mother introduced Marian to a man on the set. Marian found him to be very interesting, and a bit mysterious, but she didn't know why.

Joc Fournier was an extra. He was handsome, had a beautiful smile, and dressed impeccably. No one knew much about him.

Marian's outstanding good looks immediately made him take notice. After talking with her, he realized she was not only beautiful she was smart, and had a great sense of humor.

Much to her delight, he pursued her relentlessly with flowers, and dinners out in some of the finest restaurants in Hollywood.

This was the first man she had dated since seeing Pete, who much to her relief was serving time in prison. Pete and Joc had nothing in common. Pete was violent, jealous, and without class. Joc was kind, self-confident, and a gentleman to his very core. This was a completely new experience. Marian was still unsure of herself in her new life, so she took it slow, which only made Joc more attracted to her. Usually women threw themselves at him. Here was a woman who didn't seem that interested in him. The more time Joc spent with Marian the more he appreciated her. Here was a woman who seemed to have it all. For the first time in his life, he was experiencing genuine feelings of caring for a woman.

One Friday, he stopped by the set to see if she was available for lunch. They were finished shooting so Marian was free, and gladly accepted his invitation. He wanted to know more about her. When he brought up the subject of her past, Marian would just laugh and say, "It was interesting to say the least. The past doesn't matter much. I mostly concern myself with today, just taking one day at a time. What about you?" she said smiling at Joc.

Realizing Marian was not going to indulge his curiosity, Joc moved on to the more immediate. "Speaking of today," he said. "I thought we might go to San Diego for the weekend, if you don't have other plans, of course. I have a quiet little place not far from the ocean. We can relax away from the hustle and bustle of Hollywood for a change. What do you think?"

"Oh that sounds wonderful Joc. I would love to get away for a couple of days. I don't have to be back on the set until Tuesday morning," Marian said excitedly.

"Okay, then it's settled. I'll pick you up around two o'clock. We can drive down, and get there in time for a quiet dinner," Joc said confidently.

The ride to San Diego took them about three hours and as they drove they talked, laughed, and stopped along the way to look at the ocean.

The little place Joc said he had was not so little. It was three stories, with lots of very large windows facing the ocean, and not far from the ocean meant it was really on the beach. There was a huge stone fireplace on one wall of the great room, with big over stuffed sofas facing it. A very large kitchen and dining room were also on the first floor, and an office that was masculine, but warm. The second floor had three large guest rooms and a library in the center that looked down on the huge room below. Joc opened the door to one of the guest rooms and said to Marian, "Will this room be alright for you?"

Marian smiled and said, "I think this will do nicely, thank you."

The top floor was a master suite with windows facing the ocean view. "This is my room," Joc said. "But I rarely make it up here. I usually fall asleep on the sofa in front of the fireplace."

Marian laughed and said, "I can see why."

An elevator was available from the underground garage to service all floors. The house's décor was very masculine, but very tastefully done. There was lots of stone and natural wood throughout. The house reminded Marian of her house at Tahoe, only much larger and far more elaborate. It had been a long time since Marian had been in a home like this. She was comfortable with wealth, and it didn't intimidate her, nor was she unduly impressed by it.

Joc stopped the elevator on the second floor. "Marian would you like to freshen-up while I get the house opened up for the weekend?" Joc said.

"Thank you Joc that will be fine. I won't be too long," Marian said.

They had a quiet dinner in a small restaurant next to the ocean. After dinner, Joc suggested they walk back to the house along the beach. It was a beautiful warm night, and the moon was just a slit of silver in the clear sky filled with a million stars. Marian had taken off her sandals and was carrying them in one hand. Joc took Marian's other hand in his as they walked along the shore. The water steadily lapped against the sand. They were both quiet as they walked. Each of them secretly hoping they were meant to be together.

It had been a long time since Marian felt so happy, in fact, she was not sure she had ever had a day like this. Who was this man, an extra? Not likely. Why was he pursuing her, after all, there were many beautiful and talented women in Hollywood? She was a beautician, a recovering alcoholic, what did he see in her, she thought to herself.

As they reached the house, Joc looked into her beautiful brown eyes, and said, "Marian, you are everything I have ever dreamed of in a woman. I want to make you happy, and I don't want to do anything you don't want to do." Then he kissed her gently on the lips.

Marian kissed him back, not saying a word, but she was trembling a bit.

"Oh you're chilly," Joc said. "Let's go inside, I'll light the fire and we'll get you warmed up."

As they moved inside Joc led Marian to one of the big sofas nearest the fireplace and gave her a soft afghan to put on her. He lit the fire, and headed to the kitchen and was gone for a few minutes. Marian just sat cuddled up in the afghan, staring into the fire, watching the flames dance up and down between the logs.

Joc returned with two big mugs filled with steaming hot tea. "Do you take anything in your tea?" He asked.

"No, just tea will be fine, thank you. Joc. "Marian replied.

There were a few minutes of silence as Marian sipped her tea and then she said, "I feel I need to tell you about myself, but I don't want to ruin this beautiful night or our weekend."

"Well, then let me start. I know you are a recovering alcoholic, and you have been married and divorced. You have two grown daughters, the older of the two has a daughter also, I believe. You lived with your mother in Stockton that is before earning the position at the studio. How am I doing so far?"

Marian was shocked, "How do you know so much about me?"

"Lana's mother is a dear friend of my family, and if you remember she introduced us the day we met on the set.

That was not a chance meeting by the way. She has never approved of anyone I ever dated. She said it was about time I met a woman of substance, and I better not mess it up."

Joc took the mug of tea from Marian's hands and put it on the coffee table in front of them. Then he placed both of his hands on her cheeks and said, "She was right." Kissing her gently on the forehead, he said, "Now what do you want to know about me?"

Marian laughed and said, "Maybe I better just ask Lana's mother."

Relieved she no longer needed to wonder about Joc's motives, she relaxed. She told him about Janie and Joad, and Janie's little girl Kate. He told her about his younger brother Wes, and his family, and his sister, Marilyn, who had lost her husband in the war and never remarried. Both of his parents had passed away leaving a small fortune to each of the children. He had plenty of money, if he didn't get work it really didn't matter. He worked as an extra because he loved the movies and he loved the excitement of the business. Most important to him was he felt somewhat productive by having work to do.

They talked and laughed until the wee hours in the morning. Marian fell asleep in his arms on the big sofa. Joc carried her to her room, kissed her goodnight, and went up to his room on the top floor.

When Marian awoke in the morning, she dressed and went downstairs. She could smell coffee and headed to the big kitchen.

"Good morning sleepy head!" Joc teased. "I made coffee would you like some?"

"I most definitely would, what time is it? I didn't see a clock anywhere," Marian said.

"They're not allowed in this house, that's the rule, no clocks we just do what we want when we want," Joc said.

"I could see where a person could get use to that kind of a schedule," Marian smiled.

"I know this little place that serves the very best breakfast you can imagine. Are you hungry?' Joc asked.

"I'm starved," she said.

"Okay, we'll have to walk because we left the car at the restaurant when we decided to walk home along the beach," Joc said.

After breakfast, Joc took Marian on a tour of San Diego, showing her some of his favorite spots before returning to the beach house.

"Would you like to go for a swim?" Joc asked.

"I'm not much of a swimmer, but I'm a great sun bather," Marian replied.

"Okay Miss Sunbather, you can do the sunning and I'll do the swimming. How does that sound?" Joc quipped.

"You're on, Marian said excitedly. I saw a book in your library I thought I might enjoy. Do you mind if I take it on the beach?"

"You may take anything you want. I'll get some things and meet you on the deck in about ten minutes," Joc said smiling.

Marian got the book, put on some shorts and a halter-top and headed for the deck. Joc was waiting with a blanket and a towel in one hand and a picnic basket in the other.

"I thought we might need a little snack. Reading and swimming can make a person real hungry," Joc teased.

Marian laughed and said, "I'll race you to..." and she took off running toward the ocean.

Joc raced after her making sure he didn't catch her. When she stopped, she said breathlessly, "You let me win, didn't you?"

"No I was just admiring the view." As he spread out the blanket, and put down the picnic basket he said, "Should I go to the house and get you a back rest?"

"Oh no, you don't need to do that. I read a lot lying down, "Marian said.

"Well I'm going in for a swim and I may be a while, I swim here a lot when I get the chance." As Joc headed to the water, he turned back and said, "Don't eat without me."

Marian smiled, waved to him, and picked up her book. It took her a few minutes to start to read because she was thinking about what a wonderful time she was having and how perfect Joc seemed to be. Maybe too perfect, she thought to herself.

chapter 8

WHEN JOC RETURNED he dried himself and lay down beside her on the blanket.

"You didn't get very far on your book," Joc said.

"Oh the sun is so warm and I was listening to the waves on the shore. I guess I fell asleep," Marian said sleepily.

He touched her face gently and kissed her. Marian responded by kissing him more deeply. He ran his fingers through her hair, and gently pulled her body next to his. Kissing her more passionately now, he could feel her body responding to his as they were wrapped in each other's arms.

"Oh Marian, I want you," Joc whispered in her ear.

"And I want you, but it has been so long since..."

"It's okay, we can take our time. This probably isn't the best place. I think we might want a little more privacy," Joc whispered.

"We haven't even tasted our picnic," Marian said with a smile.

"We can have our picnic later," Joc smiled, helping Marian up from the blanket and still holding her tightly.

They kissed playfully on the way to the house, laughing as they went. When they reached the house Joc became more serious and said, "Are you alright with this? I don't want to rush you."

Marian just nodded and smiled at him. Joc picked her up and carried her to the elevator, pressed the button for the third floor, and gently laid her on his bed.

"I should wash this salt water off of me. I'll just be a few minutes." Kissing her again he said, "ummmm... you taste so good."

When Marian heard the water in the shower running she took off her clothes, and as she slipped between the sheets in Joc's bed, her only thoughts were how much she wanted to be loved, really loved.

They made love several times, each time he was so tender, making sure all of her needs were met. She had never had a man treat her with such care.

The next morning Marian awoke to Joc sitting on the bed next to her with a hot cup of coffee. He was just smiling at her, and he said, "Who was that woman in my bed last night? She is perfect in every way."

"Oh I think it was the man who was the perfect one. Is that coffee for me?" Marian asked. "It smells wonderful."

"It is, and when you get dressed, come on down I have breakfast ready for you. You must be starved we never did have our picnic," Joc laughed.

"I am starved! I could eat a horse," Marian teased.

"Come on and get dressed before I'm tempted to get back into bed with you and start all over," Joc said as he kissed her on the forehead.

Joc left, and Marian returned to her room, showered, dressed, and headed down stairs to the kitchen. Joc had set a table on the deck complete with fresh flowers, coffee, fruit, and toast.

"I didn't know what you wanted so I made everything, bacon, sausage, eggs, and hash browns. I'm really a pretty good cook," Joc said.

"In that case I'll have it all, remember I'm starved!" Marian laughed.

After breakfast, they did the dishes together, and then went for a drive along the ocean, stopping now and then to admire the views. It was a beautiful day and Marian wished it would never end.

When they returned to the beach house, they spent the evening in front of the big fireplace, laughing and talking. Then they returned to Joc's bed, making love repeatedly. They showered together, then raced to the kitchen and raided the refrigerator, after which they both fell asleep on the big sofa in front of the fire.

Monday, in the late afternoon they started to drive back to Hollywood. In the weeks that followed, Marian spent every spare minute with Joc. *Bachelor in Paradise* was nearly through shooting, and both their assignments would be ending soon. Marian had earned the respect of MGM's management in her position as a support beautician, and they assured her of continuing work if she wanted to stay. She had some big decisions to make. She loved her job and wanted to continue, but her mother was in her late seventies and living alone in the house in Stockton. Janie's family and Joad all lived in Sacramento, and she did miss them very much. She knew she had fallen deeply in love with Joc, and she knew he cared for her, but could it last, she thought to herself. She would have to talk to Joc about all of this. She knew he would be staying on still looking for work as an extra. He had told her several times he didn't need the work, he just loved being a part of movies. She knew how he felt because she loved the movie business too.

"Would you like to go to the beach house after the shooting is over on Friday?" Joc asked. "We have a lot to talk about, and probably some decisions to make. That's always a good place to think and put things into perspective."

"Could we Joc?" Marian responded. "We do need to talk. I have so much to think about now that the movie is finished."

On the ride down to the beach house in San Diego, Joc explained how the movie industry worked. The transition from movie to movie, the different ways they staffed for them, and how it affected the different groups of people involved.

"Some extras have hired agents. As I have," Joc explained. "Abe Burton, is my agents name. It is his job to find work for me on another picture. Your contract with the studio is complete with this picture, but if you want to work on the next film at MGM you can sign a new contract. You also have the option of floating. Television needs cosmetologists too, so MGM can loan you to other studios if you would like. You might like that option, as your time is more your own, but the pay isn't as steady. In any case you have a couple of weeks before you'll have to make a decision."

"That is good." Marian replied. "Because I miss seeing my family and I might like to go for a visit. I'm not sure what I want to do next. I just know I want to spend more time with you."

"And I want to spend a lot more time with you," Joc said as he smiled.

They pulled into the garage at the beach house, and Joc took their luggage into the house, and began the routine of opening up the house for their stay. Marian walked out on the deck looking out at the big rolling waves hitting the shore. She was so deep in her thoughts she didn't notice Joc behind her.

"You look like the weight of the world is on your shoulders," Joc said as he placed his arms around her waist.

As Marian turned toward Joc he could see her eyes filling up as she said, "It's just there is so much to think about, I have to make a lot of decisions. I'm not sure where to begin. I have been so happy these last months since we met, and I don't want it to end."

"Who said anything about ending? We are only beginning. You don't think I'm going to let you go now, do you?" Joc said as he kissed her gently on the lips. "Now come on inside. I have a nice fire going and a cup of my famous tea."

As they sat by the fire watching the flames dance between the logs, Joc said, "We are going to spend some time down here and give you a chance to work out all the decisions about what you want to do next. Anyway, what happened to the girl that told me she only concerned herself with today?"

Marian laughed and said, "You are right, one day at a time."

After a couple of hours of talking, laughing, and reminiscing Joc said, "I put your things in my room. Is that okay? I love reaching over in the night and feeling you next to me."

Marian just smiled and nodded approvingly. That night was wonderful, they made love, talked, and laughed, and made love again. They just couldn't seem to get enough of one another.

The next morning they had a light breakfast out on the deck , and then Joc said, "I was wondering if next week you would like to invite your family to stay with us for a few days, or do you think it's too soon for that? I know you would like to see all of them."

"I would love it, but I don't know if they could all come on such short notice," Marian replied.

"Well, what if you go visit them?" Joc said.

"Alone? Will you go with me?" Marian said.

"I thought you would never ask!" Joc said jokingly. "We can fly to Sacramento, and rent a car to visit your mother in Stockton. We'll make all the arrangements after you decide when you want to go. I have some other business to do today, so I thought you might like to do a little shopping while I take care of business."

"That sounds like fun. I would love to snoop around down town. When we were here last time, I saw some shops I wanted to explore," Marian said excitedly.

Marian had a wonderful time going into all the little shops, talking to people as she went. Joc took care of the business he had planned to do, and they went back to the beach house. They were sitting in their favorite spot, the big sofa in front of the fireplace, with cups of tea when Marian said, "I had such a good time today Joc, I met the lady who owns a little dress shop just off the main street. Her name is Maria. It turns out she makes most of the clothes she sells. She just makes things that inspire her, and they are all one of a kind. They aren't very expensive either. She got into it when her daughters were little girls. She made all of their clothing, and then friends started asking her to make things for them. It just expanded over the years into this little retail shop. Isn't that interesting?" Marian said." You know when I had my first beauty shop at Tahoe that's how it evolved. When I first began, I only had one or two regulars, but as the years went on it grew and grew. People would refer their friends, and eventually they would be regular customers too. Some of the women became very dear friends. I really enjoyed it when I just had the one shop. Then it became a lot of work when I had both the shop in Bijou, and the one at Camp Richardson. I enjoy working on the movie set, but there is a lot of pressure to get everything done fast. It doesn't allow for as much creativity, and of course, the style must fit the movie. It's fun, but it does become routine. I don't have any time to become friends with co-workers. Do you know what I mean?" Marian asked.

"I think I do. It sounds like you miss having a closer relationship with your customers, and the time to create just the right style for each person. Even though you like your current position, it's just a job. Is that what you are feeling?" Joc asked.

Contemplating it a bit, Marian said, "Yes, I guess it is."

"Well maybe that could be one of your options, opening up your own salon again?" Joc said.

Marian sat quietly for a bit and then said, "Yes, I should give that some thought. There would be the question of where there is a need, and where do I want to live and of course all the financial concerns. It's an interesting thing to think about. What about you? Did you get your business taken care of, and how did your day go?"

"Mine was interesting too. I did a little shopping myself," Joc said, smiling.

"Oh, what did you get?" Marian said excitedly.

"That's a secret, and no, I'm not going to share just yet," Joc teased. "Are you hungry? I made reservations at that little place where we had our first dinner down here. The night we walked home on the beach, remember?"

"Of course I remember, I have thought of that night so often. I was so unsure of myself, and you put me completely at ease. You know I always feel so relaxed and happy when we're together. You have a calming effect on me, and that's just one of the reasons I love you so much!" Marian said, as she leaned over to kiss him.

"I love you too Marian, I have never been so happy, I can hardly wait to be with you. I hate it when we are apart," Joc said as he kissed her again. "Now go get ready. Our reservation is in forty-five minutes."

When they arrived at the little restaurant, Joc had arranged for a table off by itself looking out at the ocean. They continued to laugh and tease each other, and neither of them ate much dinner.

When they returned to the beach house, Joc suggested they take a blanket down to the beach and watch the sunset over the ocean.

As they sat watching the waves, Joc turned to Marian, and gently kissed her forehead, then touched her nose with his finger and said, "Marian, I love you more than you will ever know, and I don't want to live without you. I'm sure you feel the same way about me. It will make me the happiest man in the world if you will marry me?"

Marian was both thrilled and terrified at what she was hearing. Of course, she loved Joc, and she was sure he loved her, but she was an alcoholic.

"Joc, are you sure about this? You know my history. Doesn't that concern you?"

"No, It doesn't," Joc stated emphatically." We've been together now for almost a year. You attend your AA meetings religiously, you've had many opportunities to drink. You have handled a job that carries a lot of stress, and you never turn to alcohol. So no, I'm not concerned."

"Joc, I'm so honored you would ask me to marry you, I would be a fool to say no," Marian said tearfully.

"I hope that means yes," Joc said, as he wiped the tears from her face.

"Oh yes, yes," she said, laughing a bit.

Then he pulled the small box from his jacket lying next to them on the blanket showing her a beautiful diamond engagement ring. "I hope you like it," he said. "This is what I went shopping for today, as he placed the ring on her finger."

"It's so beautiful," Marian said.

He took her in his arms and kissed her deeply. Then he picked her up in the blanket and carried her to the house.

They cuddled up in their favorite spot on the sofa in front of the fire, drinking their tea, and making plans for their visit to Sacramento and Stockton. They would need to set a date for the wedding because everyone would be asking. They discussed the option of living in San Diego vs. Hollywood, or maybe somewhere else. They didn't make any decisions that night. They just agreed to take first things first. The first order of business was calling the girls and Marian's mother to arrange a time to visit.

chapter 9

MARIAN CALLED THE studio and they assured her that her job would be waiting when she returned from Northern California. Joc let his agent know he would not be available for a couple of weeks.

They decided to drive to Sacramento. That would give them plenty of time to make plans, and it would be easier to drive to Stockton to see Lillian.

The next morning Joc said, "All packed?"

"All packed, but I'm excited but nervous, isn't that crazy? These are my children and mother, not strangers," Marian said.

"It will be fine. I can't wait to meet all of them. I've always wanted my own family, and now I will have the one. I don't know if you noticed, but I'm pretty good with women," Joc chuckled.

On the trip to Sacramento, they decided they would set the marriage date for six months out. That would give everyone time to get to know each other, and more importantly, time for Joc and Marian to decide where they would want to make their home. They decided it was a good idea for them both to return to work in Hollywood, at least for the short term. This trip would be strictly a vacation, which they both needed. The short time at the beach house was wonderful, and they were looking forward to more time together alone after the trip.

"Let's leave all our options open," Joc said. "We can take our time about long-range plans. You know my agent told me we don't even have to be in Hollywood for our kind of work. Some of the studios are glad to have people they can trust to travel on location for them. Many of their people are unwilling to do that."

"Really," Marian said, a bit surprised.

"That's what he said. So you see, the world is open to us," Joc said.

When they arrived in Sacramento, they checked into a hotel and called Janie and Bob, and Joad to see if they could meet for dinner. Janie suggested they have dinner at their house instead. It was still hard for Janie to believe Marian was no longer drinking, and she knew nothing about Joc. This way if there were a scene, at least it wouldn't be in public. Marian and Joc were thrilled at being invited, and this way they could see Kate too.

As Marian dressed, Joc could see the stress she was feeling and he came up behind her as she was applying the last of her make-up. "Remember sweetheart, one day at a time," Joc smiled.

Marian turned and put her arms around Joc and said, "I'll be fine because you're with me."

When they arrived at Janie and Bob's, the girls were delighted to see how good Marian looked, and Joc was so handsome.

"Joc these are my daughters, Janie and Joad, and Janie's husband Bob. Of course this is little Kate," Marian said proudly.

"Your mother talks about all of you often, I feel as though I already know you. I'm pleased to finally meet you," Joc said.

"Oh please, come in the living room and we can all talk, it will be about fifteen minutes before dinner is ready," Janie said.

"So Joc, what do you do in Hollywood?" Bob inquired.

"I'm an extra. You know, one of the people who don't have a speaking part in a movie," Joc said.

"Really, I never thought about it but I guess there are a lot of people in the movies who don't have speaking parts. Is that how you and Marian met?" Bob asked.

"Yes, we were introduced when we were both working on the set of *Bachelor in Paradise*. Lana's mother introduced us," Joc said.

"Lana?" Janie said quizzically.

"Yes, Janie. Lana Turner is who I was working for the first couple of months," Marian chuckled.

"Mom really, you really know Lana Turner!" Joad screeched.

During dinner, Marian and Joc told them about their jobs in Hollywood, their engagement, and their plans to get married in September.

"We hope we can all be together for the wedding. Do you think it is possible?" Joc inquired.

"Of course," they all said.

Then Joad asked, "Where are you planning to have the wedding?"

"We haven't decided on a place yet. We're going back to work after this little vacation and then we will work it all out in the next month or so," Marian said.

"We're going to Stockton to see mother tomorrow and we thought it might be nice if all of us went. That's, if you don't have other plans," Marian said.

"Bob what do you think? I can go with Kate if you don't want to drive down there," Janie said.

"No, I don't have any reason not to go, what time do you plan on leaving, Joc?" Bob said.

"Why don't you meet us at the hotel for breakfast? My treat of course, would nine o'clock work for you?" Joc said.

"Free breakfast always interests me," Bob said." Joad, we can pick you up on our way to the hotel and you can ride with us, or Joc and your mom if you would like."

They all visited a while longer and then before calling it a night Marian called her mother to let her know they were coming the next day.

Janie, Bob and Kate were the first to arrive, because Joad and Marian wanted to stop and buy some flowers for Lillian. That gave Janie a chance to tell Lillian how good Marian looked, and about the engagement. Lillian was not surprised because Dr. Branford had been giving her updates over the last few months. The engagement was a surprise because no one knew Joc and Marian had become that serious.

When they arrived, Marian introduced Joc to Lillian right away and of course, he was charming as always. Lillian loved him.

Marian was so happy to be with her family, and they were thrilled to see her healthy and sober for the first time in many years. Everyone laughed and had a wonderful time. Lillian had fixed a picnic lunch and they went to the park where Kate could play in the wading pool with other children her age. As the day was ending, Marian told the family she would be returning to Hollywood for a time until she and Joc could decide where they were going to live and work. Joc told them about the beach house in San Diego and invited all of them to come for a visit whenever they could make it.

They all said their goodbyes. Janie, Bob, Kate, and Joad headed back to Sacramento in Bob's car. Joc and Marian stayed a while longer with Lillian, and then they headed back to Hollywood. They drove a couple of hours until it was getting late. Joc stopped at a hotel in Fresno where they had dinner and planned to stay the night.

While they had dinner, they continued to talk and laugh about the last couple of days. They were totally enthralled with each other, and oblivious to everyone around them. They didn't notice the angry man leering at them from the bar.

chapter 10

THEY FINISHED DINNER and went to their room, still laughing. They were so much in love.

"Joc thank you so much for taking me to see the kids and mother. I was a little concerned because...well...you know all that took place before I went into treatment. I was especially worried about how Joad would react. She was with me during the worst of my addiction, and she just shut me off. She had to I guess. I was afraid I could never get her back. Having you with me made it easier for all of us...don't you think?"

"It's going to be fine now sweetheart, the first time back together is the most stressful. I like all of them. I think they actually liked me too," Joc said, with a smile."

Marian yawned and said, "It's been a long day, I guess we better get some sleep," Joc agreed and they climbed into bed. Marian fell asleep almost instantly.

About two in the morning the phone rang, a groggy Joc said, "Hello, who is this?"

The man's voice on the other end said, "You're both dead"... and then dial tone.

Joc was instantly awake...who would say such a thing, he thought.

Marian now starting to wake said, "Joc, who was that?"

Not wanting to worry Marian, Joc replied, "Someone calling the wrong room sweetheart, now go back to sleep, we have a long drive tomorrow."

As they drove Marian talked about their upcoming visit to meet Joc's sister and her children in Santa Barbara, and how she hoped his family would like her.

Joc, pre-occupied with the telephone call from last night, was half listening. He was thinking was it a wrong number, who would say such a thing?

"Joc," Marian said. "Am I talking too much?"

"Oh no sweetheart, actually I was just day dreaming. My sister is going to love you, so stop your fretting because our families have a lot in common, you'll see."

They continued to talk a while longer until Marian fell asleep. About twenty minutes later Joc noticed a car seemed to be following them. I'm probably just imagining it he thought to himself.

"Hey sleepyhead," he said, gently touching Marian's arm to wake her.

"Oh I must have dozed off," she said.

"I thought we might stop for gas and maybe a little lunch. There's probably a place not far ahead. Are you hungry?" Joc said.

"I could eat. How far are we from Hollywood?" Marian asked.

"We have a good three hours," Joc replied.

Marian pulled her mirror out of her purse and touched up her make-up in preparation for their stop for lunch.

"You look beautiful as usual," Joc told her.

A short while later Joc pulled into the gas pumps and had the attendant fill the car up with gas, wash the windows, and check the oil. He pulled away from the pumps and parked at the little restaurant where they went in to have lunch. There was no sign of the car Joc thought was following them, so he relaxed a bit. I've just been around the movies too long he thought.

After they were seated and the waitress brought the menus, Marian said, "This club sandwich sounds good. Would you like to split it with me?"

"Sure, that way I can have a milk shake and not feel guilty," Joc laughed.

After lunch, they walked out the door toward their car. Joc noticed the car he thought had been following them. The man behind the wheel appeared to be watching them. He was sure this was not a coincidence. Someone was following them. Did this have anything to do with the phone call last night? He thought to himself.

When they arrived at Marian's apartment in Hollywood, she opened the door and said, "It's good to be home. I loved seeing the girls, and mother but it was a long trip. I would like to freshen-up a bit, do you mind? I'll just be a few minutes," Marian said.

"No, take your time sweetheart. I just remembered I promised to call my friend Ron Bailey. He's a detective with the Hollywood police department. I can do that while you freshen-up, and then we can do whatever you want," Joc said.

"Okay, but don't be too long, I have plans for you tonight," She said, kissing him as she headed for the shower.

"I won't, and what kind of plans?" Joc winked, teasing her a bit.

Joc waited until he heard the water running in the bathroom, then he picked up the phone and called his friend Detective Ron Bailey. He told Ron about the phone call, the car following them, and that he had no idea who it might be.

"Doesn't sound good," Bailey said. "I know you well enough that you don't overreact. Could it be some crazy fan from the movie set?"

"Maybe," Joc said.

"Let me check it out for you. I'll get back to you, where will you be?" Detective Bailey asked.

"You can reach me at this number. I better stay with Marian, should I tell her about this?" Joc asked.

"I think you better. She could be in danger, if this guy is after her. You probably don't need to tell her about the phone call just yet. No use in having everyone scared stiff. It may be nothing," Detective Bailey said.

Joc gave Detective Bailey the details on the car, make, model, color, and as much of the license plate as he could remember. He could only give a vague description of the man himself, bald and dark eyes.

When Marian came out of the bathroom, now at home, and feeling relaxed, she put on her favorite lounging pajamas and joined Joc in the little living room of her apartment.

"Sweetheart, we need to talk about something," Joc said seriously.

"Okay"... Marian replied with hesitation.

Joc told her about the man in the car following them from Fresno. He left out the part about the phone call, as Detective Bailey suggested.

"Do you know anyone who would want to harm you or us?" Joc said.

"No... why would anyone... want...Oh no!" Marian suddenly exclaimed, "Maybe it's Pete."

"Who is Pete?" Joc asked with surprise.

Marian began to cry. "Pete was a man who I had an on and off relationship with for a couple of years when I was drinking. That was before I went into treatment. In fact, he was part of the reason I finally accepted I had a problem. He beat me, left me in Gilroy, and took my car. When I finally got home I reported him for stealing my car, and he was arrested, tried, convicted, and sentenced to four years in prison. He must have gotten out by now. Oh Joc, I'm so sorry, he is a very violent man and he is insanely jealous. He probably wants to get even with me for putting him in jail. We need to call the police!"

"Okay sweetheart, I'll call Ron back and give him this information, and if it is the guy, it will help Ron run him down. Now what is his full name and what does he look like?" Joc asked.

"His full name is Peter J. Connor, and he lived in Stockton, before he went to prison. He was about five feet-ten inches tall, and weighed about one hundred-ninety pounds. He was muscular, and he had a tattoo on his left shoulder of a dragon that ran down his arm to his wrist. I hated that tattoo. He was bald, with dark, black, piercing eyes. His teeth were straight, but yellowed from smoking, and he wore jeans and T-shirts most of the time. He owned a roadside fruit and vegetable stand. He had family in the Fresno area. Do you think that's where he saw me? I don't know how he could have seen us," Marian said worriedly.

"We only stayed at the hotel the one night, and we ate dinner right there. It doesn't sound like that's the kind of hotel he would frequent," Joc replied.

Joc called Detective Bailey and gave him the information on Pete.

"Thanks Joc, maybe you two should go down to the beach house for a few days and wait this out until we can pick him up for questioning. If it hasn't been long since his release from prison, he may have some parole requirements. On the other hand, if he had been a model prisoner, then he will have paid his debt to society and no restrictions will be applicable. Be careful until we find out more. Do you still have that .45 I gave you a few years ago?" Detective Bailey inquired.

"I keep it at the beach house, but do you think this is that serious?" Joc said.

"Don't know, but better hope for the best and plan for the worst. Don't you think?" Detective Bailey replied.

When Joc hung up the phone, he repeated to Marian what Detective Bailey had said.

"We can go to San Diego for a few days until Ron has a chance to see what we're up against. We couldn't be in a better place for this because many of the movie stars have this kind of problem. Many of them have private security guards. We can hire some if that becomes necessary. All the movie studios have security people, so we're safe there. We'll get through this, try not to worry," Joc said, and put his arms around her and kissed her gently.

"I just feel responsible for this, if only I had done something earlier about my drinking, we wouldn't be dealing with this. I was so stupid and irresponsible," Marian said, tearfully.

"Now let's not go there, sometimes a person is just deranged, and you don't even have to know them for them to target you. They're just crazy. It is not your fault sweetheart," Joc said lovingly.

They were still at Marian's apartment when the phone rang, and it was Detective Bailey, "Joc, I got a line on that Connor, creep. He served his time, and was released three months ago. His last known address was at his mother's house in Fresno, and the car registration is in her name. Therefore, it fits that this might be the guy. The police there said he took a job as a maintenance man for the Fresno Hotel. Just your bad luck you decided to stay there for the night. He must have recognized Marian. I can't bring him in for questioning unless he actually makes a threat. Sorry man, you might think about hiring a couple of bodyguards for the time being. Maybe the beach house isn't the best place right now. It's isolated down there. At least until we know how much he knows about your routines and what this guy is going to do."

"Will do Ron, and thanks, I sure appreciate it," Joc said, and he hung up the phone.

Joc repeated the conversation to Marian, and then called his agent. "Abe, this is Joc, I'm going to need to hire a couple of good bodyguards for a while. Will you arrange that for me?"

"Sure, will you need them just during the day?" Abe asked.

"No, around the clock, they will be protecting Marian and me. We will be staying at my place, the big house on Mulholland, where my brother lived. Can you have them there in a couple of hours?" Joc asked.

Abe said he would take care of it right away.

"We'll be safe there, and I can't be worrying about you staying here. He probably knows this is where you live. The house on Mulholland is in the name of the family trust, so there is no way he can get that address and connect it to me. The only address he will find for me is the apartment in Hollywood," Joc said.

"But Pete followed us from Fresno so he knows my apartment and he's probably watching us. He will just follow us when we leave here, he knows your car," Marian said, concerned.

"Stop worrying, I have a plan to get us out of here that will work. Just go pack your things...on second thought don't pack anything. A suitcase might tip him off," Joc said.

A couple of the make-up artist lived in Marian's apartment building and Joc had them do a makeover on both of them. They became an older couple. Joc was gray with jowls, heavier, and walked with a cane. Marian was very heavy with a gray wig and wire rimmed glasses. They hardly recognized each other. He called a cab and had the driver come to the door to help them out to the cab, If Pete was watching the building he only saw an old couple leave and get into a cab. Just to be sure, they had the cab take them to a local restaurant frequented by senior citizens. After a half hour had passed, they took a different cab to the house on Mulholland. Joc was sure no one had followed them.

The bodyguards arrived at the house a couple of hours later, and for the first time in several hours Joc felt Marian was safe. He had never told her about the phone call, but he was sure it was Pete Connor. He knew it was just a matter of time before Pete would find Marian. Bodyguards or not, he knew if this man was determined to make good on his threat he would.

Detective Bailey called Joc to tell him he would do what he could, but as long as Pete didn't break the law, there wasn't anything he could do but wait. The police department was always shorthanded, so for them to keep an eye on Pete was out of the question.

"Joc, you know by tonight he is going to figure out you are not at Marian's apartment, and he's going to try to get into the studio," Detective Bailey said.

"We can't live in fear forever. We are both due back at work the first of the week, and Marian wants to go to her AA meetings. How can I keep her safe there? We want to go to Santa Barbara in a few weeks to visit my sister and the kids. I refuse to let this creep ruin our lives," Joc replied.

"Let the bodyguards do their job, they're good at this, try to relax and live as you normally would. He will either go away, or make a move. If he tries anything, we will have him," Detective Bailey said confidently.

For the few next days nothing happened. Joc and Marian went to and from work at MGM studios. Marian attended AA meetings on the studio property, and when they left the studios, it was always in different cars, taking different routes to the house on Mulholland. They managed to go and see Joc's sister in Santa Barbara, and they had a wonderful time. Joc's sister Marilyn and her two children Becky and Bill Jr. had a modest home in a wooded area. Marilyn stayed home full time with the children. Marilyn loved Marian and she told Joc how happy she was that he had found someone he loved.

The date for the wedding was set for the first week in September. It would be held at the beach house in San Diego, which would work well for everyone. When Marian called Janie and Bob, then Joad,, and then her mother. "We wanted you to be the first to know the wedding is going to be the first week in September at the beach house in San Diego. Joc will make the plane reservations for everyone, and if you wouldn't mind picking-up mother and bring her to Sacramento, you can all fly together, that would be great," Marian said.

None of the family members knew about the problem with Pete. Joc and Marian felt sure that problem would be resolved long before the wedding.

Pete was still staying close to Marian's apartment building and outside the studio gate across the street so he knew where she worked. It appeared he was not going away, but he was unable to get closer than across the street due to the tight security on the set. After a time it seemed as though, Pete had given up. Joc was not so sure.

Marian gave up her apartment, left no forwarding address, and moved her things into the house on Mulholland, and Joc did the same. They kept the bodyguards, but other than that, life went back to normal. Joc remained vigilant.

Marian was now fifty-one years old. Since she had quit drinking and smoking two years ago, she looked like a woman in her early forties. She was thankful for the good genes. She was a talented woman, but planning a wedding was not something she had ever experienced. Janie and Bob had eloped, much to her dismay, and Joad was not yet thinking of marriage. She asked the one person closest to Joc and her, Lana's mother, to help her with the plans.

Lana's mother was a great help with planning the wedding. Between her daughter's multiple marriages, and that of close friends, Lana's mother had lots of experience. That, and the fact she thought of Joc as the son she never had, made her the perfect wedding planner. The two of them, complete with Marian's bodyguard, headed for the beach house in San Diego. There were still several months before the big day, but it was not too early to make arrangements for the caterer, flowers, the cake, invitations, and of course her dress.

After they were settled at the beach house, the two women sat down at the breakfast table and proceeded to plan.

"Okay Marian, the first order of business is the guest list. You and Joc have decided to have just family and close friends. Is that right?" Lana's mother asked.

"Yes, that is what we have talked about. The family part is easy, but how do we decide about which friends?" Marian asked.

"Well we'll start with a list of everyone who immediately comes to mind, see how many that entails, and then we can either add or delete as we feel is appropriate. The studio will have a reception for you later, for members of the cast of whatever movies you two are working on at the time. That's sort of standard procedure because the Hollywood types always love to have an excuse for a party," Lana's mother said.

They made the list and there were about thirty adults and ten children total. That seemed to be a perfect amount of guests to Marian. It would be a nice size to be able to enjoy everyone and Lana's mother agreed.

The next morning they arrived at the bakery and selected a modest but beautiful cake. The caterer made it easy because they had different packages to choose from simple to elegant. All priced accordingly. Lana's mother suggested they take the one that provided a buffet style luncheon of fresh seafood and numerous salads. An open bar, and champagne for the toast, coffee and tea would be provided, and of course the cake. The invitations were simple. When it came to the flowers, the decision was much more difficult because they were not going to be married in a church. Marian and Joc decided the ceremony would be on the beach. The large deck on the front of the beach house would accommodate that number of guest easily so the buffet would be set up inside and guest would be able to eat outside and enjoy the beautiful ocean view. For the ceremony, Marian would come down the stairs from the deck escorted by her brother to the beach below where Joc and his brother would be waiting with the minister who would perform the ceremony. The rest of the family and guests would be seated so they could see the bride and groom's faces. Lana's mother had made it so simple.

"Now tomorrow we will have the real fun of picking out your dress. I know of two or three shops that have gowns to die for," Lana's mother said excitedly.

"Okay, you have done great so far, I have every confidence in you. I thought this was going to be so much work and stress, but you have made it very easy," Marian said smiling. "Thank you so much."

"It's my pleasure dear, you are so easy to work with, and Joc is going to love everything you have chosen," Lana's mother said.

The next day they went to look for the wedding dress. Marian tried on what she thought was every dress in San Diego. She was tired and getting discouraged. Nothing was quite right. This was her second marriage, Joc's first. She was not a young woman, and it seemed most of the dresses were made for girls in their twenties. In the last shop they entered, Marian recognized the woman she had talked with the day Joc was shopping for her ring. "You're name is Maria isn't it?" Marian asked. "I met you a couple of months ago. You told me how you got started here, and I found it so interesting."

"Oh yes, I remember you are the beautician. How are you? Which one of you is the bride to be?" Maria said.

"Marian here is the bride to be," Lana's mother said. "I'm afraid we have just about given up finding the perfect dress."

Maria's shop was quite small and she had only a few dresses on display. Lana's mother told her they had been looking all day and were unable to find something appropriate for a more mature woman.

"I think I might be able to help you, she said kindly, as she took Marian by the hand. Come with me dear and sit right here," Maria said, as she disappeared through a curtain in the back.

Marian was glad to get off her feet, but she really didn't think this little shop could possibly have anything. She kind of shrugged and looked at Lana's mother who did the same. A few minutes later, Maria came out with a dress over her arm.

"Come dear. Let's try this one on you," Maria said, as she opened the door to a tiny dressing room.

As Marian stepped into the gown she could see the beautiful detailed stitches, with tiny pearls adorning the lace around the bodice. The dress was satin and was form fitting, the color was an antique white. Maria took a few pins from the little pin cushion attached to her arm and began pinning in a few places for a perfect fit.

"Okay dear, let's go out and show your friend, and you can see yourself in the big mirrors," Maria said.

As Marian stepped out of the dressing room, Lana's mother gasped, "That dress is stunning, no you are stunning. It's perfect!"

Marian turned and looked in the big mirror and she could hardly believe her own eyes. It was perfect! The dress clung to every curve of her beautiful body, yet it was not risqué in any sense of the word. The sleeves were long satin with a two-inch wide lace insert that ran from the shoulder to her wrist. The back was open to her waist, and the dress clung to her perfectly shaped bottom, falling to the floor with a very small train. At the front, the satin material crossed her flat tummy to fall down her right leg to the floor. The left side of the dress was straight and form fitting. Marian couldn't believe her eyes.

"This is the dress, how did you know? It's perfect!" Marian exclaimed.

"It's the same dress design I wore at my wedding, modernized a bit of course. I'm so happy you like it. All of my dresses are one of a kind because I make each one myself," Maria said.

"I will take it." Marian said. "Thank you so much, and to think I was just about to give up."

Maria helped Marian out of the dress and asked her if she could come in for a final fitting later in the week. Marian agreed to return the following Wednesday.

With most of the plans underway, Marian felt this was going to be a wonderful, yet simple event. She wanted everyone to have a good time, especially Joc.

"Oh Marian, we almost forgot, you are going to want some sort of music, are you not?" Lana's mother asked.

"Yes, of course. Let me talk to Joc and see what he prefers. He hasn't had a chance to make any decisions about this wedding," Marian said.

"I'm sure he is delighted he doesn't have to be in on all the planning. Men don't care about weddings as much as we women. At least that has been my experience," Lana's mother replied.

"I suppose you are right. Thank you again for helping me through this whole process. It would have been quite overwhelming alone," Marian said, gratefully.

Jake, Marian's bodyguard, was bored going from store to store, but he was always there, watching and insuring her safety. Marian had gotten used to having him with her every day. By now, she had almost forgotten about Pete, and that was a serious mistake.

chapter 11

After returning to Hollywood and the house on Mulholland, Marian couldn't wait to tell Joc about everything she and Lana's mother had done. She showed Joc the guest list and of course, he thought it was fine.

"I need to go back to San Diego next Wednesday, for a final fitting on my dress. Is that going to be a problem?" Marian asked.

"No, I'm not working next week, so maybe we could spend a couple of days down there if you can take the time off," Joc said.

"Do you think we still need to have the bodyguards? I know that's very expensive and I feel terrible you're paying for that," Marian said.

"Detective Bailey is making some off the record inquires about this Connor guy. We don't want to take any chances. The money is not a problem," Joc answered.

Joc never told Marian about the phone call in Fresno from someone saying, "You're both dead." Joc was sure the call was from Pete, but he had no way to prove it. Any man who was insanely jealous, would beat a woman, and then steal her car, was not someone to take lightly. Joc would wait to hear what Detective Ron Bailey found out before making any decisions about the bodyguards.

While Joc and Marian were in San Diego, Joc received a call from Detective Bailey. "Joc, is Marian there with you?" he asked.

"No Ron, she is in town having the final fitting of her dress. Is anything wrong?" Joc asked.

"I'm not sure but someone matching Connor's description is in town and has been asking questions about you and Marian. I think he may have found out about the beach house. Are you going to stay down there this week?" Detective Bailey asked.

"Yes we planned to stay until Friday, unless you think we should come back sooner," Joc replied.

"Do you still have the bodyguards and that .45? Could you use a little extra company?" Bailey inquired.

"Yes to both questions," Joc answered. "I would really appreciate your coming down, and I would like you to get to know Marian."

"Okay, I have a few loose ends to tie up here and then I'll head on down. Probably won't get there until late, so don't shoot me when I show up," Detective Bailey said jokingly.

"Great Ron, I'll see you tonight and thanks again," Joc said.

When Marian came out of the dress shop after the final fitting of her dress, she didn't see her bodyguard. Out of nowhere, a car pulled up beside her. The door flew open and she was instantly pulled into the car as it sped off.

"Pete, what ... do you want?" Marian said surprised and a little frightened.

"Shut-up you bitch, you'll find out soon enough. Did you think you're going to throw me in prison, then go off and marry prince charming? Well you aren't going to marry anyone, you hear me? When I'm done with you no one will want you!" Pete yelled.

"Pete this is crazy, you're the one who left me. Remember the night you beat me up and stole my car, and left me in Gilroy to find my own way home? What did you think I was going to do ... just give you my car and forget about it?" Marian shouted.

"We loved each other," Pete screamed.

"No, Pete we got drunk together, that's all we had and that's not love. Marian said, sadly. Now stop this car and take me back to town, and where is Jake?"

Pete laughed, "You mean that stupid bodyguard? You won't be seeing him again!"

"Pete, what have you done? Is he okay? You know the police know who you are, you can't get away," Marian said, trying not to show her fear.

"Shut-up, just shut-up, if I can't have you no one else can either!" Pete shouted.

Joc wasn't aware of what had happened in town. He prepared dinner for Marian and was waiting for her to get home from the dress fitting. He was looking forward to having Ron stay with them for a few days. About an hour had passed since he had talked to Detective Bailey when the phone rang.

"Joc, this is Ron. That guy Connor got ahead of us. He stabbed Marian's bodyguard and he has taken her and an old couple who lives just out of town as hostages," Detective Bailey reported.

"What ... are they okay? Where is Jake, her bodyguard? Has Pete hurt Marian?" Joc yelled.

"No, as far as we know she is okay. We don't know about the old couple. Jake is in surgery now at the hospital in San Diego. We don't know if he will make it. We don't think Connor will harm Marian, but you know there are no guarantees. The bad news is, he has all of them in the old couple's house." Detective Bailey replied.

"This can't be happening!" Joc shouted.

"Hold on there Joc, take it easy. I'm coming in an hour. A police helicopter is flying me in to help since I'm familiar with the case. Just hope Marian doesn't say anything to set him off, they had quite a violent history in Stockton. Meet me at the San Diego police department. " Detective Bailey said, and he hung up the phone.

Joc was at the police station when Detective Bailey arrived. Everyone was briefed on what had taken place so far. Because of the knife assault on Marian's bodyguard, Jake, Pete was going back to prison and everyone knew it, including Pete.

Pete forced himself into the old couple's car the night before, made them drive to their home, and tied them up. Then he stole their car and went after Marian. When he pulled the car into the garage, he forced Marian into the house, and tied her up with the old couple. Marian could see Pete was panicky he was sweating, and pacing, the knife shoved in his belt had blood on it. Marian guessed it was from her bodyguard Jake. Pete had not hurt the old couple, at least not yet.

"Marian whispered to the old couple, "Are you okay?"

The old man nodded, and the woman just had tears running down her cheeks. Marian felt so bad for them. How could Pete do such a thing to innocent people? She remembered how violent Pete could become, and she remembered he got worse if she argued with him. Better, keep her mouth shut she thought to herself, and see what happens.

The police had the old couple's house surrounded and a plan in place to rescue them. A negotiator was brought in and everyone headed to the house where Pete held Marian and his hostages.

"Pete Connor, we know you are in there, let the people go and we can talk," the negotiator said calmly with a bullhorn.

There was no response from inside the house, but Pete became more agitated. He pulled Marian away from the old couple. The husband grabbed his wife's hand, and she started to cry.

"Pete!" Marian screamed, "stop, let them go, you are scaring them to death."

"No, they are our way out of here, don't you see? You and I can go to Mexico, get a little place down there. They are our ticket out of the country," Pete said in a whisper.

At that moment, Marian realized how crazy Pete was and how much danger she and the old couple faced. Pete was out of his mind to think she was going to go with him anywhere, but the look in his eyes told her he really believed what he was saying. I better just play along, not try to upset him, so he doesn't hurt these people, she thought.

Pete went over to the window to look out and see where the police were. While he was out of earshot Marian told the old couple, she was going to pretend to go along with his plan. "Try not to worry, the police know who he is, and they will get us out of here safely," Marian whispered.

The old woman was still terrified and her husband held her hand tightly, they just nodded, too frightened to say a word.

"Mr. Connor, let the hostages go and you can tell us what you want," The negotiator said.

Pete was more agitated now. Marian could see he didn't know what to do. What she didn't know was how far he was willing to go. Maybe she could get him to let the old couple go. However, if Pete really believed they were his ticket across the border, that wouldn't happen. Keep quiet she told herself, let the police do their job. Surely, they had a plan.

At that moment, Pete grabbed the old woman and pulled her to the window where the police could see her. He held the knife to her throat as he yelled, "We're getting out of here. You're going to get us to the Mexican border, or I'll kill her," Pete screamed.

The negotiator was calm, "Okay, Mr. Connor, we can make arrangements for that, but you will have to let one of the people go," He said.

"Pete, let her go, she is so scared she will just be a problem. Just keep her husband. We don't need both of them. There's less of a chance of something going wrong without her," Marian said.

Pete thought for a minute, and then he pulled the old woman over to the door and yelled, "I'm sending her out."

He shoved her out the door, and then one of the police officers grabbed her just before she fell. Good, one out one to go, Marian thought. Now how can we get the old man to safety?

"That's good Mr. Connor," The negotiator said calmly.

"Okay, now we are going to leave here in the car, and nobody is going to stop us," Pete hollered.

Holding the knife to the old man's throat, Pete yelled at Marian, "Come on Marian you're driving us out of here."

Marian did as she was told, not wanting to see the old man hurt. Pete pushed him down in the back seat and told Marian to get in the driver's seat.

"Okay Pete, but you have to untie me so I can drive," Marian said.

Pete cut the rope he had tied her with and said, "Don't try anything or I'll kill this guy, you hear me?"

Marian didn't say anything she just got in the driver's seat. Pete got in the back on the floor and held the knife to the old man's throat.

The garage door opened and she started to back the car out, she could see the police all around the property. She was terrified they didn't see Pete was in the back seat on the floor holding the knife on the old man.

Once the old woman was safe and had calmed down, she told the police Marian had whispered to them that she was going to pretend to go along with Pete's plan of going to Mexico with him. She also was able to tell them Pete was unarmed except for the large hunting knife. This made the job of the police much easier, since Pete didn't have any other weapons, but he still held two hostages who were very much in danger.

The police also learned the old couple's names were Andrew and Isabel McDonald, Andrew's nickname was Mac. They had been married fifty-three years. The car had a full tank of gas because Mac had filled up yesterday just before Pete forced himself into their car and made them drive him to their house. They did what he said because he was holding a knife on Isabel. Isabel was very worried about Mac because he had a serious heart condition. This information made it harder for the police to capture Pete, as any gunfire might frighten Mac to death. They only had about a half hour before the car would reach the border. They had to alert the border officials of the hostage situation and get their cooperation.

The plan was when the car reached the border, to let it go through. Since Pete had let Isabel go without harming her, it appeared he just wanted to get out of the country with Marian. He would probably let Mac go after he was safely across the border. They were also counting on Marian to persuade Pete to let Mac go since he wouldn't need him anymore.

Joc didn't like this plan because this left Marian alone in Pete's hands and he didn't trust the Mexican police to help to free her once Mac was safe. What assurance did Joc have Marian would be unharmed. Joc remembered that call from Pete saying, "you're both dead." It seemed there was no other choice and Detective Bailey assured him this wasn't only the best plan, but also the only one.

The San Diego police followed the car to the border and the car went through as planned. Pete told Marian to stop at the first cantina she saw.

"There is one ahead on the right I'll stop there," Marian said.

When the car came to a stop, Pete did just what the police thought he would do. He opened the door, shoved

Mac out on the ground, jumped in the front seat, and shouted, "Get going Marian."

Pete directed her to drive out in the countryside and she did as he told her. When they were about twenty miles out, he said to her, "Pull off into that orchard, stop the car, and get out."

"Where are we going Pete?" Marian asked trying not to show her nervousness.

"We have to ditch this car, and find a place to hide out," Pete said.

"But Pete we are in Mexico. The police can't come after us here," Marian said.

"Are you an idiot, they didn't let us cross the border without having the Mexican police in on it. Pete shouted angrily. Now get moving, this is all your fault and you're going to pay."

At the border, Joc and Detective Bailey were trying to get the Mexican police to let them hunt for Pete and Marian. The Mexican police were not convinced Marian was not Pete's partner, and now that Mac was free it was over as far as they were concerned. The assault on Jake, Marian's bodyguard, wasn't in their jurisdiction, so it wasn't their concern. As long as Pete and Marian didn't break any laws in Mexico, they were free to stay in the country. If the Mexican police found the stolen car, it would be returned to the United States to the owner's, the McDonalds.

Joc was furious, "I knew this would happen he told Detective Bailey. Now how are we going to get Marian back safely?"

"We will Joc, but we have to go back to Hollywood, where I can get the FBI involved in this," Detective Bailey said calmly.

When they reached San Diego, the San Diego police informed Detective Bailey, Marian's bodyguard, Jake, didn't survive the surgery. This was now a murder case.

The helicopter took Joc and Detective Bailey back to Hollywood. Joc never said a word on the way back, all he could think about was Marian. How could I let this happen to her he thought?

Back in Mexico, after about two hours of walking, Pete and Marian reached a small house. Pete spoke Spanish to the man who was working in the field, so Marian couldn't understand what Pete told him. After a short time, the man took Pete and Marian to the house to meet his wife, Rosa Alverez. They spoke in Spanish, but everyone seemed comfortable and friendly. Apparently, Pete gave them some story they believed. Pete was calmer now and seemed less threatening toward Marian.

Rosa looked to be in her fifties, and didn't speak any English, and Marian knew only a few words of Spanish, so the women just smiled at each other as Rosa continued to prepare a meal. Pete and Juan went outside and they both worked in the fields until dinner. There was no telephone in the little house, and Marian didn't even see a car so she knew no one would ever find her here.

Joc knew he had to let Marian's family know what had happened, but he couldn't just pick up the phone and say, "Pete has kidnapped your mother and he has taken her to Mexico."

Detective Bailey had notified the FBI and everything was being done to try to get Marian home safely, but it was going to take time.

Joc decided to fly to Sacramento and tell Janie and Bob, and Joad what had happened. When he arrived at Janie and Bob's house, they were surprised to see him of course.

"Where is Mom?" Janie said when she saw that Marian was not with him. "Is everything all right?"

"May I come in?" Joc said solemnly. "Your mom is all right but there is a problem."

"Of course come in Joc. Don't tell me she started drinking again," Janie said dejectedly.

Bob was in the living room watching television. When Joc sat down Bob turned off the television.

"Well Joc, this can only be bad news or you wouldn't come here alone," Bob said.

chapter 12

As JOC TOLD Janie and Bob, what happened, Janie started to cry, "Poor mom, she finally got her life together. She is so happy and so much in love ... I hope ..."she just looked away as a tear fell down her cheek.

"I thought maybe I would pick Joad up and tell her what is going on, and then we could go down to Stockton to see Lillian. Do you think that is the right way to do this?" Joc asked.

"Sure that's fine, but what can we do?" Bob inquired.

"I don't think there is anything we can do right now, that's what makes this so damn frustrating. I never should have let the police take her out of the country," Joc said in frustration.

"It sounds like no one had any choice in the matter, remember two people were saved. Marian is tough and she's smart too, with the FBI involved I'm sure it's going to all work out," Bob said.

"I'll call Joad and have her come over. You can both stay here tonight and we can go see grandma in the morning," Janie said.

"After you call Joad, I would like to use your phone to call Detective Bailey. Maybe he will have some news," Joc said.

"Sure Janie said you can call now," handing Joc the phone.

"Ron, I'm at Marian's daughter's home in Sacramento. I believe you have the number. We are going to Stockton tomorrow to tell Marian's mother what has happened. I'll be back in a couple of days. Do you have any news from the FBI?" Joc asked.

"Yes, they have located the McDonalds car. It had been abandoned in an old orchard. There was no sign of Pete or Marian though, sorry," Detective Bailey reported.

The next morning Janie, Bob, Joad, and Joc drove to Lillian's house in Stockton. After hearing the story of what had happened, Lillian said, "Joad you probably know more about Pete than any of us. Can you remember anything that might help the FBI find him?"

"Lillian, that's a great idea. Joad, would you be able to take some time off from your job and come back with me to Hollywood so the FBI can talk with you?" Joc asked.

"Sure, I know my boss would let me do that under the circumstances," Joad said.

Lillian decided to go back to Janie and Bob's home until Marian was found. Joc and Joad left for Hollywood the next day.

While meeting with the FBI investigators, Joad was able to tell them a great deal about Pete. The most positive news was Pete had never been violent toward Marian unless they were both drinking. Now that he was wanted for kidnapping and murder, no one could predict what he would do. She explained he spoke Spanish very well and the migrant workers always liked him. This gave the FBI the lead they had been looking for. Obviously some of the locals had taken them in. In the Mexican countryside, there was little communication with the outside world, except for occasional trips into town for supplies.

While in Hollywood, Joc took Joad to the studios in an attempt to take her mind off her mother's kidnapping. No matter how they tried neither of them could think of anything else.

Two days later, the FBI reported they had information Pete and a woman fitting Marian's description were staying with an older couple out in the countryside. The locals said Juan Alverez usually came into town about every three weeks for a few supplies, and this was his week to come into town. The FBI agents would be ready, and if Pete was with him, they would take him into custody. They were sure the Alverez's were not involved.

Joc told Detective Bailey he would take Joad down to the house in San Diego, to wait for further news and hopefully Marian's rescue. Detective Bailey said, "That would be fine Joc, I've got your number down there, and when we get Marian back in the United States you would be close to the border."

When they arrived at the house in San Diego, Joc showed Joad the house. When they got out on the deck, Joad asked, "I think I'll take a walk down by the ocean if you don't mind?"

"Sure," Joc replied. "I'll give Detective Bailey a call to see if there is any news, then I'll come down and join you."

"Everyone is in place. The FBI is just waiting to see if they show up in town. This is the hard part, just waiting," Detective Bailey said.

"Okay, I'll take Joad to town and have some lunch. I'll check back with you when we get back to the house, probably be a couple of hours," Joc replied.

After Joc hung up the phone, he walked down to the beach where Joad was waiting. "Wow Joc," Joad said, "this is such a great place, I love it here. I don't know if my mom told you we lived at Lake Tahoe when I was a kid. I sure miss the water.

Joc smiled, "I'm glad you like it, your mom loves it here too. In fact, this is where she wants to have the wedding, so I assume you approve?"

"What do you say we go have some lunch since there was no news from Detective Bailey. We just have to wait. We might as well not do it on an empty stomach. There is no way of knowing when we will be able to eat if we get a call from him or the FBI," Joc explained.

"Okay, I don't have much of an appetite, but what else can we do?" Joad sighed.

The FBI had four men staked out dressed like locals so as not to arouse suspicion incase Pete was with Alverez. If Alverez were alone, they would have to follow him home without being seen. They couldn't depend on any help from the locals. The fact was the locals didn't trust federal agents, and they would probably try to help Pete. The FBI didn't think Pete had access to any guns, but they would have to assume that was a possibility. The tough part was to make sure no innocent people got hurt if Pete did come into town. They already knew Pete had no problem-taking hostages.

About two o'clock that afternoon, an old truck rumbled into town. Alverez, was the lone passenger of the man who owned the truck. After Alverez and the man who had driven him into town left, one of the agents speaking in

Spanish, and posing as a worker asked the shopkeeper "Is anyone looking for workers."

The shopkeeper said, "I don't know of anyone, most around here do all their own work, they are too poor to hire anyone."

"What about the men who just left? It looked like they could use some help. I will work for a place to stay and food, don't need to have money," the agent said.

"Alverez, one of the men who just left here said, he has a man and his wife who are helping out at his place now. Just for food and a place to sleep, but they aren't staying for long. Maybe he could use you after they leave," the shopkeeper replied.

"Where is his place?" the agent asked, "I'm new around here, don't know much about the area."

The storekeeper gave him directions to the Alverez place and the agent thanked him.

The FBI needed a new plan. The agent reported to headquarters about what had taken place, and a new plan would have to be put into place quickly because the shopkeeper indicated Pete would be leaving the Alverez place fairly soon. The further Pete got into the countryside the less chance they had to get Marian out alive. They had to move quickly and with force.

The next morning the FBI team was ready to act. They would go in on foot because any other method would cause them to be seen. Pete might use the Alverez's as hostages, just as he had done with the McDonalds. Detective Bailey, Joc and Joad were waiting at the border for Marian to be rescued.

The FBI waited until they were sure the women were in the house, and Pete and Juan were in the field working.

"Pete Connor, this is the FBI, lay down on the ground with your arms out to your sides. You are surrounded by federal agents," one of the agents shouted.

Pete was startled but he started to run toward the house. "Stop or we will shoot!" the agent yelled.

Pete kept running toward the house. "Stop I said!" the agent repeated.

Pete was almost to the door of the little house when four bullets rang out, each one of them hitting its mark. With his hand on the door, Pete fell to the ground.

When the agents reached him, he was dead. One of the agents shouted, "Marian Roberson are you in there and are you all right?"

"Yes," she yelled back.

"Open the door, it's over, you're safe now," the agent said calmly.

When Marian reached the border and saw Joc and Joad waiting for her she ran to them with tears running down her cheeks.

"It's all right sweetheart, it's over, and you are safe now," Joc said, holding her tightly.

"Mom are you okay? He didn't hurt you did he?" Joad asked.

"I'm fine now honey lets go home," Marian said.

When they reached the beach house they called Janie, Bob, and Lillian and told them everything was fine. Joc called his sister Marilyn and his brother Wes, to let them know too.

That night in bed, as Marian lay in Joc's arms, he told her again, "I love you so much. If anything happened to you my life would over."

Marian told him, "I've never been so happy in my life. What kept me going through this whole ordeal with Pete, was I needed to see you again. I feel so awful Jake lost his life in such a senseless way."

"Yes, it's too bad about Jake, but that was his job to protect your life, and if he wasn't protecting you he would have been protecting someone else. He chose that work. Remember, Isabel and Mac McDonald are alive today because of your quick thinking," Joc reminded her.

"Yes, but if… I …" Marian started.

"No what if's sweetheart," Joc reassured her." Let's just be grateful that we are alive, and we have loving families. We can look forward to our beautiful future together."

"By the way, Joad approves of this house," Joc said with a chuckle.

Marian laughed for the first time since she was rescued. "Yes, I'll just bet she does."

After spending a few days together with Joad, Joc and Marian took her to the airport so she could go back to work in Sacramento. Except for a few nightmares, life returned to normal for Joc and Marian and the plans for the wedding were going forward.

"I never thought there was so much planning that went into just getting married. Andy and I eloped. Much to my sadness, so did Janie and Bob. One of the great joys for a mother is seeing her daughter getting married, in the traditional way, you know, the dress, her father walking her down the aisle, etc. Well I guess it's going to be me this time. I hope Joad will find the right person someday, and maybe she will have a nice wedding. Maybe, that's why I want this, to set a good example for once in my life," Marian mused.

"I think you have set many good examples for the girls, it shows in how loving, and caring they both are towards you. You did a good job raising your girls, anyone can see that," Joc said.

"No Joc, I wasn't a very good mother. I was too young when Janie was born. Then Joad came along when Janie was already eight years old. I just never had a chance to ... well ... no that is no excuse. There were many young mothers during the war years, and they didn't turn into alcoholics. The girls turned out to be good people because of the choices they made, better ones then mine, thank god. There was a time after Pete shoved Mac out of the car, and told me to drive out into the countryside, I was sure he was going to kill me. While I was out there at the Alverez's, I had time to think about how I wished I had done more for all the people I love. Maybe now I will have time to make it up to them," Marian said.

"I think I know what you mean. It gave me time to reflect on my life too. We all have regrets Marian, the time I spent with your family made me realize how much I've missed by not having a family. Now I feel like I have one with you at my side," Joc said, smiling as he touched her cheek.

By September, the ordeal with Pete was just a distant memory, and people were arriving in San Diego for the wedding. Joc and Marian had planned several activities for the families to get better acquainted. The big day had finally arrived. Marian and Joc made a beautiful couple, and everything went as planned. The guest list included the two families, Dr.and Mrs. Branford, Thelma and Evert, and Rowena, all from Stockton. Guest from Tahoe included Daffy, Peg, Maddie and Chester, Nat and Mimi. Mrs. Rich, now in her nineties was too old to travel, but she sent her love and best wishes. Sadly, Bell wouldn't be there either. Marian had learned Bell had taken her own life a few months ago.

Marian's brother Bob gave her away. Joc's best man was his brother Wes. Charles from San Francisco was also a guest. Lana and her mother, Abe Joc's agent, and Detective Ron Bailey were the only Hollywood people invited. It was a beautiful private affair and everyone had a wonderful time.

Joc took Marian to Paris, France for their honeymoon. He made reservations for the honeymoon suite at Le Bristol, and for three weeks, they toured Paris. Marian loved history, but she had never left the United States, she could only have dreamed of such a romantic trip. To be in Paris standing next to the Eiffel Tower, touring The Louvre, The Tuileries gardens, Notre Dame Cathedral, and perhaps the best was a private dinner cruise on the Seine, that Joc had arranged with a friend of his who owned a large yacht. When they returned to the suite a couple of days before they were scheduled to leave for home, they were in each other's arms when Marian said, "Oh, Joc this is such a beautiful place and I'm so lucky. Most people will never be able to experience this kind of a trip. Thank you so much."

"This is only the beginning sweetheart, when you were kidnapped, all I could think about was how much I love you, and if you were brought back to me safely... Joc stopped, as tears welled up in his eyes... I was going to make sure every moment we had together counted."

They both sat quietly for a while, not saying anything, just holding each other, and absorbed in their own thoughts. Joc spoke first saying, "We need to think about where we are going to make our home, besides Paris, that is." Joc teased.

"Where do you want to live?" Marian asked.

"Well, we're not limited to any one place you know. The house on Mulholland belongs to the family, but I can purchase it from my brother and sister if you want to live there. The beach house in San Diego belongs to me so we can make that our permanent home, or we can just keep it as a vacation place. Maybe you would like to live closer to your mother and the girls. You know a lot depends on if we are going to continue to work in the movie industry," Joc told her.

"Yes, I know I've been thinking about that too. I really enjoyed working on the movie sets, but I miss being with you. I think I should continue to work, but I'm not sure I still want to do hair. You know so much has happened in such a short time. I'm not sure what to do… " Marian said.

"I have been feeling the same way, I don't think I really want to go back to being an extra, it was fun when I didn't have anyone to come home to, but now, I don't miss it at all. So let's just take our time, do a little more traveling spend more time together. I'm sure we'll come up with the right answers. What do you think?" Joc said.

"That would be wonderful, can we really do that? I know you have said money isn't an issue, but Joc, this is very expensive, and I haven't contributed at all," Marian said.

"Marian you are my wife now, and you will never have to worry about money again. Even if something were to happen to me. I've setup a trust that will take care of you for the rest of your life. You see we really can do whatever we want, there is so much money we really can't spend it all, even if we never work again," Joc smiled as he kissed her.

Before they left Paris, they notified the studios about their intentions to travel for a couple of months. The studios had plenty of people to draw from so it wasn't a problem. They wished them well, and told them anytime they wanted work, the door would be open.

Marian had never been to the Northeast, and Joc had only been to Boston for about a week and that was several years ago, so they decided to rent a car and visit several of the New England states, taking in all the historical sites. They stayed in bed-and-breakfasts so they could meet people and have a more relaxed atmosphere. After all they had been through in the last few months, this was a welcome relief. In Hollywood, everyone is always on the go. There is little time to sit quietly. Paris was exciting, but also a very busy lifestyle. Here one could relax and enjoy nature.

One morning as they sat on a little patio of a bed-and-breakfast, Marian whispered, "Look over there, Joc, do you see that deer? I think she has just given birth, the baby is just to her right, over by that tree."

"Your right," Joc whispered excitedly," I see them."

They sat very quietly as they watched the mother deer clean her new born fawn, carefully licking and nudging the baby to its feet. The baby was so adorable. The fawn was wobbly at first and then it became stronger. Within a very short time, it started to nurse. The mother seemed to know humans were there, but didn't appear to be frightened at their presence. After about an hour, the mother deer started to move into the forest with the new fawn close at her side.

At dinner that night, they told the other guest about what they had witnessed. James, one of the owners of the bed-and-breakfast said, "We have several deer that roam this area, but we have never been lucky enough to see any being born. We usually don't get to see the fawns until they have almost lost their spots."

"Do you think they will be back in the morning?" Marian asked.

"Oh, I doubt it, like I said, they are pretty reclusive creatures," James answered.

Marian was up before Joc the next morning and she took her coffee out on the patio hoping she would get a glimpse of the mother and her fawn again. Joc joined her about a half hour later, and they started to plan their day.

"Marian," Joc whispered," look."

There they were, mother and fawn, back in the same place as where the baby had been born the day before. The mother looked at Marian and Joc, and again didn't seem to be fearful of their presence. This time the deer only stayed about ten minutes before wandering off into the woods.

"Well, I don't know how we will top this," Joc said jokingly.

They had spent the last three weeks in New England, and now the chill of fall was in the air. "Do you think we should head back to San Diego, or would you like to go somewhere else Marian?" Joc asked.

"Maybe we should go back for a time. We've been gone for over two months now, and it might feel good to put our feet in the sand," Marian said.

"I can make reservations as soon as you would like to leave," Joc said.

On the flight home, they had bad weather in Denver, and had to stay for a couple of nights before it cleared enough to fly back to San Diego. This gave them a little time to see the area. "This is beautiful here," Marian said," it reminds me a little of Tahoe."

"Well, maybe we should stay for a time." Joc said.

"No, not now, "Marian said, "I think I'm ready to go home."

Marian fell asleep on the plane ride back to San Diego, but it was not a restful sleep. She knew she was dreaming, but she couldn't recall what it was about. Only whatever it was, it was disturbing.

chapter 13

THE DAY AFTER returning to San Diego, Marian called Janie to let her know they were back in San Diego.

"Hi honey, I just wanted to let you know Joc and I returned home yesterday," Marian said.

"Did you have a wonderful time? What was Paris like? We can't wait to hear all about your trip," Janie said excitedly.

"And I can't wait to tell all of you about it. Has everything been okay while we were gone?" Marian inquired.

"Yes, but grandma hasn't been feeling too well. Dr. Branford has been keeping an eye on her... but mom ... I think you better come see her soon," Janie said hesitantly.

"What do you mean Janie, what's wrong?" Marian said.

"About a week after we got back from the wedding, she was not feeling too well, and... mom, she had a small stroke. She was all right because there wasn't damage from it, but Dr. Branford is concerned it may happen again," Janie said, in a worried voice.

"Okay honey I will make arrangements to come right away," Marian replied.

As soon as Marian hung up the phone she called to Joc, who was walking down on the beach. He waved to her, and smiled. However, she just motioned for him to come back to the house. He knew something was wrong, and ran up the beach to the house. "What is it sweetheart, what's wrong?" Joc said, in a worried voice.

Marian repeated the conversation she had with Janie. "Call Dr. Branford and find out how she is. We can leave in the morning for Stockton," Joc said.

Marian called Dr. Branford, and discovered Lillian had a bad heart condition, there was no way of knowing how long she had to live. She was seventy-four years old, and in good condition except for this heart problem. Actually, it wasn't so much her heart, as her arteries were badly blocked, and at her age, there wasn't a lot they could do for her without putting her in more danger.

"Marian, she really should not be alone in that house," Dr. Branford said.

"We will leave here tomorrow, and be in Stockton, by nightfall," Marian said.

"Good, I think that's a good idea," Dr. Branford replied.

After Marian hung up the phone, she said, "Joc can we leave tonight? I'm so worried I won't be able to sleep anyway."

"Why don't we go in the morning very early, we'll still be there before dark," Joc replied.

Marian was almost hysterical, "No, no I must go now... you don't know..."

Joc interrupted, "What is it sweetheart? Tell me what has you so upset."

"My father, he died before I could see him…he was in a coma, and I waited until I was done with work, just like this, there is no time to waste," Marian cried.

Seeing how upset Marian was, Joc said, "Okay, I will call a pilot friend of mine and see if he can fly us there today."

One hour later, they were at the private airfield getting ready for takeoff, and two hours later, they were pulling into Lillian's driveway at the little house in Stockton.

Joc grabbed Marian's hands tightly before she could get out of the car. "Stop Marian, you don't want to frighten your mother. She's not expecting us. You must calm down. You need to tell her we are on our way home and we wanted to stop to tell her all about the trip, or something like that," Joc said firmly.

Marian was frantic, "Let me go!" she said, pulling away.

As she opened the door of the car, Joc was beside her, he took her hand gently, and said, "It is okay, everything is going to be fine."

Just then, Lillian appeared on the little porch, "My stars look at you two, what are you doing here?" Lillian asked.

Marian ran to her mother, and held her so tight that Lillian said, "Marian, you're going to squeeze me to death. What is wrong?"

Realizing her mistake, Marian said, "It's just so good to see you. We have been gone over a month, and I'm just so happy to see you."

"Well come on in, and Joc, you look handsome as always," Lillian joked.

"Thank you Lillian and you're looking fit as usual," Joc quipped.

"Can you stay, or are you on your way home today?" Lillian asked.

"We would like to stay for a few days, if that's okay with you mom?" Marian asked.

"Of course you can stay. The spare bedroom is all made up for visitors, even though I don't get too many anymore," Lillian said.

It was getting close to dinnertime. "Mrs. Reister, I heard you have one of the best Chinese take-out restaurants right here in Stockton, is that true?" Joc said smiling and giving her a little wink.

"Joc you may call me Lillian, no need for Mrs. Reister, we are family now. Yes, Marian knows the place well," Lillian, answered.

"How about if I go and get us a nice Chinese dinner. Do you two have any favorite dishes?" Joc asked.

Lillian went to the little desk and pulled out a menu from Minnie's Chinese and the three of them picked out the items they wanted.

"Now don't you girls talk about me behind my back," he said, as he headed out the door.

After Joc left, Marian thought about asking her mother about the stroke, but she knew if she did, Lillian would know their showing up unexpectedly was actually planned. Lillian was a quiet person who never liked to be the center of attention, and this was even truer about needing others to care for her. Marian would have to keep up the façade until Lillian chose to tell her about the stroke herself. In the meantime, she would just enjoy spending a few days together.

By the time Joc returned with the food, Lillian and Marian had set the little table in the kitchen. "That food smells wonderful," Marian said.

"I know," Joc replied. "I almost pulled over and got into it on the way home," He laughed. "The people who own Minnie's are really nice. When I mentioned your name Lillian, they told me to be sure to say hello."

"That's nice they think of me. You know they are the second generation running the restaurant, and I think some of the younger folks are third generation. Sweets and I started going there in the twenties," Lillian replied.

They were quiet as they ate. "Mom, Joc and I are trying to decide what we are going to do about work now that we are married .We want to spend more time together and also with our families, but we're so spread apart, we're not sure just how to do that. How did you and Frank manage it?" Marian asked.

"Times were different. Remember the war was on then. After it was over everyone settled in different places. Bob had the apple ranch in Arnolds, but he really didn't need our help. You and Andy were building the house, with you working, it seemed reasonable for Frank to help Andy, and I could find a job in Tahoe easily. When the house was finished, we decided Reno would be a nice place for us to settle. We rented out these houses in case someone in the family needed a place to live. You know we remembered the great depression, and of course, we planned to live out our old age here together. I guess we went where we were needed most," Lillian said, thoughtfully.

"Mom, I know Stockton has never been your favorite place to live. If you could live anyplace in the world, where would that be?" Marian asked.

"Oh my, I never thought about that. At my age, it doesn't matter much where I live. I've gotten accustomed to it here and things are familiar. I do worry sometimes about keeping up the places. My renters in the back are moving out next week. I hate to go through finding new ones. It's so hard to tell about people now-a-days," Lillian said.

Joc knew that anything needing to be done to the houses was easy for him to have it done. He also knew Lillian was proud and wouldn't want him to pay anyone, or, for him to buy materials. He would have to think how this could be worked out without embarrassing Lillian.

That night as he and Marian lay in bed, Joc said, "Marian, what if we stayed in the back house, and we fixed it up real nice, you know new appliances, roof, siding, and the works. Do you think your mother would like that, or do you think she would be insulted?"

"Oh I don't know Joc, do you know what you are saying? That place is a wreck," Marian replied.

"Nothing is beyond repair, and if we lived here for a while you could be close to your mother, now when it counts. That's, if she wants us. If you don't want to be right here, we could rent a place close by. What do you think? It would give us something productive to do while we decide what's next," Joc said.

"We can see how it goes for the next few days, see if she tells us about her health issues, and then we can talk to her about it. I would love to stay here, but are you sure?" Marian asked.

"Sure. I think it would be fun, and more importantly, it's useful," Joc said.

The next couple of days they all enjoyed themselves, Lillian got along with Joc better than she did with Marian. He kidded her but always respectfully, and she loved his easygoing manner. One afternoon Lillian and Joc were alone while Marian had gone to the store. Lillian was talking about looking for a new renter, but she was concerned about finding someone who would live in a house that old and still be able to pay the rent on time, keep the place clean, etc. This was Joc's opportunity to present his idea. He had given this considerable thought over the last few days, about just what to say and how to say it.

"Lillian," he began. "Marian is real happy here close to you and the girls, and I've been thinking about something that might help us all. While we were on our honeymoon we talked a little about what our future would look like, but we never really came to any decisions. You need to know I've set up a trust for her so no matter what happens to me she will be well taken care of. I want to make sure she is happy. As I'm sure you know, money alone can't make one happy. Neither of us want to go back to work in Hollywood, at least not right now. So I was wondering if you would allow us to fix-up the house in the back before you rent it again," Joc stopped and tried to read Lillian's reaction to his plan.

"That would be nice Joc, but I really don't have the money to put into fixing it up right now," Lillian said.

"Oh, I didn't expect you to spend any money on it. I thought Marian and I could do the work and live there as we did it," Joc said.

"Well, let me think about it. I would love you two to stay a while longer. Maybe that would keep Marian busy to have a project to work on. That might be a good thing," Lillian said.

Joc changed the subject not wanting Lillian to feel pressured into anything. After all, she had still hadn't revealed her medical problems to either of them. That weekend they decided to drive to Sacramento to see the girls. Janie was pregnant with her second child and due in a few weeks. They had a great time, and returned to Stockton before dark on Sunday.

Monday morning Lillian was up early and had coffee ready when Joc got up. Marian was still in the bathroom doing her make-up.

"Joc," Lillian said." I have been thinking about what you said regarding fixing up the house in the back. I think it would be a good idea because I'll be able to attract a better renter if the house is more modern. I have the places willed to Bob and Marian when I die, and Bob keeps telling me these places would fall down around me if the termites quit holding hands," Lillian laughed.

Joc laughed too, and just then Marian came into the kitchen. "What's so funny you two?" Marian said with a smile, happy her mother and Joc were getting along so well.

"Well, it's a long story but how would you like to go into the contracting business for a while?" Joc said with a chuckle. "Lillian would like to hire us to fix-up the back house. What do you think?"

"You want us to stay for a while mom? That's great, I wasn't sure if we were getting on your nerves," Marian said.

"Well, there is something else you need to know. When you were on your honeymoon, I had a small stroke, nothing too serious, but Dr. Branford said I have... I can't say the medical word for it, but my arteries are getting plugged-up and I could have another stroke or worse anytime. I'm too old to do much about it, so it's one day at a time. You need to know this, and you need to know I've taken care of my will, and I'm prepared for whatever God has in mind for me," Lillian said, matter-of-factly.

Marian looked at Joc with tears in her eyes, and took her mother's hand. "Mom are you sure there isn't anything... maybe we need to get a second opinion."

"No Marian, we did all the tests. I've had a real good life, and maybe I still have more time, who knows? I just want you to know since you will be right here, if my time comes, you aren't to be upset. I'm so happy you and Joc are going to stay for a while. Now, let's have breakfast. Joc, you can tell me all about what you have planned for the back house," Lillian said, cheerfully.

"Well, since winter is upon us, I think it will be best to start on the inside first. When did you say you and Frank built that house?" Joc inquired.

"Nineteen-twenty-five, I think," Lillian said.

That afternoon Joc began to checking out the old house and made plans for the remodel. He could hardly wait to get started. He would try to do most of the work himself, but would hire a professional for wiring and plumbing.

Thanksgiving was just a week away and everyone was very busy, Joc offered to take the family out for dinner in Stockton. Janie, Bob, Kate, and Joad all came down Thursday morning, and they had dinner at the Stockton hotel. Marian invited Rowena to join them. After dinner, they went back to Lillian's before going home. Everyone was surprised to see so much progress on the house. The walls were stripped down to the studs. The electrician and plumber were scheduled for the following Monday to rewire and plumb the house completely. Then the fun would begin. There would be new sheetrock, paint, and appliances.

Christmas that year brought a special present, on December 26, Janie gave birth to her second child, a boy, who would carry on the family name.

By the end of March, the back house was complete. Lillian was thrilled, and Joc never told her how much it cost. It really didn't matter because he and Marian had worked together and they were able to spend a good deal of time with Lillian. Joc convinced Lillian to move into the back house so he could hire a contractor to remodel her house. The doctor said she was doing better than expected and maybe she was going to be fine.

When Joc and Marian said their goodbyes to Lillian, they headed to Lake Tahoe on their way back to San Diego. "I'm looking forward to seeing Tahoe. Believe it or not, I've never been there," Joc said.

"Really," Marian said. "I'm surprised because you have been just about everywhere."

"Well, I don't know about that. Maybe we should stay a few days, and you can show me the house you and Andy built, your beauty shops, you know all the sights," Joc said.

Marian was quiet for a moment. Am I ready to relive all of that? She thought to herself.

Joc noticed her hesitation and said, "Sweetheart, if you would rather not, that's okay. We'll just take in a few of the tourist spots and head for home."

"No Joc, I would love to share those sights with you. This is the first time I will have been back since Joad and I moved to Stockton. I think my emotions were just overwhelming me a bit," Marian answered, smiling and snuggling up to Joc in the car.

"Let's get a room in one of the hotels and then maybe we should call Daffy or Peg, and let them know we are here," Joc said.

After checking into the hotel, they called Daffy and told her they were in town for a few days and they would love to see everyone.

"I'll take care of everything Marian. You can show Joc around and I'll arrange for all of us to take the paddle-cruiser- luncheon tour to Emerald Bay. All tourists have to take that trip you know," Daffy laughed as she hung up the phone.

Marian and Joc had breakfast at the hotel and then headed out for their adventure. First stop was the house she and Andy had built.

"I don't see it," Marian said, very puzzled. "It was right here. I know this is the place, because that's the Burnside's right over there. All these houses are new. This apartment building is on the lot were the house was. That's our old fence. What do you suppose happened?"

Joc got out and knocked on the door of the apartment house, and a woman came to the door. "Can you tell me when this building was built?" Joc inquired.

"Yes about two years ago. There was a big house here before, but there was a fire and it burnt to the ground, no one was hurt, thank God," the woman replied.

"Okay, thank you very much," Joc said, as he turned and walked to the car.

Joc repeated what the woman had told him. "Are you okay sweetheart?" He said.

"Oh yes, Marian said hesitating a bit. It's just a shock that's all. We already know the beauty shop in Bijou is gone, but the one I rented at the end of the street should still be there," Marian said.

As they drove around the South Shore, Marian couldn't believe how much things had changed in just ten years. Many of the old places had been torn down to make way for new businesses, large homes, and apartments. The traffic was much worse too. It took them almost an hour to drive from the Stateline to the "Y" and the turn off to Camp Richardson. As they drove along Marian pointed to places she remembered, or where someone she knew use to live. They had called Mattie the night before and she had invited them to her house at Fallen Leaf for lunch. When they arrived, Chester took Joc to show him the property, which encompassed several acres reaching down to the lakeshore. The two women were like schoolgirls, so excited to see one another again. They stayed at the house as Mattie prepared lunch for the four of them. Marian and Joc told Mattie and Chester about the honeymoon in Paris, and then the remodeling of Lillian's little house in Stockton.

"I will bet there were some good stories about that project," Mattie said with a big laugh.

"None that we can repeat here," Joc said quickly.

"Marian, did you ever tell Joc the story about Frank and the sub-flooring of the house up here?" Mattie said giggling a bit.

"I don't think she did," Joc said. "What happened?"

Marian repeated the story about Frank nailing his coveralls to the floor and thinking he was paralyzed. They all laughed once again at how funny that story was. After they all stopped laughing Marian said, "We went by the house, or at least where it used to be."

"Oh Marian, we were all so sad to hear about the fire. We all had so many nice memories attached to the building of that house. It was like losing an old friend," Mattie said, sadly.

"We only lost the house Mattie, not the memories," Marian said, as she smiled.

They were all quiet for a few minutes as they finished the lunch Mattie had prepared for them.

"You're right. Marian by the way, Daffy has arranged for a private dinner on the paddle wheeler, to tour Emerald Bay. She has threatened all of us with our lives if we don't show up. I'm sure there will be a lot of reminiscing. I hope you boys will not be bored to death Joc," Mattie said.

"Quite the contrary Mattie, I love hearing everything about Marian. Lillian and I had a great time, she told me things about Marian when she was a little girl, but she swore me to secrecy," Joc said, smiling and chuckling a bit.

"Joc, you never told me!" Marian said, surprised and a little embarrassed.

"I said she swore me to secrecy. I'll never tell, even if I'm tortured," Joc replied.

"Well if things get too boring for us Joc maybe you can share some of the better ones with the boys," Chester said, teasing Marian.

"Joc, I'm not too old to tell my mommy on you," Marian said.

"Okay, okay I will be good," Joc promised.

When their visit was over and as they drove back to the hotel, Joc said, "Mattie and Chester are really wonderful people. You are so lucky to have such good friends."

"Yes, I know Joc, and to think they never judged me. Mattie stood by me even when others were fed up with my drinking. Chester tried to help me, but it was no use, I just wouldn't listen to anyone," Marian said, as she thought about the many times they stood by her. "I wish there was some way I could make it all up to them."

"I think they're just happy you stopped drinking and have made a good life for yourself." Joc said.

"Yes, thanks to you too. I don't know how I would have survived without all the love and support you've given me, and still do," Marian said.

"I'll always be with you as long as you want me," Joc said, squeezing her hand as they drove along.

The next afternoon everyone arrived at the paddle wheeler around four in the afternoon. Included in the group were Nat and Mimi, Chester and Mattie, Daffy, and Peg and Sam. Mrs. Rich's son brought her, as she was very frail, but mentally still very sharp.

Joc, was fascinated with Tahoe and was asking a million questions about the area. All the men were natives of Tahoe and were delighted to share their knowledge of the lake and the surrounding area. For the women it was as though Marian had never left, they caught up on old gossip, things like who had left, and who was still there. They told Marian about the tragic way Bell had taken her own life just a little less than a year ago. As they approached Emerald Bay, the sun was starting to set over Mt. Tallac. When everyone was seated for dinner Chester said, "Quiet everyone, I would like to propose a toast, to Marian. You have brought so much happiness to each one of us over the years you lived and worked at Tahoe. Here is to those memories, and wishing continued happiness for you and Joc."

"Here! Here!" They all said in unison.

Overwhelmed with emotion, all Marian could manage to get out was a very quiet, "Thank you,. You are my dearest friends."

"Well Chester, I think you are the first person to actually render Marian speechless," Joc said, as he hugged Marian tightly, and smiling at her lovingly.

After dessert and coffee were served, Joc and Marian went for a walk on the deck. It was a beautiful, clear night, and the lake was as smooth as glass. As Joc held Marian in his arms, they watched the lights twinkle on the shore. Neither of them would forget this wonderful night together with these fine friends. When they reached the dock, everyone said their goodbyes and once again went their separate ways.

At breakfast the next morning Joc said, "Marian, Chester and the other men were telling me that their wives are always complaining they don't have a good beautician here anymore. I guess there are several shops, but they cater to the tourist and the entertainers who play at the clubs. They asked me what our plans were for the future. I told them we really haven't had a chance to make any real plans. I think they were hinting that maybe we would settle here."

"Oh Joc, I don't know. They are just remembering the old days. Things have changed here a lot. You know in life you can't go back," Marian said.

"Yes I know and you are right, but it is really a beautiful place. It would be so much closer to the kids and Lillian. I could see us living here at least part of the year. Maybe we could live here in the summer and San Diego in the winter. What do you say we just look around at houses today? We don't have anything else planned, we could just look. We don't have to make any decisions," Joc said.

"I guess looking around could be fun, just seeing what is new would be interesting," Marian said.

They spent the day looking at houses. They looked at everything from older one-room cabins to beachfront estates. Marian tried to picture living at Tahoe again, but she couldn't chase away the ghosts of the past.

As they had lunch, she said,"Joc, I don't know if this would be good for me. I have always loved Tahoe. The smell of pine trees, the mountains all around, the beautiful sandy beaches, and of course the gorgeous lake. Nevertheless, everywhere I go I seem to relive my past. I just don't think this would be a good thing right now. You know drinking and gambling is so easy here, do you understand?"

"Of course I do, sweetheart. I just want you to be happy and I thought maybe being back here might be important to you," Joc said.

"It is of course, but the thought of living here, or having a beauty shop, I just don't think so. Not right now anyway. Let's just go home," Marian said.

"You are the boss, and your wish is my command. Step into my magic carriage, and I shall transport you to the ocean," Joc said, making a sweeping gesture with his arm as he opened the door for her.

Marian was quiet for a while as they drove. Many thoughts were racing through her head. The war years, Marge, the building of the house at Tahoe, Bell's suicide, the move to Stockton, and as she remembered the kidnapping by Pete she let out a tiny gasp.

"What is it, sweetheart are you alright?" Joc said with alarm.

"Yes, I'm fine. I'm looking forward to being home with you at the beach house. I think I've been away too long that's all. I miss our quiet times in front of the fire sipping tea, and our walks on the beach, the smell of salt water, and watching the sun sink into the ocean," Marian said wistfully.

"I miss that too, and tomorrow we will be home," Joc said.

When they arrived at the beach house Marian jumped out of the car and ran to the house. "Hold on sweetheart, give me a chance to open the door," Joc laughed.

After Joc opened the house, he started a fire, and Marian made them tea. As they sat snuggled in the big sofa, Marian sighed and said, "It feels so good to be home, and this feels like home to me."

"I 'm happy you love it here too. I've always had that same feeling whenever I come here. It feels like home to me too," Joc said.

For the next week, they stayed close to home, enjoying each other and relaxing after what had been a very hectic several months.

They let everyone in both families know they were home in San Diego, and this would be home for them in the near future. She had some people to thank and she did that the best way she knew how, by writing to each one individually, starting with Mattie and Chester.

Dear Mattie and Chester,

Thank you so very much for the beautiful and most delicious lunch you made for Joc and me. Chester, you are a prince, as always. You welcomed Joc, as though you had known him forever, and that made him feel very much at ease for the rest of the time we spent at Tahoe.

Joc told me that you were the one who suggested that we consider making Tahoe our new home. We want you to know that after the paddle wheeler cruise we spent most of our free time looking for houses.

Joc loved Tahoe, as everyone does. In the end, it was my decision not to move back. It just seemed that everywhere I turned I had ghosts from the past. Perhaps, someday I will be stronger, but until that time, my time at Tahoe will have to be limited to short visits. I love all of you and I will always be indebted to you for your steadfast support of me, even when I didn't deserve such loyalty.

We are going to make San Diego our home, and we would love you to come visit us here.

Thanks again for everything,

Love,
Marian and Joc

She wrote similar letters to everyone else, especially Daffy, who put together the whole dinner cruise party.

chapter 14

"SWEETHEART, MY AGENT called and asked if we were tired of playing tourist. I told him I loved it, and I thought you did too," Joc said with a smile. "I didn't make a mistake, did I?"

"No you didn't make a mistake. We probably should think of something productive to do with our lives before we become real beach bums," Marian laughed.

"All right then let's go to town and have lunch. That's productive," Joc laughed.

"Joc you are incorrigible," Marian giggled, as she reached for her purse.

While they were eating lunch, she spotted the little bridal shop across the street that belonged to Maria. "Joc, I would like to go over and see Maria. She's the seamstress who made my wedding dress. I haven't seen her since that awful day with Pete, would you mind," Marian asked.

"No that would be fine. I have a few things to do here in town myself. I will come get you when I'm done," Joc replied.

When Marian entered the shop, Maria remembered her right away.

"Marian, how are you dear? I was so worried about you, but I read in the paper you had been rescued. Goodness what an ordeal, I heard that poor young man died of his injuries. How awful, was he married?" Maria asked.

"He was not married, Jake was his name, and yes, it was awful," Marian said sadly.

"Well on a happier note, how was the wedding? You two make a handsome couple," Maria said.

"It was perfect, it was just family and our closest friends, about thirty people total. Everyone raved about my dress, so you will be getting all of the business we can send your way," Marian said.

"Thank you dear, but I'm getting too old to work here eight hours a day anymore. I have decided to sell the shop that's if I can get a buyer. What I would really like to do is just sew a few dresses a year, for special customers, but that probably isn't practical. I own the building, so I could just rent it to someone, but they would probably want to make it into an ice cream store or something," Maria said.

"When do you plan to sell it?" Marian asked.

"I haven't decided exactly, I don't know why I'm waiting," Maria said.

Just then Joc came into the little shop. "You must be Maria, the magician," Joc said chuckling a bit.

Maria just smiled at him and said, "And you must be prince charming for Marian here."

"Joc, Maria is thinking of selling her shop. She was just telling me she would like to continue making a few dresses a year, but she doesn't want to be here the long hours anymore," Marian said.

Joc could see the excitement in Marian's eyes, but he was not sure what she was thinking.

"Well I guess that's a good idea, I must admit I don't know much about wedding dresses. I do know Marian's dress was spectacular. I can only imagine how much work goes into making a wedding dress. When do you plan on selling?" Joc asked.

"I was just telling Marian I don't know... I don't know what I'm waiting for," Maria replied.

"Well it is a big decision, so taking your time isn't a bad idea. We better be going now Marian. It was nice to meet you Maria," Joc said, turning to leave the store.

"I 'll come back tomorrow to see you Maria," Marian said, as she left with Joc.

Marian could hardly contain her excitement on the way home. This could be her opportunity to have her own bridal store and realize her secret dream.

"Joc, do you think we could buy Maria's store? I 'm sure this is something I would like to do, that's if you wouldn't mind my taking it on. I really don't see myself not working at something, but on the other hand, I don't want to tie us down so we couldn't come and go as we would like. See how you've spoiled me?"

"That's what I want to do is spoil you. We can go talk to Maria tomorrow and see just what she has in mind," Joc said.

Marian could hardly sleep that night. She had all kinds of ideas running through her mind. She was up early, and had breakfast ready for Joc when he got up shortly after her. As they sat on the deck enjoying the morning together,

Marian said, "Joc what if she wants too much money and we can't make a profit of that little business?"

"I'm not that concerned about the business being a success. If the building isn't too expensive it will be a good investment just for the real estate alone. There is always a market for little rentals in San Diego and that one is in an excellent location. I didn't look at the structural integrity of the building, but most of the little shops have been well maintained over the years. I've been thinking about making a change too. Investing real estate is one of the options I've been considering," Joc replied.

"Oh Joc, I'm so excited I hardly slept last night thinking about all the possibilities. Maria doesn't get there until about ten o'clock do you want to go for a walk on the beach after I clean-up these dishes," Marian said, as she headed into the kitchen.

"We could walk into town along the beach if you would like, that might burn up some of that excess energy," Joc said, with a little grin.

While Marian was cleaning up in the kitchen, Joc slipped into the other room and made a call.

"What do you think would be a fair price? I don't want to cheat the woman, he said to the voice on the other end. Okay, that sounds good, and I appreciate your help," Joc said, as he hung up the phone.

When Joc and Marian arrived at Maria's little shop she was happy to see them.

"What a pleasure to see you both," Maria said with a smile.

"Maria," Joc began. "You mentioned to us yesterday you may be considering selling your shop if you could find the right buyer. Is that correct?"

"Yes, I'm just getting too old to work the long days, but I still love making dresses. I don't want to stop doing what I love. Does that make any sense?" Maria asked.

"Yes, it makes a lot of sense. That's why we stopped by, we have a proposition for you to consider. Marian thinks she would like to buy your little shop, but she doesn't make dresses so she would need you to take on the custom work. Frankly, my interest is in the real estate as an investment. Do you think selling to us would work for you?" Joc asked kindly.

"That sounds perfect. However, I have no idea what the property is worth. The property was paid for several years ago. The taxes keep going up every year, and that is a worry for me. What were you thinking it is worth to you?" Maria asked.

Joc told her about his conversation this morning with a real estate investor he knows.

"I would feel better if you would ask one of the realtors here in the area, or perhaps have an appraisal. I can pay you cash or if you prefer payments we can arrange that."

Marian had been quiet as Joc spoke with Maria, not wanting to confuse her.

"Why don't you sleep on it Maria, we're not going away. If you need a little time to decide that would be fine," Marian said, kindly as she took her hand.

"Thank you dear. That's probably a good idea. I can give you an answer by the end of the week," Maria said. "Are you going to open your own beauty shop? You know we could use another one in town."

"No, I don't think so. I would like to carry on with what you have here. Perhaps, change things some but not much. That will depend on if you are willing to stay to do the custom work. I promise you NO ice cream," Marian said, laughing a little.

As Marian and Joc left the shop Maria called to them, "I will call you as soon as I make up my mind, and thank you both."

Joc and Marian walked around the town a little before they headed back to the beach house.

"Are you still excited about starting a new business? You know the beauty shop idea isn't a bad one," Joc said.

"I know Joc, but I've been thinking more along the lines of a wedding shop for the stars. I thought I'd call Lana's mother and get her thoughts. Do you think she will think I'm crazy?" Marian asked.

"No, that's not crazy at all. Give her a call and see what she thinks," Joc said with enthusiasm.

Maria called Marian on Thursday to tell her she was accepting their generous offer. She would be delighted to make three or four custom dresses each year. Perhaps more if time permitted and if her health continued to be good.

Joc arranged to complete the purchase, and three weeks later Marian had a new business. There were many decisions to make including fresh paint, a bigger dressing room, and some interior changes were needed. She decided to keep the name MARIA'S. On the new front entry doors, she had etched in the glass under Maria's name, *Custom Wedding Dresses for the Stars*.

Five weeks following the purchase, the remodel was complete and the grand opening was a fabulous success.

Marian booked her first wedding dress for Maria. Joc was delighted to see Marian so happy. He hadn't seen her excited like this except at her own wedding. Following the opening, Joc took Marian to dinner at their favorite restaurant where the owner led them to a table looking out at the ocean.

"This was quite a day today, and a successful one as well, don't you think?" Joc said smiling as he watched Marian's excitement.

"It was really great, wasn't it? Maria said she was so proud to have her name on the door and she is pleased with all the changes. She said it was no longer just another dress shop. Now we would be catering to an exclusive clientele who demanded the latest in fashion and design. I hope that's a good thing," Marian said laughing a little.

"Well Mrs. Fournier, I guess I'm going to have to make appointments with you if I want to spend time with you in the future," Joc said chuckling.

With a mischievous little laugh, Marian said, "Well, Mr. Fournier, as luck would have it I'm free ALL night and I know this really nice house by the ocean if you would like to join me there."

"You don't have to ask me twice," Joc said getting up to leave.

When they got home, they went straight up to the bedroom. Marian went into the shower and a few minutes later Joc was beside her. He gently began kissing her and as he pulled her next to him, he became more aroused. He lifted her up and she wrapped her legs around him kissing him deeply feeling him inside her as the warm water ran over their naked bodies.

"Oh Joc she moaned, I love you so much and you are such a good lover."

"You have such a beautiful body," Joc said, as he gently began to wash her he whispered, "I love you more than you will ever know."

After they showered, they got into bed and continued making love. When Marian woke in the morning Joc was still lying next to her, gently stroking her hair, as he said, "Good morning beautiful, did you sleep well?."

"Oh yes, and I had this wonderful dream about the most handsome man who made love to me, it was wonderful," Marian said wistfully.

"So now I have competition,." Joc said pretending to be alarmed.

"No, you will never have any competition you are the very best," Marian said, kissing him deeply.

"You better not start that young lady. Remember you have a business to run now. No more lying around, I'll fix us some breakfast while you get ready for work," He said.

As the days and weeks went by Joc and Marian were settling into their new routine. Joc had started a real estate company in San Diego, which was doing quite well. He had five people working for him, and Marian had hired two employees to help at Maria's. This was giving them a little free time to share their experiences of the two new businesses with each other.

One evening Joad called to tell them she was seeing Bill, someone who she had gone to school with at Tahoe, and she would like to have Joc meet him.

Joad said, "We have vacation in August, would that time be convenient for you and Joc?"

"We would love to see you, and of course, we'll have time," Marian said.

When Marian hung up the phone she said, "Bill is a very nice young man, I always liked him. Joad never paid much attention to him because he wasn't a skier. I think he always liked her. Then we moved to Stockton, and she lost contact with everyone from Tahoe."

Lana's mother was in San Diego every couple of weeks, and they had the first wedding for one of the movie stars scheduled for the middle of June. This would be the first big wedding they would do and Marian was a nervous wreck.

"Joc, what if something goes wrong? It will ruin the business. I don't want to let Maria and Lana's mother down."

"Everything is going to be fine, stop worrying. All of you work together like a well-oiled machine. Do you remember our wedding? It came off without a hitch. All you have to worry about is those two prim-donnas don't get into a fight and call it off."

"Oh no, I never even thought about that!" Marian exclaimed.

The wedding was beautiful, and everyone was very pleased. Everything went as planned and the custom dress Maria had sewn for the bride was truly spectacular. Now Joc and Marian's lives could get back to normal.

Joad and Bill arrived the first week of August and the real reason for their trip was to announce their engagement. They planned to be married the following July and wanted Joc and Marian's advice as to where they should have the ceremony. Since most of their friends, and Bill's family still lived at Tahoe. They decided that would be the best location.

"Would you like us to make all the arrangements for you?" Marian asked. "You know that's what we do at Maria's. Do you have a dress picked out, or perhaps one you have pictured in your mind? Would you like to come with me to the shop tomorrow and talk to Maria, she's really good at helping with that."

"I really liked the dress you wore when you and Joc got married. Do you think she could make one like that for me?" Joad said.

"How would you like to wear that one? I saved it for you, in case you might be willing to wear it. Maria would alter it for you of course," Marian said.

"Oh mom, that would be wonderful!" Joad exclaimed.

Maria and Lana's mother sat down with Joad and they helped her plan the wedding. Lana always believed in starting with the guest list. Her saying was, "We need to see how big the elephant is before we start carving it up."

By the time the list was completed, it looked like there was going to be about two hundred people invited. Marian asked Joc if he would handle the logistics of making all the travel arrangements, as that would be difficult for Lana's mother to do. He was delighted to be of help.

"Bill, let's take the guest list and see who will need to fly, then we can deal with hotel reservations, and other transportation," Joc said.

"They will need to fly into the airport in Reno. There is a small airport at Tahoe, but it's limited to private aircraft," Bill said. "Joc, there is one other problem. I don't know how to put this but my mother is a real pain, if you know what I mean. We haven't even told her about the engagement. As soon as we do, she will want to take over everything. She only remembers Marian when she was drinking, and she didn't like her much, so when she hears Marian is handling everything...well...God help us all."

"That's good to know but don't worry I will talk to Marian, and she can have Lana's mother take charge. Believe me Lana's mother has handled the most difficult of situations. She has a way of making difficult people think they have done all the planning, and she even gets them to do most of the work," Joc laughed.

"What a mess Joc. If it were up to me, we would just elope. But the thought of having Joad and my mother both mad at me at the same time...well that's just too scary," Bill said a bit embarrassed.

Joc started laughing and he put his arm around Bill and said, "I sure do Bill, and I'm afraid you would have to add one more to that list. Marian. She has been dreaming of this day, and hoping Joad would have a real wedding. Don't ask me what's so important about weddings to women. I guess it is just one of their complexities we will never understand. When Marian wanted to buy Maria's little bridal shop I didn't object because I knew it would be a good business. Money is no object when it comes to weddings, and it also happens to be a good piece of real estate."

"Joc there is one other big problem. Joad would like to invite her father. However, Marian and Andy haven't spoken to each other since they divorced. Joad hasn't seen him since she was in the sixth grade. She is really much closer to you than she is to her real father. Her thoughts are, she doesn't want our future children to be denied knowing all of their grandparents. How can we deal with that?" Bill asked.

"I think Joad should invite her father. She should call him first to let him know your plans to be married. If he seems pleased about being contacted, then she should ask him if he would give her away. If for some reason he says no, I will be delighted to step in. However, I can't imagine any father turning down that opportunity, a bitter divorce or not," Joc said.

The next day Joad made the call to Andy. "Hi dad, this is your daughter, Joad, I'm calling because I've just gotten engaged to Bill Lambert. I think you know his father, Tom. And..."

"Joad, what a surprise, and congratulations, when is the big day?" Andy said excitedly.

"Well we haven't set the exact date yet, but July for sure, and at Tahoe. I was hoping you and Thelma would come, and..."

"Of course we will come, we wouldn't miss it. How does your mother feel about us coming? How is she doing these days?" Andy said hesitantly.

"She's great. You know she quit drinking a few years ago, and then she met a wonderful man, his name is Joc. In fact, he's the one who encouraged me to call," Joad said, feeling more confident now. "Oh, one other thing, I would like very much for you to give me away."

Andy was choked with emotion at being asked, so he took a moment before he could speak. "Baby, there is nothing I would be more honored to do, thank you for asking me," Andy said, gaining his composure a bit. "Tell me about you, where do you live now? Do you have a job? And what does Bill do?"

Joad answered all of his questions and gave him her phone number and address. They agreed to talk soon. Now the ice was broken, things went smoothly in planning the rest of the wedding. The wedding was held at Bill's parent's house near Cave Rock. It was a large home with three acres of property going down to the lake. Joad and Bill took their vows standing on the boat dock with the lake in the background. Andy, as promised was there to give Joad away. Janie was maid of honor, Kate was the flower girl, and Bill's sister was a bridesmaid. The reception was held at the same location following the wedding, and Lana's mother made sure Bill's mother was the center of attention. Marian was so happy to see both of her daughters in such a beautiful setting, and she and Andy actually had a nice time. Thelma and Joc got along well. They were both relieved Andy and Marian's first face to face meeting after almost ten years had actually gone quite well. Some of the family stayed on at Tahoe to vacation and Bill and Joad went to Hawaii for their honeymoon.

Marian and Joc returned to San Diego. When they settled in their favorite spot on the sofa, Marian said to Joc, "Wasn't it a beautiful wedding?"

"Yes it was," he replied. "Everyone I talked to thought you ladies had done a wonderful job. What does Bill's father do for a living? He seems to have done quite well."

"I'm not really sure. They moved to Tahoe from somewhere in Los Angeles I think, but no one knew much about him. They built a motel and he had a liquor store too. I think he's kind of a mystery. Some of my beauty shop customers said they thought he had some connections to the mob, though I never believed that was true. I must tell you my biggest fear was seeing Andy again, but with you by my side, it was really no problem. I actually enjoyed Thelma, she is a very nice person, don't you think?" Marian asked.

"Yes, we talked a good deal. She's kind of like me, never married before Andy, and no children of her own.

We agreed you both did well for yourselves," Joc chuckled and then gave her a kiss.

"Joc, you are such a tease, but you are right I'm very lucky to have you. I do miss the girls though. I love it here but I would like to spend a little more time with Janie's children, then when Joad has children I would like to be close to them as well. Do you think we could visit a few times a year?" Marian asked.

"We can do better than that. We can buy a home in Sacramento and live there part of the year," Joc replied.

"What would we do about our businesses?" Marian asked.

"Perhaps we should start looking for some competent managers for both of us. I would like to do a little more traveling, wouldn't you? Maybe we could even do a movie or two," Joc said looking to see Marian's reaction.

"Oh Joc, I don't think I could go back to doing hair again," Marian said.

"Well how about being an extra? There're always looking for good looking women," Joc replied.

Marian laughed, "They would never want me," she said. "I've never done any acting. Well a little in high school, but that was a long time ago."

"That's the great part about being an extra. You don't have to know how to act, all you have to do is follow directions, and I know you can to that. Come on, let me give my agent a call, just out of curiosity," Joc said.

"Okay, call if you want but don't expect much," Marian said.

The next morning Joc called Abe, to see if there were any new movies coming up away from Hollywood.

"Joc, good to hear from you, how is married life treating you? How's that beautiful woman you married? I heard all about the kidnapping, she wasn't hurt was she? "Abe asked.

"No, she was fine, a little shook-up but unharmed, thank God. Married life is wonderful. The reason I called was to see if you still have a need for extras on locations other than Hollywood, and if so, do you think you could use Marian too?" Joc asked.

"I always have work for you Joc, I was afraid I had lost you forever. I thought Marian was a beautician on the sets?" Abe responded.

"Yes, that's what she did, but she doesn't want to do hair and make-up anymore. You know that's very hard work and long hours too. So I suggested she might want to become an extra," Joc replied.

"I would love to have her as a client, she's good looking, and I know she can follow directions. I will mail out new contracts to both of you today," Abe said.

"Great and it is really good talking to you," Joc said.

"Same here," Abe said and he hung up the phone.

Joc picked Marian up for lunch, and they went to a little deli on the main street where they could sit outside. After they had ordered Joc said, "I talked to Abe this morning and he is sending out new contracts."

"That's wonderful Joc, I know you would love to do another movie," Marian said.

"No, I said contracts. That's two, one for you and one for me. He wants us both," Joc smiled.

"Really, he wants me too!" Marian exclaimed.

"Yes and I told him we want to work on the same movie, and on location anywhere but Hollywood," Joc said, smiling at her.

"When do we go?" Marian said excitedly.

"Hold on there, sweetheart it may be a couple of months before he calls us. In the meantime I think we better start looking for a couple of good managers for the businesses," Joc laughed.

Lana's mother had been having a wonderful time coordinating weddings. However, it really wasn't enough to keep her as busy as she liked to be. When Marian shared the plan that she and Joc were going to be extras, Lana's mother could hardly contain herself.

"Marian, don't look any further, I want to manage Maria's for you. It would be perfect. You know you can trust me, and I have a few ideas about growing this little place into a gold mine," Lana's mother said. "That's if you don't mind."

"Mind, are you kidding me? You were my first choice, but I didn't know how to ask you. I was afraid you might be insulted. Anything you want to do to make this little place better, you have my blessing," Marian said. "Joc will be thrilled too."

Just then, Joc came into Maria's. "Well would you look at the two of you. From the smiles on both of your faces, you must have booked another big wedding. Who is it this time, Elizabeth Taylor getting hitched again?"

Marian grabbed Joc and kissed him. It's much better than that. Lana's mother is going to manage Maria's for me isn't that wonderful!" Marian exclaimed.

Joc was all smiles, "That is really wonderful news. You couldn't have asked for anyone better. I'm starved, let's go have lunch and celebrate."

At lunch Marian and Lana's mother were so excited they were both talking at once. "I'll start looking for a place to stay this week. It will have to be somewhere that allows dogs. I want Duke to be with me," Lana's mother said.

Joc said, "Why don't you stay at the beach house? There is no need for you to rent a place, and it would be better to have someone living there rather than just leaving it empty when we're gone. Of course Duke would be a great watch dog."

"Yes, that's a great idea, that house is so big, there is plenty of room for all of us," Marian said.

"If you two are sure," Lana's mother said hesitantly, "I wouldn't want to intrude."

"It's settled then. You and Duke are coming to live with us,"Joc said.

Marian got busy preparing one of the rooms for Lana's mother and Duke, while Joc installed a doggie door. That way Lana's mother wouldn't have to let him in and out all the time. It only took about a week and Lana's mother moved in.

It was fun having Lana's mother staying with them, they played cards, and board games, and Lana's mother and Marian talked about new ideas for Maria's. Joc took Duke for runs on the beach and taught him to fetch sticks in the ocean. He was becoming a very good watchdog too.

About three weeks had gone by and Joc received a call from Abe, their agent. He had a movie that they were going to shoot in Colorado during December, and he wondered if they might be interested.

"That sounds great, I'll ask Marian tonight, and I will let you know in the morning. Will that work for you?" Joc asked.

"Sure thing Joc, that will be fine, I will look forward to your call," Abe replied.

That night at dinner, Joc told Marian and Lana's mother about the offer from Abe.

"I think, Lana told me about that movie. It is set in Colorado. I think it's a murder mystery involving skiers caught in an avalanche or something like that. MGM is producing it I think." Lana's mother said.

"That's the one," Joc said. "Skiing should be right up your ally Marian, maybe they will be looking at you for a staring roll."

"Now Joc, what would we really be doing?" Marian asked.

"I don't know but you can be sure it won't be hard, except for standing around in the cold. It should be fun, what do you say sweetheart? What do you want me to tell Abe?" Joc asked.

"Yes of course! I can hardly wait," Marian said.

Joc called Abe and told him they wanted the jobs.

"That's great news Joc, it will be good working with you again. Do you want me to make arrangements for a place for you and Marian to live while you are in Colorado?" Abe asked.

"No, I can handle that myself, just let me know when they will start filming and where in Colorado. I assume it is going to be someplace near one of the ski resorts," Joc said.

"Probably, but I'll get the details and get back to you as soon as I have more information," Abe replied.

That night Marian was so excited. "What do you think I should pack? I don't have any clothes for cold weather anymore. Will we be staying in a hotel or what?" Marian asked.

"I was thinking maybe we would rent a vacation house, maybe something large enough for all the family to come and spend Christmas in the snow. What do you think?" Joc asked.

"That would really be fun, having everyone together. They would have a lot to do there too, but we don't even know where yet," Marian said.

"Your right, it's just a fun thought. We'll wait and see where and when before we plan too much, and Mrs. Fournier the same goes for packing cloths. We will probably need to buy things when we get there," Joc smiled and kissed her on the end of her nose.

By late October, everything had been decided about the new movie MGM was filming. A murder mystery was to take place at a ski resort in Aspen, Colorado. The plot was a common one as it involved a famous skier being murdered. The usual number of suspects would be involved, with the real murderer not being reveled until the very end of the film.

Joc's part was a bartender in the local ski lodge, and Marian's part was a pretty ski bunny that frequented the lodge.

Joc was able to locate a six-bedroom house to rent while they were in Aspen. This would allow them to have all the families come for Christmas. It was a beautiful house and reminded Marian of the beach house in San Diego. They contacted Janie and Bob and the children, Joad and Bill, Lillian, Marilyn and her children, Wes and his family, and of course Lana's mother. Everyone accepted and all were looking forward to Christmas in Aspen.

Marian found the movie to be very exciting because as a beautician, she had always worked off stage. She had never been involved in the actual shooting of scenes.

They took a break from filming over Thanksgiving so everyone could be with their families. Joc and Marian invited those in the cast who were not going home, to have Thanksgiving with them. The day after Thanksgiving a few of the cast members joined Joc and Marian to go cut a big Christmas tree. They helped decorate the tree and the rest of the house so it would be ready when the families arrived for Christmas.

Filming began again on Monday. They were on a tight schedule because everyone wanted to be finished before Christmas. When the only beautician broke her leg skiing, Joc told the director Marian was a licensed beautician and had worked on *Bachelor in Paradise*. Perhaps she could fill in until they could get someone else. Marian happily obliged and the director took notice of this very talented woman.

They finished filming just four days before Christmas and everyone was thankful they would be spending Christmas at home with their families. Joc and Marian's families all arrived two days before Christmas and stayed through New Year's Eve.

chapter 15

THERE WERE PRESENTS for everyone and it was such a treat to see how these two families blended as though they had always been one. Of course, Joc had a surprise for Marian.

When everyone had finished opening their presents on Christmas morning Joc said, "As all of you know Marian and I have been working on a film here in Aspen for the last couple of months. I have a little film to show all of you that I'm sure you will love. Wes will you hit the lights for us please? Joc walked over to Marian and said, Mrs. Fournier, I would like to show you the Christmas present I have for you."

The film started with some candid pictures of Marian on the set. She said, "Oh no," everyone laughed. As the film continued there were a few shots with her in her part as an extra, and a few with her doing hair for the main stars in the film. Everyone clapped. There was one of her in the kitchen taking the turkey out of the oven at Thanksgiving, then helping with the Christmas tree decorations. Then on the screen came an address sign 1901 9th Ave, Sacramento, California, with a picture of the outside of a home. The home has four bedrooms, living room, and formal dining room with French doors to the yard. The kitchen is a chef's dream, with a separate breakfast area. A spacious family room with a bath, and French doors to the yard . The Master suite has a walk-in closet, tiled bath with dual sinks. There are dual pane windows and a marble entry.

The final picture was a huge bow with a card that said, Merry Christmas Sweetheart this is your new home in Sacramento!

Everyone was saying things like wow, and that is so great, and Joc you are a prince. Marian was speechless, as the tears ran down her cheeks. "Oh, I'm so sorry. I thought you would like it, It's okay I can sell it tomorrow if you don't want it." Joc said teased as he held her close.

Marian started to laugh, with the tears still coming down, she said, "Joc I love you so much, but sometimes..."

Joc interrupted, and put his arm around Lana's mother on one side and Marian on his other side as he said to, "I can never thank you enough for bringing this wonderful woman into my life. Then pulling Marian closer he looked into her eyes and said I had no idea such happiness was possible, Thank you and Merry Christmas sweetheart."

Everyone started talking at once, about when they were going to see the new house, who was leaving first, and as they were all caught up in the excitement of the moment, Joc and Marian slipped away to the little den in the back of the house. "Would you like to go to the house from here or do you want to go home first?" Joc asked.

"I would love to see the house first, but what about everyone else?" Marian replied.

"They will probably want to see the house as soon as they get back. There's not a stick of furniture in the place, so there's no worry of anyone staying too long," Joc chuckled. "We could stay a few days and see how you want to furnish it or we can hire a decorator to work with you on that."

"Okay, let's go see it on our way home and stay for a bit in Sacramento to decide what to do about furnishings, and then go home to San Diego. I want to see the changes at Maria's too. Lana's mother has been working on it and what she has described to me sounds wonderful. She says Duke misses you playing with him," Marian said.

Joc laughed, "I miss him too, and my job of throwing sticks in the ocean. He sure is a great dog."

"Lana's mother told me he has become a great watch dog too. One night someone was walking up to the house from the beach, and he raised such a fuss, whoever it was left as soon as she turned on the outside lights," Marian said.

When they arrived in Sacramento, the first three days were busy showing family members the new house and meeting with decorators. Marian finally decided she would like to do the project herself.

"When Joad was here she told me an old friend of mine, his name is Darryl, has opened an interior decorating store in Stockton. He was a good friend to Joad and me. We worked together as beauticians at Smith and Lang. In fact, if it wasn't for Darryl I wouldn't have been hired in the first place. When I was drinking he looked after Joad too," Marian said.

"Okay, we can go see Lillian and then we can look-up this Darryl fellow," Joc said.

The name of Darryl's business was simply DESIGN BY DARRYL, and it was a beautiful studio, modest but very up scale. It took Darryl only a minute to recognize Marian. He took her hand turned her around and around and said, "Look at you Kid you look fabulous! This beautiful man must be Joc. Little sister has told me how much she likes you. I sure wish I had been in the country at the time of your wedding. What brings you two to Stockton?" Darryl asked.

"We just purchased a house in Sacramento and Marian would like you to do the decorating for her," Joc said.

"That would be my honor. Where in Sacramento is the home located?" Darryl asked. "Just look at you Marian, I'm so happy to see you looking so well."

"I know, the last time you saw me I was pretty much a mess. I haven't had a drink in over four years eight months and two days now. The house is near William Land Park. It's one of the older homes that have been completely remodeled inside, but no furnishings of course," Marian said.

"I'm sorry I missed little sister's wedding, but we were so busy here. There was no way I could get away. I did get to see them after the wedding though. She has grown-up into a pretty woman, just like her mother," Darryl said.

Joc liked Darryl right away. He could see why Marian wanted to hire him. He had nice pieces in the studio. He showed them his portfolio with some of his finished homes and Joc knew he would do an extra special job on Marian's house. Darryl told them he would be able to start the following week. "How would you like to arrange the details? Do you want to pick out things yourselves, or do you want me to select for you?" Darryl asked.

"At first I wanted to do this myself, but that isn't practical, and after seeing what you have done with all these other homes, I want you to do everything. We need to go back to San Diego because we both have businesses there. We have been away for over two months now and we must get back and spend a little time there. We've had an extra key for the house made for you," Marian said.

"We can keep in touch by telephone, and if needed we can come to Sacramento for a day or two at a time, if you would like. We have plenty of room at the house in San Diego too if you want to come there," Joc said.

"Well that sounds very tempting Joc. Marian, what kind of business do you have? Did you open your own salon?" Darryl asked.

"No Darryl, quite by accident I found this little bridal shop owned by a lady who was getting ready to retire, so Joc bought it for me. It's been so much fun. You must come and visit. I can hardly wait to show it to you and hear all about you completing your dream," Marian smiled and gave Darryl a hug.

Marian and Joc spent a couple of days with Lillian, who was doing well. She was already talking about getting the ground ready to put in her garden as soon as it warmed up.

Darryl drove to Sacramento to look at his new project. After seeing the house, he couldn't wait to get started. Joc and Marian returned to San Diego.

chapter 16

BILL'S FATHER, TOM, was working on securing investors for a new casino that was to be located near the base of Kingsbury grade. It was all very secret, but Tom made several trips to Sacramento and other cities in an effort to get the project underway.

One afternoon Tom appeared at Maria's asking for Marian. She was taken by surprise to see him there. "Oh for heaven's sake Tom, you are the last person I expected to walk through that door. It's great to see you, what brings you here?" Marian said. She was smiling and genuinely surprised to see him.

"I have some business here in San Diego. I had a little spare time and Bill and Joad told me where to find you," Tom replied.

"Joc's business is just a couple of blocks from here. We can go get him and then grab a bite to eat. You haven't had lunch yet have you?" Marian asked.

"Well no, but I don't want to intrude," Tom said.

"Don't be silly, I'm so pleased to see you. As they walked down the street toward Joc's, Tom asked, "What business is Joc in?"

"He does real estate investing. It's a small office with a few guys who do sales also," Marian said.

When they reached Joc's, Marian said, "Look who I found wondering around town, and we are both very hungry. We heard you were buying lunch," Marian quipped.

Joc kissed Marian and said, "Tom, how nice to see you, and as a matter of fact I was just about to come get Marian for lunch. What brings you to our fair city?" Joc asked.

"I have a meeting tomorrow with a fellow who is considering investing in my new casino project at Tahoe. I've brought him the plans and other information for him to review," Tom said.

"That sounds promising. Where are you staying while you are in San Diego?" Joc asked.

"I just got here and I haven't had a chance to check in yet, but I have a reservation at the Hyatt Hotel," Tom said.

"Why don't you stay with us, we have plenty of room, and you can call and cancel your reservation," Joc said.

"Oh I couldn't do that, and really the hotel will be fine," Tom replied.

"We can't let someone in the family stay in a hotel when we have so much room. You'll have plenty of privacy, and it's much quieter. We insist," Marian said.

"After lunch we can go to the house and get you settled," Joc said.

"Well okay, sounds like you two are not taking no for an answer. The car I rented is parked in front of Marian's store," Tom said, smiling and looking a bit embarrassed.

Tom was amazed at the beach house. His home at Tahoe was a show place, but this home was every bit as nice.

Tom came to America as a teenager and worked in the coalmines in Steubenville, Ohio. Dean Martin, Frank Sinatra and the boys came from this same town. Tom was a short man, who had all the mannerisms that his Italian background stereotyped.

Having worked on a film once with Frank Sinatra, Joc was well aware of the ego these men liked to display. Still he found something he liked about Tom, he seemed to have a little more humility. That evening Joc decided to ask Tom about his project.

"Are you at liberty to tell me a little about your project Tom?" Joc began.

"Well there's not a lot to tell just yet. It's still in the planning stages. I have secured the land, and I've had some preliminary drawings made up of the proposed project, but I've never done anything this big before. My background has been in automatic screw machining. I'm still learning the ropes of this business, so to speak," Tom volunteered.

"I know a little about how that feels. When I started my real estate investing business, I didn't know much more than the word real estate. As you go along you pick up a little here and a little there, and pretty soon you're surprised at what you do know," Joc mused.

"Yeah, the fellow I'm meeting with tomorrow is supposed to be the owner of some big electrical company here in San Diego. He claims he wants to be a major stockholder in the project," Tom said skeptically.

"Oh do you mind telling me his name? I may know who he is. This is a pretty small town here, as it probably is at Tahoe," Joc said.

"No it is no secret, his name is Wilson, and his company is Wilson Electrical," Tom said.

"Dave Wilson, I know him well, he is a good man, and he is real all right. He's made a fortune in the electrical business. He started out in residential housing, and then branched out into the commercial field where he has made a killing," Joc said.

"That's good news. Some of the people I've talked with are just talkers, all smoke, and no fire, if you know what I mean?" Tom said.

"I think you'll like Dave, he's no nonsense. If he agrees to be part of your project, he will do what he says," Joc said.

"Okay you two, dinner is ready. It's so nice out we've have set a table out on the deck. Lana's mother has made a wonderful salad to go with our steaks," Marian said.

At dinner, Marian told Tom all about how Lana's mother introduced them when they were working in Hollywood. She also told Tom how they just finished working on *Murder for Hire* in Colorado. Then she told him about her Christmas present of the house in Sacramento. She served Tom wine with his dinner, and Lana's mother joined him. Marian explained she was an alcoholic and she hadn't had a drink in over four years so she and Joc toasted their friends with ice tea instead of wine. Marian inquired about Ann, Tom's wife, but mainly just to be polite, as she didn't care for Ann. When dinner was finished, they showed Tom his room and the rest of the house, and returned to the big comfortable sofas by the fireplace.

"This is a great place you have here," Tom said. "How do you like living by the ocean? This isn't a lot different from Tahoe, except it's a lot warmer and I like that," Tom said with a slight grin.

They continued to talk for an hour or so and then Tom said, "I should excuse myself, I have a long day tomorrow and I want to be at my best. You understand."

"Of course, I think we will be turning in soon ourselves. We enjoyed having you, and you are welcome anytime and the best of luck tomorrow," Joc said.

"Thank you both and it was so nice meeting you meme," Tom said to Lana's mother, not knowing what to call her. She had a name of course, but she chose to introduce herself as Lana Turner's mother, so everyone else did as well.

The next morning Marian had fixed a light breakfast for everyone. Lana's mother headed to Maria's, Joc to the real estate office, and Tom left for his appointment with Mr. Wilson. Marian stayed behind and cleaned up the house, went for a walk with Duke and played his favorite game of fetching a stick from the surf. Then she sat out on the deck to sunbathe and read one of her favorite mysteries by Erle Stanly Gardner.

A few weeks had passed since Tom had visited Joc and Marian., when Dave Wilson stopped by the real estate office to see Joc.

"Dave nice to see you, what brings you by this morning?" Joc asked.

"I would like to pick your brain a bit, if you don't mind," Dave said.

"Anything up here, pointing to his head, is all yours Dave," Joc quipped.

"Well I'm considering investing a good deal of money into a casino at Lake Tahoe. I understand you know the fellow who has approached me, Tom Lambert," Dave said.

"I do know Tom. In fact, his son is married to Marian's youngest daughter, Joad. He told me a little about his project and that he was going to meet with you. Beyond that I don't know much more," Joc answered honestly.

"Well I'm having him checked out by my people. So far he seems to be on the up and up. There's a little question about who he associated with in his younger years in Steubenville but his connections to those boys don't seem to have been deep or long lasting. You know you have to be so careful these days about going into business with someone. You know what I mean?" Dave said candidly.

"I do, and I understand completely, but I'm afraid I don't know any more about him than I just told you. He stayed with us over night before he met with you and he seemed to be a nice enough fellow," Joc continued.

"Oh no, I'm not asking that. I'm asking what you think about investing in a casino at Lake Tahoe?" Dave said.

"I don't know anything about the casino business, but I can tell you I nearly bought a home up there. It's a beautiful resort area, and it's grown a good deal in the last several years, so the location is great," Joc replied.

"What stopped you? From buying the home, that is," Dave asked.

"Marian lived there with her ex-husband for several years and she just didn't think she wanted to re-live the past, if you understand," Joc said.

"I didn't mean to get too personal. So it wasn't anything about Tahoe, more just personal issues right?" Dave said.

"Exactly, I may still do some investing there anyway in the future. I don't want to wait too long because I think it's going to continue to grow. I think it's still what you would call a ground floor opportunity. But the casino business, that's way above my expertise," Joc said shaking his head.

"Okay then, I still have a few I's to dot T's to cross but I appreciate your input. Thanks Joc," Dave said, as he turned to leave.

"Sure thing Dave, anytime, and keep me posted will you? It sounds intriguing," Joc said.

A couple of months went by and Joc ran into Dave in the deli in San Diego.

"How is everything, Dave?" Joc said with a smile.

"Couldn't be better, Dave replied. We'll be signing final papers in two weeks for the project, and then start construction before the end of next month."

"Congratulations, I guess all your questions were answered satisfactorily," Joc replied.

"Yes, and I feel so good about this project, everything just seems to fall into place. You know some deals are a struggle every minute. This one, well it just seems right. Have to run Joc, I have a million things to do today. Good seeing you," Dave said.

When Joc got home that night, he told Marian about his conversation with Dave.

"Have you heard anything from Joad about the deal?" Joc asked.

"No, just that she's not included in any discussions about it. I guess Tom is quite the chauvinist, you know the type, women are to be barefoot and pregnant. God help Bill if he tries that stuff on Joad. You know when that girl was about ten she told me she didn't want to be a Catholic anymore because she couldn't be an altar boy. In case you hadn't noticed, she is not a Catholic. When that kid makes up her mind, it's made up," Marian said shaking her head.

"Hum, I wonder where she gets that," Joc said smiling and chuckling a bit.

One afternoon, Joc heard on the news, Dave Wilson had had a massive heart attack. He was expected to live, but it had done severe damage to his heart. Joc went to see him at the hospital the following week.

"Dave, I'm sure sorry. How are you doing?" Joc said sincerely concerned.

"I'm alive, but that's about the extent of it Joc. The doctors tell me I'll never be able to go to Tahoe. I guess the altitude is too tough on the ole ticker," Dave said weakly." I'm going to have to back out of the casino deal. No use investing in something I'll never be able to see."

"I'm sorry, Dave. The important thing is you are alive," Joc said.

"Yea, but I sure hate to let Tom down. We have become good friends over the last several months. You know he has everything he owns tied up in that project. If it doesn't go through, he might lose everything. What makes a guy do that, put everything on the line like that?" Dave said sadly.

"I don't know Dave, but don't worry about that now. You need to take care of yourself," Joc said.

Marian could hardly wait to see Joc to tell him the news. "Joad called today, and she is pregnant, isn't that exciting. She is due in December," Marian exclaimed.

"Yes that's wonderful news. Darryl will have the house done long before December so we can plan to spend a month or two in Sacramento if you would like too," Joc said.

"I was hoping you would say that. Maybe we could have everyone for Thanksgiving or Christmas," Marian said excitedly.

"Okay, we'll plan on it. I think it will be fun," Joc said.

"I went to see Dave Wilson in the hospital today. He had some bad news about the prognosis for his health. The damage was so bad to his heart he won't be able to go to Tahoe again. I guess the altitude is the issue," Joc said sadly.

"Oh that poor man, it sounds like he's lucky to be alive," Marian replied.

"Yes he certainly is. He told me something else that is concerning. Tom mortgaged everything they have for that casino project. He'll lose it all if he doesn't get another investor," Joc said.

"Oh no!" Marian exclaimed.

"What do you suppose prompted him to do such a risky thing?" Joc asked.

"I don't know, but when you are around gambling all the time, people just take risk as a normal thing. I know Andy and I sure did. We spent everything we made, and we were doing very well, both of us. We didn't even have our house paid for, and we could have done it easily. I guess we just convinced ourselves things were always going to get better and better," Marian said.

"I don't know how much he needs, but I have a feeling it's a lot more than I'm capable of raising. Getting into business with family or friends can be very risky no matter how well things go. I don't like gambling anyway, kind of a dirty business I think," Joc said.

"You weren't seriously thinking of investing with him were you?" Marian said concerned.

"No, no I just feel badly this is going to be hard on him. He's not a young man anymore, and starting over, well, that's no picnic no matter what your age," Joc said.

Tom had only three months left to find another investor for the casino project before the bank would start foreclosure proceedings. That would mean he would lose the big house on the lake, a couple of smaller homes he had as rentals, and of course the land where the proposed casino was to be built.

He asked everyone he knew if they knew anyone who had the funds to invest in such a project. Finally, someone told him to have ten thousand dollars in cash and he was to give the money to a priest, as a donation, after which a meeting would be arranged with the investor. Tom knew this was risky business so he insisted on the meeting being in a busy public restaurant in downtown Sacramento. He decided to take his son Bill with him. After donating the money, Tom received a telephone call from the priest giving him the time and place of the meeting with the investor. The meeting took place in New York the following week. The investor was the Teamsters Union, and this was to be a loan, the terms of which would be at the Union's discretion. Tom met with Mr. James Hoffa Sr. himself. Tom was concerned about the outcome of the trial Hoffa's upcoming trial, but Hoffa was not. He didn't believe he would be going to prison. Of course, he was wrong.

The papers for the loan were never signed. Having no more money to proceed with the project, Tom was unable to get any more extensions from the bank and they foreclosed.

Devastated by the failure, Tom and Ann left Tahoe and moved to Palm Springs where sadly he went to work managing a machine shop for fifty dollars a week.

chapter 17

DARRYL FINISHED THE decorating of the house in Sacramento by the end of September. Marian could hardly wait to see the finished product. She and Joc flew to Sacramento and met Darryl at the house. Darryl opened the front door and when Marian stepped inside the entry, she was speechless.

"Don't you like it?" Darryl said with some concern.

"Like it, it's so beautiful. Darryl, I could never have imagined this in my wildest dreams. You are fantastic!" Marian squealed.

"Wow, you are some talented guy," Joc said, amazed at what Darryl had accomplished.

"Let me take you on the guided tour," Darryl said. "The crystal chandelier in the entry is from Austria as are the two in the dining room. The dining room table and the twelve matching chairs are made of exotic woods from different regions in South America. The credenza incorporates some of the same woods with the top made from copper. I remember you told me how you loved copper and wood. There are also twelve matching copper place mats. When you open this door of the credenza, you will find a small refrigerator. The other side and the center drawers hold your china and silver service for twelve. I hope you like the china. The color is sand, and you can see the lightly etched fir trees in the center of each piece. So what do you think so far?" Darryl said proudly.

Marian was grinning from ear to ear and she said, "Darryl it's perfect. Joc, can you believe what he has done?"

"It's fantastic," Joc replied. "I can hardly wait to see the other rooms."

"Well then without further ado let's go," as he led them to the living room, he said, "This was simple after I found this Persian rug, everything else fell into place."

The fireplace mantel held two elegant crystal candle-holders with green pine boughs between. A large comfortable sectional was covered in light tan suede, with darker brown decorator pillows. The coffee table and end tables were wood that matched the fireplace mantels color, and the end tables held copper lamps with mica shades.

As Darryl continued his tour he said, "I remember how much you like music, and I think you told me you could play."

Darryl pointed to the small grand piano on one side of the room. The other wall of the room was filled with books. "The library is for you Joc, and I found a couple of nice chairs because Marian said you liked to read. Am I still doing okay?" Darryl asked, smiling broadly now.

"The kitchen was done, so all I had to do was outfit it for you. This was fun, because unless you've changed, I know cooking is only something you like to do on occasion. Continuing with the copper theme, you have a complete set of Revere Ware with copper bottoms. All the back-splashes are a simulated copper to prevent spotting and stains. Glasses, everyday dishes, flatware, etc. etc. it's all here," Darryl explained, using a sweeping motion with his arm as he spoke.

"Now for the fun stuff, this first bedroom I let little sister pick out the items."

As he opened the door to the first bedroom, there was a complete nursery. The whole room was decorated in a circus theme, bright colorful and fun. It had brightly sparkling circus animals decorating the walls, the crib had a mobile had a tightrope walker as the top, with an elephant, a tiger, a dancing bear, and a seal hanging below. There was a rocker with an afghan adorned with circus animals, and a dresser with a top for changing. There was also a small child size twin bed, and a toy box.

" I think she did pretty well don't you? As you can see nothing is permanent here, so as the grandchildren grow it's easily transformed with little expense," Darryl said.

Marian was astounded, "I would never have thought about a nursery until one of the grandchildren stayed overnight, and with the baby coming and Robby only a year old, this is perfect," Marian said.

"Next stop is a children's play room. I believe you said Joc's families have little ones too."

As he opened the door, two sets of bunk beds with matching dressers were on one side of the room, and the window seat had little pillows in bright colors. There was a long desk with four child size chairs, and the desk slid open into a large game table. There were shelves in the walk-in closet that held several board games.

"Janie picked out the items for this room. Also a good job, I believe." Darryl said.

There were three other guest rooms, each had a different theme, one was decorated with an ocean and seaside theme, and the other two were traditional décor.

"Now for the master bedroom," Darryl said, proudly. "The first thing you see as you open the double doors to the bedroom is the king-size bed made from natural birch logs, sanded smooth and protected with a clear sealer to maintain the natural beauty of the wood. The same is true of the dressers and nightstands. The fireplace just needed two comfortable chairs. I took the liberty of choosing shades of blue and green. They are restful colors and most people don't object to either," Darryl continued.

As Darryl opened the French doors that lead to the balcony, which overlooked the back yard, Marian spotted a beautiful fountain made from copper leaves with fish that appeared to be jumping. A small bistro table with two chairs was in the opposite corner. Plants and flowers completed the feel of the outdoors, and Marian bent over and touched one of the copper fish as Darryl watched her. The walk-in closet and the bath were what one would expect. It was perfect in every way down to the scented candles. The best part for Marian no doubt, was the built-in make-up table with fabulous lighting and a very comfortable chair.

"I knew you would need this, and Joc told me that was the most important thing for you to have, since you spend so much time in the bathroom," Darryl said, laughing and teasing Marian.

"I can see I don't have a chance with you two," Marian joked. "Honestly, Darryl I'm so impressed with what you have done. You really have thought of everything, I can't wait to come back and move in. Joc, thank you my love, I don't deserve to have all of this."

"Yes sweetheart you do deserve this and more, I love you," Joc said as he kissed her.

As they walked back through the house, Marian and Joc would notice other small details Darryl hadn't pointed out when he showed them through to begin with. He was thrilled they had noticed. It meant a lot to Darryl to see Marian so happy. He had never seen Marian completely sober when he knew her in Stockton. What an outstanding women she is, he thought to himself as they walked to the cars and said their goodbyes.

On the flight back to San Diego, all Marian talked about was the house in Sacramento. How beautiful it was and how much she loved what Darryl had done.

"Maybe we should consider making Sacramento our permanent home and use the beach house as a vacation place," Joc said.

"Oh, I don't know Joc, I love the beach house too!" Marian said a bit whimsically.

"Well then we'll just go back and forth between the two, since you can't make up your mind," Joc laughed. They both laughed and sat back and enjoyed the flight.

When they arrived in San Diego, Marian could hardly wait to tell Lana's mother all about the house in Sacramento, but as she was talking, she sensed Lana's mother wasn't as enthusiastic as she usually was.

"What's wrong is everything alright?" Marian said concerned.

"Oh no everything is fine and that's so exciting, but I was just thinking, with the new house, and grandchildren on the way, I may not be seeing much of you," Lana's mother said

Marian laughed and said, "Me playing the grand-mother roll? You must be kidding. Don't get me wrong I love the girls, and of course, any children they have will have my love too, but I'm a worker. I always have been and I always will be. I love working at Maria's with you. I also had so much fun being an extra on the film in Colorado, and then there is Joc. Can you picture him just hanging around playing grandpa? No, we have decided to stay here. Perhaps we will spend holidays at the house in Sacramento. We plan to do any films that look interesting and of course you and Duke are always part of everything we do."

Once again, life returned to normal in San Diego. Maria's had become a thriving business doing custom weddings for the stars, and Joc's real estate business was very busy. Lana's mother bought a smaller house in town, but she couldn't have Duke there. Joc gladly adopted Duke, and Lana's mother agreed to house sit for them anytime they were on a film or in Sacramento.

Over the next several years, Marian's life was happy and full of good times. Joad, like Janie, had two children now, a boy and a girl. Marian was there for all of the special occasions and most holidays were spent either at the house in Sacramento or at the beach house in San Diego, with both families in attendance. Lillian was close to eighty now, and was happy in Stockton in the houses she and Frank had built. With the houses updated, she was able to attract good renters, and she was able to take the bus to Reno on occasion to visit slot machine number eight, at Harold's Club. Her son Bob and his family lived in Carson City so she would visit with them too.

Life for all of them was good since Marian had stopped drinking and Joc came into her life, but once again, all that was about to change.

chapter 18

IT BEGAN WITH the stranger who came into Joc's office inquiring about a house for sale just down the beach from where Joc and Marian lived.

"I'm Joc Fournier, and you are?" Joc said, putting out his hand to greet the man.

"Ah Vince, the man said, coldly. When can I see the house?"

"Would you like to see it now?" Joc answered. "My car is outside. That property is on the market for six-hundred-fifty thousand. It has beach frontage, and being at the end of the road, it's very private. It is a bit dated but structurally it's sound."

"I'll take my own car, I'll just follow you," Vince replied.

"Okay. Suit yourself it's only about a half mile from here," Joc said, smiling and giving a slight shrug.

When they reached the house, Joc unlocked the front door saying, "It's been a while since anyone has lived here. Go ahead and take a look around." Sensing Vince didn't want Joc giving him a tour, he said, "if you have any questions I'll be out here on the deck."

Vince took a quick look at the house and then said, "I want to see the garage."

"Sure, right through the kitchen, over here is the door to access the garage from inside," Joc said as he opened the door.

Vince was not the typical buyer for a San Diego beach-front property. Joc wondered if he was wasting his time, but what could it hurt if he wasted a half hour or so. Vince seemed to take a special interest in the garage, especially since there was a door leading out to the beach. "Good," Vince said," This will work fine, how long will it take before I can move in?"

Somewhat surprised at the speed at which Vince decided on the property Joc said, "We can go back to the office and write it up, then it just depends on the lender and title company to draw up the papers."

"No lender. I'm paying cash," Vince snapped.

"In that case no more than a couple of days," Joc said.

"Good. Go write it up and I'll be back at your office in an hour to sign," Vince replied.

On the way back to the office, several things were running through Joc's mind. Was this guy real, was he married? Did he have a family? What was it about this house? What was so interesting about the garage? When he sat down to fill out the paperwork he realized he didn't know Vince's last name, address, or anything about him.

Just then, Sam, one of Joc's agents pushed through the front door of the office.

"Good morning Joc, how are you this morning? What a great day to be alive," Sam said happily.

"Sure is Sam, and I'm fine... but the strangest thing just happened. You know that house down the beach from my place?" Joc said.

"Sure the older one, kind of dated, for six-hundred-fifty?" Sam replied.

"That's the one. Well, I just showed it to a guy, and he told me to come back here and write it up. He's buying it for cash today, and he wants to move in ASAP. Can you believe that?" Joc said still puzzled by this man.

"Geez Joc, you live a charmed life," Sam said.

"Yeah, well we'll see if he actually shows up. When I started to wright it up I realized I don't even know his last name, or his present address," Joc said, shaking his head a bit. "How many years have I been doing this now?"

Joc and Sam sat and talked a while waiting to see if Vince returned. About forty-five minutes later the office door opened and Vince walked in, looked around warily, saying, "You got the papers ready for me to sign?"

"All set, I just need to have your last name and a mailing address for you. We can go over to the title company and you can give them a check, and then you have a deal," Joc replied.

"Donatello is the last name, and general delivery San Jose, is the address," Vince said, still looking around the office.

Joc filled in the blanks, had Vince sign the papers, and said, "Okay, that's it. Let's go to the title company," Joc said.

Vince handed Joc a certified check made out for six-hundred and fifty thousand dollars and said," No you go. I have other things to take care of right now."

He handed Joc a small piece of paper with a number written on it. "Here's my number call me when I can move in. Won't be more than a week, will it?" Vince scowled.

Joc handed Vince a receipt for the check and said, "No, it shouldn't take more than a day or two at the most, just like I said," Joc replied.

With that, Vince was gone. "Wow, Sam said, after Vince was gone. "Can you believe that, who is that guy anyway?"

"Got me." Joc said puzzled, "This check looks real to me. Do you want to go to the title company with me?"

"Sure, I wouldn't want to miss this," Sam said.

Vince had only been gone a few minutes when Joc and Sam left the office walking toward the title company. "Look Sam, he's gone, he just disappeared. This is really strange," Joc said, worried a bit.

"Well you'll know soon enough if this guy is real or not. My guess is he's just strange, you know someone who can round up six-fifty K in an hour with a certified check ... well you got to take that seriously," Sam said.

"You'er right Sam. I guess I shouldn't be concerned. But you know he's going to be my neighbor so that's probably why I'm even talking about him," Joc said relaxing a bit.

By the next week, the house had closed and Vince took possession right away. He had some men there, who were working on updating the house. There was a lot of noise. Hammering, saws running, and trucks were coming and going. There was even a few times when work was being done until the wee hours of the morning. Joc was pleased to see Vince was updating the house because it would only improve the land around it. He soon forgot his initial concerns about Vince.

One afternoon, while in the hardware store downtown, Joc ran into Vince. "Hello Vince, how is the remodel coming?" Joc said cheerfully.

"It's slow, but what I really need is an interior decorator. I know what to do with the structural stuff, but putting it all together with furniture, paint and that kind of thing, well I can't do that," Vince said.

Immediately, Darryl came to mind and Joc said, "You know, I can recommend someone for that, but he's in Stockton. Might be a bit expensive to have him come here, but I'd be happy to check for you. That's if you would like me too."

"Can't hurt, I've spent so much money already, I've quit keeping track," Vince said giving a slight smile.

"I'll give him a call today and let you know what he says," Joc said as he turned to leave.

That evening Vince walked over to Joc and Marian's, but as he came up the stairs to the deck, Duke started growling and snarling behind the glass doors.

"Duke, stop that!" Joc commanded, as he opened the door for Vince.

"Great watch dog you have there," Vince said, still a bit leery of Duke.

"I've never seen him like this," Joc said, holding on to his collar tightly as Duke's hair was standing up on his back and his lips were curled back showing his large teeth.

"Sit!" Joc commanded, and Duke obediently responded, but kept watching Vince.

"Sorry about that, Vince, would you like a drink or a cup of coffee, or tea?" Joc asked.

"Coffee if you have it made," Vince said politely.

Joc headed for the kitchen to get the coffee, asking Vince if he wanted anything in it.

Just then, Marian came down stairs and said, "What's Duke making such a fuss about?"

"Marian, I'd like you to meet Vince. Were you able to get in touch with Darryl today?" Joc asked.

"It's my pleasure to meet you Vince," Marian answered politely. She could hear Duke was still growling very low. "Yes, I did call Darryl and he's going to fly in on Saturday. I invited him to stay a few days with us, then he can meet Vince and they can talk."

"That's so very nice of you, I didn't mean for you to go to all that trouble," Vince said.

"Oh it's no trouble. Darryl and I are old friends. I've wanted him to spend some time here with us anyway. This was just a good excuse," Marian said, smiling her beautiful smile. "If you don't come to any business agreement it's no problem. He has plenty of business in the valley."

Joc brought in the coffee, and Duke never took his eyes off Vince. They talked a little, but the conversation was somewhat strained. Vince finished his coffee rather quickly and said, "Well I better go now, and I'll look forward to Saturday."

As Vince got up to leave, Duke followed him still making a low growl. Joc walked with him to the door and said, "See you Saturday Vince."

When Vince was gone, Duke was back to his old self, playful, and tail wagging. "What was that all about?" Marian said to Joc."I've never seen Duke act like that before, have you?"

"No, I sure haven't. He must have startled Duke when he came up the stairs of the deck." Joc said somewhat puzzled.

"But Joc, did you hear him growl the whole time Vince was here? He never took his eyes off him," Marian said. "You know animals have a six-sense for things sometimes, and Duke doesn't like him."

"Well, let's not make too much of it right now. Maybe after he sees him more often he will calm down," Joc said dismissively. "Now tell me how you got Darryl to come down here?"

Marian just laughed and said, "I hardly got the words out of my mouth. He said he would be on the first flight Saturday morning. You know Joc, regardless of what Vince decides, maybe we could have Darryl do some of his magic on the beach house."

"I was thinking the same thing. This place could use some modernization. It's been over ten years since anything has been done here," Joc said, "If he stays with us, and has both jobs we might be able to save a little money in the process."

"Be thinking of what you want done, because I don't know what I would change. I fell in love with this house the first time I saw it, so I don't know what would improve it." Marian said.

"Oh, you fell in love with the house? I thought you had fallen in love with me!" Joc teased.

Marian just laughed and cuddled up next to Joc on the big couch in front of the fireplace. "I know one thing I don't want him to change and that's this spot!"

When Darryl arrived on Saturday, Marian and Joc picked him up at the airport. After all the hugs were exchanged, they took Darryl to Maria's, the real estate office, and then took him to lunch at their favorite restaurant by the ocean.

After lunch, they arrived at the house and Duke was there to greet them, tail wagging, and sniffing Darryl.

"What is your name boy?" Darryl said petting Duke's big head.

"This is Duke," Marian said. "He sure seems to like you Darryl."

"Of course, dogs, kids and old ladies, all love me," Darryl laughed, "And on occasion, I find a nice boyfriend too," he said winking at Marian.

"Wow this is a great place, no wonder you love it here kid. Joc how did you find this place?" Darryl said enthusiastically.

"It was about fifteen years ago Darryl. We were doing a movie in San Diego. I was walking along the beach one evening and saw a for sale sign on the house. I checked on the price, and the rest is history," Joc replied.

"Who is this fellow Vince?" Darryl asked.

"Well he lives alone. Has plenty of money, and beyond that I don't know much about him accept Duke apparently hates him," Joc laughed.

"Hum ... so you don't think much of this Vince person Duke? I better take it slow," Darryl said to Duke.

Marian took Darryl upstairs and showed him one of the guest rooms, then Joc and Duke joined them.

"Marian and I were thinking regardless of what happens with decorating Vince's house, we would like you to redecorate this house," Joc said.

"Great, show me around the rest of the house," Darryl said, now very interested.

As they went from room to room, Darryl was mentally taking notes of the room sizes, and the building materials that had been used in the homes original construction.

"I like this house," he said. "You did a good job of selecting quality materials Joc," Darryl said.

"Oh I didn't have anything to do with that. The house was already built when I bought it. I bought it just as you see it, furnishings and everything. I just liked the feel of it," Joc said.

"Well I think we can modernize it without destroying any of its classic charm," Darryl replied.

Duke was running from room to room with them, and Darryl was playing with him as they went.

"You're a good boy, Duke, what do you think about redecorating your digs?" Darryl said, rubbing Dukes big head.

Marian showed Darryl the kitchen last. "I want you to make yourself at home here Darryl, so help yourself to the refrigerator, and most other food is in the pantry over here," she said, pointing to the door of the pantry. "I guess you and Joc better go over to Vince's and get acquainted. Duke you stay here with me," Marian said.

Joc and Darryl went down the deck and walked along the beachfront to Vince's property. They decided to go around to the front door by the driveway and ring the doorbell. No one came to the door, so they rang the bell again. Just as they were about to leave, Vince opened the door.

"It's you Joc, I'm sorry I was on the other side of the house when you rang the first time," Vince said.

"This is Darryl Hammond, the interior designer we told you about. I thought I would introduce you. He will be staying with us for a while, as we are going to have him redecorate our place. However, if you decide to use his services your house will take priority," Joc said.

"Darryl, nice to meet you, and there is no question about using you. You come highly recommended," Vince replied. "Please come in and I will show you around the house."

As the men entered the house, Joc was surprised to see how much had been done since Vince bought the property. Walls had been removed, and tile and wood floors had been replaced throughout the house. The bathrooms had Greek columns. Marble adorned the entire bath walls, counter tops, showers, and tubs. The place was very ostentatious, not Joc's style at all, but Vince seemed very pleased with it all.

"Very nice," Darryl said. "When will you be able to sit down with me for a few hours so I can get a feel for what you would like the final look to be?"

"Anytime you're ready, I know you just arrived so you may want to wait until tomorrow, but I'm available anytime you want," Vince said.

"Well, what do you say we start now?" Darryl said. "Joc is that okay with you?"

"Of course, I've plenty to do at the office, and I think Marian wants to cook for you tonight. You two get right at it. We usually have dinner around seven," Joc said, as he was leaving.

Darryl stayed behind, and he and Vince started with the great room discussing the kind of furniture Vince found most comfortable. They progressed from room to room as Darryl took mental notes.

"Do you want to write any of this down?" Vince said to Darryl. "I can get you a pencil and paper if you like."

"No thank you, this is the way I always do my preliminary work. I have pictures in my mind of each of the rooms. When I write it down it just seems to distract me," Darryl said. "You will be consulted on anything before I actually purchase, unless of course you don't want that. There will be many materials delivered. Shall we just store them in the garage?"

"No." Vince said quickly. "Not the garage. The kitchen and dining room would be best for that. You can work on those rooms last."

Darryl thought that strange, as the two men talked, he thought to himself, Duke old boy, I think you're right. I don't like this person either, but it will be a good job and I'll be able to spend some time with Marian and Joc.

When Darryl returned to Joc and Marian's he felt relieved. Their home was warm and inviting, not at all like Vince's, which was cold and uncomfortable.

Marian sensed Darryl's concern and said, "What is it Darryl? You seem distracted. You must be tired after such a long day."

"No, I'm fine kid. It's just that place of Vince's is so cold and uninviting. It's going to be a challenge because I think he likes it like that," Darryl said. "Maybe it's just him, I think Duke nailed him."

"You know that was so strange, Duke is never like that, and he just wouldn't stop growling until Vince was out of the house. What do you suppose made him like that?" Marian said, puzzled.

Just then, Joc came in. "How was your day you two? Did you get a chance to catch up?"

"Actually, Darryl just got here himself, and we were just saying how strange Vince is," Marian answered.

"That's an understatement. That guy gives me the creeps. He sure needs your skills Darryl, that place feels as cold as a mausoleum," Joc, said, pretending to shiver.

"I've seen worse believe me, but I think it's Vince that gives the house that feel, not just the marble," Darryl said.

After the first couple of weeks, Darryl asked Joc and Marian if he could devote full time to Vince's project. "I just want to get this job behind me. It's draining me. When I get a room finished I'm happy with it until Vince comes in to see it, and then ... It's as though it's all wrong ... it seems dark and gloomy, I don't get it, but it's getting me down," Darryl said.

"We're so sorry Darryl. We didn't mean to get you into something that's not enjoyable," Marian said sadly. "Of course you can do ours anytime."

Joc said, "There is something wrong over there. I'm going to have Ron Bailey look into Vince's background. I'll call him tomorrow morning."

The next morning Joc called Ron. "Hello stranger," Ron said cheerfully. "How is that beautiful bride of yours?"

"She's great Ron, the best thing that ever happened to me," Joc replied.

"Well did you call to invite me down for a vacation? Or is this a business call?" Ron joked.

"A little of both I guess. You know you have an open invitation to come here anytime for a vacation. I wonder if you could look into something for me?" Joc asked.

"Sure man, anything as long as it's legal," Ron joked.

Joc explained briefly about Vince, how he bought the house, the remodel and all of their uneasy feelings about the new neighbor.

"Are you sure you just don't want to share your little paradise Joc," Ron said. "What exactly do you want me to do?"

"Just check his back ground, you know, does he haves a record or anything shady in his background," Joc said.

"Sure I can do that, at least a routine background check," Ron said. "I can get back to you by the end of the week. I'll need his full name and any addresses you have for him beside the current one of course."

"It's Vincent Donatello. At least that's the name on the title for the house. He gave me general delivery San Jose for an address," Joc said. "When are you coming down here to visit us?"

"I have some vacation time coming, so now that I have an official invitation, I will put San Diego on my wish list. Trouble with my business is the crooks pick the most inopportune times to do their business," Ron said with a laugh.

"I sure appreciate your help Ron and I'll look forward to hearing what, if anything, you find out on this guy," Joc replied.

Darryl was beginning to show the strain of working on Vince's house, but he was so close to being finished. He just had two more rooms to decorate, he was sure he could finish by the end of the week.

Meanwhile, Joc was doing a little detective work on his own. He went over to the title company and asked the title officer if they had a copy of the check that Vince deposited with them. He said he would like to have a copy for his records. Since it was such a large amount, the auditor might have questions about the transaction. The title officer obliged and Joc had a copy of the six-hundred -fifty thousand dollar check drawn on a large bank in Chicago. Maybe Ron would be able to use that information. If not, then maybe he would hire a private investigator to look into Vince's background. In any case, Joc was going to get to the bottom of this. Then there was Duke, he liked everyone. Normally he was a pussycat, but he hated this guy, why?

Ron called Joc at the office on Friday morning. "Joc, I said I'd get back to you by the end of the week, but I'm afraid I don't have anything to report. There's no one with that name in San Jose or anywhere in California. That is before the purchase of the house in San Diego. Everything on this guy starts and ends with that purchase. Driver's license, car registration, real estate, and an unlisted phone number, nothing more. No bank accounts, credit cards, nothing! I think I'd like to meet this character, do you think you can pull that off if I come down this weekend?"

"We can try. Darryl thinks he'll be done by Friday, maybe we can say you want to use Darryl's services, and you would like to see what he has done with Vince's. Something like that might work. Try not to look like a cop when you come," Joc teased.

Ron left Hollywood early Saturday morning and arrived at Marian and Joc's by nine o'clock. Duke was there to greet him with tail wagging, and begging to be petted.

"You're just in time for breakfast, but of course you planned it that way, right?" Joc teased.

"That's right. I could smell the bacon cooking a couple of miles away," Ron said smiling.

Marian introduced Ron to Darryl, poured coffee for everyone, and started taking orders for how everyone liked their eggs cooked. As Marian was fixing breakfast the men were discussing the plan for how they were going to get Ron to meet Vince. They decided the best way was to have Darryl go over, ask Vince if he would come over to Marian and Joc's, and meet Ron. That way maybe Ron could get some fingerprints to try to identify him. If he refused, well then Darryl would just ask if he and Ron could come over and see the results.

After breakfast, they put plan A into action. Darryl went over to Vince's and rang the bell.

"Morning Vince," Darryl began. "I wonder if I could impose on you. Marian and Joc have a friend down from Hollywood who would like to have his house redecorated. They have told him about me, and that I've just finished your home. I wonder if you would be willing to come over to Marian and Joc's house to meet him. Perhaps tell him a little about how the decorating process went. You know, what you liked and of course feel free to tell him if there was anything, you didn't like. I can leave you alone with him if that's more comfortable for you, assuming you would be willing at all. Please don't feel obligated. I would never ask you, but this was Marian's idea, and you know it put me in an awkward position in front of him."

Vince looked uncomfortable, but then relaxed a bit. "Why don't you just bring him over here? That might be better for both of us. You can stay, I like everything you did, and you accomplished it in a record amount of time."

"Thank you, Vince. When would be the best time?" Darryl asked.

"Any time before one o'clock, I have to leave for a while after that, and I don't know for sure what time I will be home," Vince said.

Darryl was disappointed he couldn't get Vince over to Marian and Joc's, but it made better sense for Ron to go over there. That's if Ron was really was a prospective customer. Darryl returned to Marian and Joc's house and told them it was all set for Ron and him to go over to Vince's, but it needed to be before one o'clock.

When they arrived at Vince's house Darryl rang the doorbell. Upon opening the door, Vince said, "Come on in Darryl, and he just nodded acknowledging Ron. Darryl made the introductions, and Vince said, "Darryl why don't you just show the place, you can explain everything better than me anyway."

"Please join us Vince. You can tell Ron how we worked from the original plan. That's if it isn't too much trouble," Darryl said.

Vince really did like what Darryl had done. As they went through each room, Vince became more interested in showing off the house. Ron played along pretending to be interested by asking questions about some of the materials they used, and at the same time, taking notes on a pad of paper.

"Vince, would you mind if I used your bathroom? I'm sorry, just a little too much coffee this morning I guess," Ron said.

"Sure, you know where it is, help yourself," Vince replied.

Ron set the pad of paper with his notes on the counter and went into the bathroom. He and Darryl had already planned this beforehand. After using the bathroom, Ron would forget the pad of paper and after they were outside, he would ring the doorbell and ask Vince to bring it to him. That's how he would get Vince's fingerprints.

The plan worked perfectly and Vince didn't catch on. Ron and Darryl thanked Vince again for being so accommodating, and returned to Marian and Joc's house.

Ron spent the weekend as planned and returned to Hollywood late Sunday night. He could hardly wait to see what the fingerprints would tell him about this guy. He certainly seemed nice enough. He knew Joc well enough to trust his instincts, and then of course there was the matter of no prior identity.

chapter 19

DARRYL WAS EXCITED to start on Marian and Joc's house. Now he could once again enjoy his work. They had decided to start from the top floor with the oversized bedroom. There was so much room up there and most of it was wasted space. The views were the best in the house, but there were not enough windows to capture the 360-degree view. Darryl drew up a plan to show to Marian and Joc. It required adding a large window seat that looked toward the ocean. From here, one could watch storms gather at sea, or see the sun sink down into the ocean at sunset. In the master bathroom he wanted to add a Jacuzzi tub with windows that facing the mountains to the north, a multi-head shower, and a built in make-up table complete with its own lighting for Marian. There was already a beautiful fireplace, which Darryl planned to provide with two comfortable chairs and a table. The bed was a lovely cherry wood four-poster which would be the center of the rooms décor.

"This is going to cost a lot to complete because of the construction work. I think it will be worth it in the long run though," Darryl said a bit hesitantly.

"I can do the construction work," Joc said enthusiastically. "That's if you don't mind working with me Darryl."

Darryl was a bit surprised Joc could do that kind of work, until Marian said, "You remember the little house in the back at mother's in Stockton? Joc put a new foundation under it, did all the sheetrock work, windows, a new roof, and everything."

"Marian, we did have a professional do the electrical and plumbing," Joc said. "The good news is I do have a complete set of the original construction plans for this house."

"When do you want to get started?" Darryl said with a big smile.

"We can go down to the lumber yard tomorrow and order any materials we need, and I can rent any tools I don't have here," Joc said.

It was Marian's job to move everything to one of the guest rooms on the second floor where they would sleep until their new bedroom suite was finished. She could hardly wait. She loved the beach house, but that bedroom always seemed like an afterthought to her. Joc must not have liked it much either, because before they were married, he said he slept on the couch a good deal of the time.

When Joc, Darryl, and Duke were at the lumber store, they ran into Vince. Duke reacted as he had before around Vince, the low deep growl, with the hair standing up on his back. "Duke, sit." Joc commanded. Duke did as he was told but never took his eyes off Vince.

Vince ignored the dog and said, "Looks like you are planning a big project."

"Yes. Darryl is starting on our place now that he's finished with yours," Joc answered. "What are you doing here? Your place is all done, isn't?"

"I'm going to be building a fence. I want a big flower garden. The fence is for privacy," Vince answered.

"I thought your place is all landscaped. Where are you going to put the flower garden?" Joc asked.

"The garden will be on the beach side in back of the garage. That's why I wanted a door out to the beach from the garage," Vince explained. "I can bring plants in through the garage and out the back door. I have a back-hoe digging it up now to put in some good soil where the sand is now."

Duke never stopped his strange behavior until Vince left the store.

"Boy, Duke sure hates him," Joc said shaking his head in disbelief. "It worries me a little if he ever came around when we weren't home. I think Duke would kill him."

The following week, Ron called Joc. "I hope you are sitting down. I sent those prints in, and your neighbor's real name is Louis DeMartini, from Chicago. He doesn't have any warrants on him. However, the FBI has questioned him in three unsolved missing person cases. The police could never pin anything on him because the people never turned up, and no bodies were ever found. He's still their number one suspect. They were very interested in the fact that he is living out here under an assumed name," Ron said.

"That explains a lot," Joc said. "Darryl and I ran into him this morning at the lumber store and Duke went crazy again. He said he was building a fence for a flower garden."

"I don't want to worry you, but this guy is real bad news," Ron said. "Each one of the victims had a large sum of money that went missing along with them. That could account for paying cash for that big beach house."

"Thanks Ron, but where do we go from here? I would rather not tell Marian about this just yet. I don't want to worry her unnecessarily," Joc said.

"Let me get more details on each of these cases, but for God's sake stay clear of him until we know more," Ron counseled.

Joc told Darryl what Ron had told him on the phone, and he asked him not to tell Marian just yet. Darryl agreed not to say a word.

From the upstairs where Joc and Darryl were working, they could see the area where Vince was building the fence. It appeared to be just what he said. A backhoe had dug up an area about twelve feet by twenty and it looked to be at least four or five feet deep, but why? Top soil for sod or a garden would only need several inches. What was he planting that needed such depth? Even mature trees weren't planted at such a depth. As they worked on the upstairs, they watched Vince working on his yard, and week by week, they Joc and Darryl became more curious. Joc decided to call Ron and tell him what was going on, also to find out if he had any new information on Vince.

"Detective Ron Bailey's office, "Ron said as he answered his phone. "Hey Ron, it's Joc. I was just calling for an update on our mysterious neighbor. Have you got anything new?"

"Hi Joc, no I'm afraid there's nothing new. The feds are over loaded, and I'm told this guy falls into the cold case category, with no bodies, there's no crime," Ron said.

Joc proceeded to tell Ron what he and Darryl had been observing for the last few weeks. "That's strange, but strange doesn't make a crime," Ron said. "Just stay clear of him, both of you. If he is up to no good, he will show himself soon enough, and then we can do something. I alerted your local police. They have agreed to keep an eye on him. That's all I can do right now, sorry man."

"That's okay, I understand. It could be nothing more than he is just an odd ball,." Joc said.

"How's that pretty wife of yours?" Ron asked. "And how is Darryl coming along with the redecorating?"

"We have made quite a mess, but Marian is still speaking to us, so things are pretty good here. We'll have you come down to inspect when we finish up, and Darryl says to say hello to you," Joc said.

"Okay, same here, and I'll come down as soon as I get a chance. Take care, and remember what I said. Stay clear of that guy," Ron repeated.

Marian kept asking about what Ron had found out about Vince, and Joc and Darryl kept stalling. They would have to tell her something eventually, so they decided to tell her the next morning.

Joc said, "You know sweetheart, I talked to Ron again yesterday and this is what he's found out from the fingerprints."

He proceeded to tell Marian everything, including the part about the garden in the now fenced back yard. He told her that Ron was having the local police keep an eye on him.

"We don't have any worries about him coming over here, because I have no doubt Duke would take him apart, limb by limb," Joc said emphatically. "You saw how he behaved toward him when he was here, and when Darryl and I ran into him at the lumber store he was just as bad."

"Marian don't worry, one of us will always be here until we get this project finished," Darryl added.

Marian sat quietly for a minute, and then she said, "So we really don't know if Vince has done anything wrong, just that Duke hates him and he is a suspect in the disappearance of these people. Is that correct?"

"Yes, that's right," Joc said.

"Okay then we will go on living our lives normally. I don't want to live like we did before. No bodyguards, no hiding, none of that!" she said looking directly at Joc.

"No sweetheart, nothing like that will be necessary, I promise," Joc said, as he held her in his arms kissing her gently on the cheek.

After Marian left for Maria's, Darryl asked Joc what Marian meant about bodyguards, and hiding. Joc told Darryl the whole story about Pete and the kidnapping.

"I never heard anything about that," Darryl said surprised. "Poor Marian, I met Pete, and he was no good for her. I'm embarrassed to say I stayed away from Marian in those days because little sister was gone, and I couldn't stand Pete."

"Well, you were a good friend then, and you're a good friend now. I want you to know how much we both appreciate you disrupting your life to do this work for us. We can never thank you enough," Joc said sincerely. "I must say though, you are a bit of a slave driver," Joc laughed, trying to lighten the mood a little.

"Speaking of slave driving, you have a lot of hard work to get done today," Darryl said laughing as he pointed to Joc.

"Okay, okay, I'll get started. Would you mind cleaning up down here? Marian won't be happy if she comes home to a dirty kitchen," Joc replied.

"Sure thing," Darryl said. "Then I will come up and help you out."

The two men went about their work. By the time Marian returned from Maria's, the upstairs bedroom construction was finished. Now it was time for Darryl to start doing his magic, and he could hardly wait.

"This project is all yours Darryl, I have to go and spend some time in the office. I hope Sam hasn't sold the place. Duke can keep you company," Joc said dryly.

"Marian I'm having some items delivered today, so would you keep an eye out for me as I may not hear them when they come," Darryl said.

"Sure Darryl, I'll be happy to do that," Marian said.

Darryl was busy all day, and the first delivery truck Darryl was expecting had come around ten o'clock. About an hour later, another delivery truck came by the house. Marian noticed because she wasn't expecting anything else, but the truck kept going and pulled into Vince's driveway. It backed up to the garage and unloaded three large freezers. Marian watched from the front deck. Why does a guy who lives alone need three freezers... Marian thought to herself. She just couldn't shake that question from her mind. She needed to tell Joc right away. She ran up the stairs to see if Darryl would go with her.

"Darryl let's go meet Joc for lunch at the deli.

"Ah okay," Darryl said with some hesitation, because he still had a lot to do.

Marian and Darryl stopped at the real estate office, and Joc suggested they go get Lana's mother to join them.

While the four of them were having lunch, Lana's mother said, "We have a new customer. You'll never guess who it is. I'll give you a hint. She's a real big star."

"Come on," Darryl said. "You need to give us more than that. Everyone you work with is a real big star!"

"Okay, the initials are L.T., but don't tell anyone because it hasn't been announced to the public yet," Lana's mother said whispering.

"Not Again!" Joc exclaimed.." Isn't this about number five?"

"Actually, I think it's number six," Lana's mother giggled.

"See Darryl, you could really do well in Hollywood, just redecorating after each of these divorces. They all have at least two or three exes," Joc said.

She couldn't contain herself any longer and she blurted out, "The strangest thing happened today. After the truck came with the materials Darryl was waiting for, a short time later another truck showed up. At first, I thought it was for us, but then it kept going and pulled into Vince's house. The driver unloaded three large freezers into Vince's garage. What on earth do you suppose a man who lives alone would need with three freezers?"

"Three freezers, are you sure Marian?" Lana's mother said with surprise.

"Oh I'm sure all right," Marian said.

"Don't you think it's real strange a man living alone has a need for not one, but three freezers?" Darryl said with a puzzled look.

"Well yes, but maybe there's a good reason, although I can't think of one off the top of my head," Joc said.

"Remember what Ron said, there were three people missing," Darryl reminded Joc. "In addition, what's the deal with that garden? No one has a garden on the beach side of their house. I have walked up and down that beach for a mile in both directions. No gardens, no fences, not one Joc."

"Darryl your letting your imagination run away with you," Joc laughed, trying to minimize any concern Marian might be having.

"Well you have to admit it certainly isn't normal, but then there isn't anything normal about Vince," Marian said.

"Remember sweetheart, Ron is having the local police keep an eye on Vince, so we don't have anything to worry about. Now tell us a little more about this secret wedding you two have booked," Joc said changing the subject.

"Marian are you free this weekend?" Lana's mother asked. "I could use your help for a day or two on this wedding. That's if you have time and Joc will let me steal you for a night or two."

"Of course I can help you. These guys just think I'm in the way most of the time anyway," Marian said.

As Lana's mother and Marian got up to leave, Marian leaned over and gave Joc a kiss and said, "I'll see you tonight my love."

Joc and Darryl waited until Marian was gone and then Darryl said, "Joc I'm really concerned about what is going on over there at Vince's place.

"You're right. We need to get a look," Joc said. "How can we do it? I don't want Marian to know anything more than she does now. She really has been through too much."

Joc and Darryl decided to update Ron and maybe the three of them could work out a plan to discover what, if anything was going on with Vince Donatello, aka Louis DeMartini. They had to know. Ron agreed to join them for the weekend and then the three of them would work out some kind of plan.

For the next few days Darryl was so busy finishing the upstairs bedroom suite he didn't have much time to watch what was going on over at Vince's. On Thursday, the master suite was complete. It was time to show Marian the results.

Darryl and Joc planned to make a big production out of showing the room to Marian. It began with Darryl having spread rose petals on the floor. Candles were lit in all the appropriate locations. Then Joc carried Marian across the threshold of the new bedroom and gently placed her on the big four-poster bed. She looked around the room in disbelief.

"Oh my, it's so beautiful. I never dreamed a room could be so perfect!" she said.

Darryl laughed and said, "Hey kid, you know only the best for you. Now come look at the rest of it, I'm sure Joc will have you in that bed soon enough."

Darryl took Marian by the hand and showed her the view from each of the windows. He explained everything about the bathroom, and then he turned on the lights surrounded her make-up table. He gave her the remote control that turned on the fireplace, and opened and closed the curtains. When he was done, Marian sat down at the window seat and Joc and Darryl joined her.

"Isn't it beautiful, sweetheart?" Joc whispered as he gently kissed her cheek.

Marian was quiet as her mind drifted back to when she was a young army wife in Georgia working as a beautician in the Ralston Hotel beauty salon. She could never have dreamed her life would be this wonderful. Joc's love was the real thing. It had little to do with the material things he showered upon her. They loved one another so deeply material wealth was nothing compared to the feelings they had for one another.

"Yes Joc it is." she said, "Your love is the most beautiful thing in the world. Thank you for loving me."

"Okay, time for me to depart this scene, it is getting too mushy for me," Darryl said getting up to leave.

They all laughed, and then Marian said, "I know your love is in this room too, because it shows in every detail. No one could ever walk in here and not feel it. Thank you Darryl."

chapter 20

RON ARRIVED FRIDAY night, and the four of them stayed up talking and sharing stories. Darryl took center stage with stories of several of his decorating jobs from the early days. They were hilarious, and Ron shared some of his funniest stories of arrests. Joc sat holding Marian close to him as they listened to their two friends. They couldn't have been happier or more in love with each other and life.

In the morning, Joc took everyone to breakfast in town and following breakfast Marian want to Maria's to help Lana's mother with the wedding plans. .

"Okay boys, let's head home, and make a plan," Joc said.

Ron looked at the garden from Joc and Marian's upstairs bedroom. Just as Darryl and Joc had said, it was a strange place seemed to have no purpose. It certainly didn't conform to any other beachfront properties in San Diego. When Darryl described the three freezers delivered to Vince's garage, Ron agreed that didn't fit with a man who lived alone and had little or no company. However, none of this really meant anything unless they could get a look inside. Vince rarely left and even if he did, the place was locked up tight, and there was a security system. They decided to try to get a closer look at the garden while it was still daylight. They would pretend to walk the beach and throw sticks for Duke. Ron would try to get a closer look while Darryl and Joc provided a distraction in case Vince was watching.

The plan seemed to be working as Joc threw a stick in the ocean and Duke would run into the waves to retrieve it. Darryl and Joc would laugh loudly enough to attract Vince's attention if he was looking. Ron went to the far side of the fence out of sight and attempted to look through the slats. He was able to see two large palm trees had been planted in either end of the deep hole that had been dug by the backhoe. Strangely, the holes for the trees were considerably shallower than the rest of the excavation. What was he planning? Could this be for a pond? Why would a pond be so deep? A couple of feet would have been sufficient for that purpose. The distraction worked well until Duke tired of the game and ran to the fence where Ron was. When he heard Duke barking next to the fence, Vince came out of the garage door and Ron joined Darryl and Joc, but Duke would not come. When he heard Vince he began to growl and jump at the fence, then he began to try to dig under the fence. Vince yelled at Duke, but the more he yelled the more Duke growled and tried to get in. Joc yelled at Duke to stop and come, but it was no use.

"Get the dog away from here!" Vince yelled.

"Sorry Vince, I don't know what's wrong with him," Joc said, as he grabbed Duke by the collar and pulled him away from the fence, still growling and pulling away.

"That dog is dangerous, keep him away from my property or I will shoot him!" Vince yelled.

"Well, that didn't go as planned," Ron said. "I do agree that is no ordinary garden, and now we know he has a gun. All we can do is wait until he leaves and try to get into that garage. I think I can defeat the alarm long enough for us to get a look, but we would be breaking the law. Can't get a warrant on what we have, which is nothing more than, well nothing."

"Ron you can't risk your career, I won't let you do this. You can show me how to defeat the alarm, and you and Darryl will need to be lookouts in case anything goes wrong," Joc said.

The three men took turns watching for Vince to leave his house, and finally at about seven o'clock that evening, the garage opened and Vince left in his car. As soon as Vince was out of sight, Joc immediately headed for the garage. Darryl and Ron stayed where they could see anyone coming toward the house. Once the alarm was disarmed, Joc entered the garage and headed to the first freezer. It was locked, all of them were locked. There was no way he could open them without breaking the locks. Joc decided to look at the garden while he was there. He opened the door leading to the garden from the garage and closed it behind him. The second he closed the door he realized his mistake, he couldn't get back into the garage. As he was looking for a way out he heard the garage door open and a car pull in. He was trapped. All he could do was wait and hope Vince would go inside the house. Maybe then, he would be able to somehow get over the fence and back to his house without being seen by Vince. Just then, the garage door to the garden swung open. Joc looked around but there was no place to hide. All he could hope was it was dark enough that Vince couldn't see him crouched against the wall next to the fence. Vince walked over to the large hole and looked in. He went into the garage again, opened one of the freezers and using a dolly took something out of the freezer and struggled over to the hole and tipped the object into the hole. It was too dark for Joc to see what it was, but it was large enough to be a body. Joc had to get closer. When Vince returned to the garage Joc waited until he could hear Vince, straining to load whatever was in the next freezer onto the dolly. Joc inched his way closer to the garage door where he could see clearly. It was a body on the dolly. His heart began to race. He knew his only chance was to get to the garage door opener. In order to do that, he would have to risk running past Vince to reach the opener attached to the wall going into the house. If he could get the main garage door open, he could yell for help. He knew if he tried to stay hidden, Vince would probably see him. Even if he didn't discover him, there was no way out of the yard tonight. Surely, Vince would cover up the bodies after they were in the hole, and that could take hours. As Vince pushed the body through the back garage door toward the hole, Joc ran into the garage pulling the door shut behind him. He hit the garage door opener and started to run. But he was too late. Vince heard the garage door opening and saw Joc running. He fired three shots, each shot hit its mark, and Joc fell to the ground not moving.

Hearing the gunfire, Ron and Darryl ran toward Vince's garage. The next second Duke jumped Vince and had him by the throat, growling a low angry growl. Seeing Joc's body on the ground, Darryl ran to help him. Ron disarmed Vince, but Duke wouldn't let him go. The officers who had been watching Vince's house heard the commotion and called for backup. Darryl could hear the sound of sirens in the distance as he knelt next to Joc's body he was saying, "Hang on Joc, help is on the way."

Joc didn't answer. His blood was seeping into the driveway next to his still body.

The police cars arrived with sirens and lights flashing, and Joc's body was placed in the ambulance, which took off immediately headed for the hospital.

Darryl took hold of Dukes collar, "Come on boy, it's okay now, good job," he said stroking Duke's head.

Vince was yelling about shooting a trespasser, but the body was still on the dolly. Seeing that, one of the police officers put the cuffs on Vince. Ron explained he was a detective with the Hollywood division. Ron told the police the FBI had questioned Vince, aka Louis, in the disappearance of three people in Chicago. The officers took their names and released Ron and Darryl telling them not to leave San Diego until this could be sorted out.

Darryl dropped Ron at the hospital while he went to get Marian. When Marian answered the door, Darryl took her in his arms and said, "Marian, there's been an accident. Joc is in the hospital. You need to come with me."

"What, what kind of accident, is he alright?" her eyes filling with tears.

"I don't know, we need to go now. Please," Darryl said.

Lana's mother took Marian's arm. They got in the car and headed to the hospital. Ron was there waiting for them.

"Ron, where is he? What has happened to Joc?" Marian cried.

"Marian, he's been shot. He's in surgery now, all we can do is wait," Ron said.

"He's been shot! What's going on?" She screamed.

One of the doctors came into the room and said," Are you Mrs. Fournier?"
"Yes, how is my husband?" Marian asked.

"He's in emergency surgery now. He's lost a lot of blood. We'll know more in a few hours. Perhaps you should go home. We'll call you as soon as we know more," The doctor continued.

"No, no I'm not leaving!" Marian exclaimed.

"Okay Mrs. Fournier, we'll let you know as soon as we can," the doctor said, as turned and walked away.

Marian turned to Darryl and Ron, "Tell me how this could have happened?"

"What were you all thinking?" Marian asked incredulously.

"Marian, he did have bodies in those freezers!" Ron said.

"I don't care what he had in his freezers. Joc may be dying!" Marian said.

Darryl and Ron didn't say anything because they knew she was right. They had no business trying to solve this without the police. Ron put his head in his hands, he felt sick. He, of all people, knew how dangerous this was, or at least he should have known. Darryl couldn't believe he had been so stupid, and now Joc lay dying because of this stupid stunt.

Several hours passed before one of the doctors came out to speak to them. "Mrs. Fournier, " he began. "Your husband was shot three times, and the bullets did a lot of damage. Fortunately, none of them damaged any vital organs. The next forty-eight hours will be critical. We have done all we can," he said.

"Can I see him?" Marian pleaded.

"He's in ICU now, and we have him heavily sedated, but you may go in. He won't wake-up for several hours. He was in excellent health. If he makes it for the next twelve hours, he has a fifty-fifty chance of recovery, barring any infection. Come with me I will take you to him," the doctor said.

Marian followed in a daze. All she could remember was the words he has a fifty-fifty chance of recovering. When she entered the ICU, Joc had tubes coming out of him everywhere. The tears poured from her eyes and she whimpered like an injured animal. "Oh my love, please don't leave me," she whispered.

Joc's skin was ashen. The machines monitoring his blood pressure and heart rate hummed beside his bed. The doctor put his arm around Marian and slowly walked her from the room. When they reached the waiting area, he told Darryl and Ron to take her home. He would call if there were any change in Joc's condition.

It was close to three in the morning when they reached the house. The police were still at Vince's, and crime scene tape was encircling the garage, and two police officers stood guard in front of the driveway. When Duke saw Marian, he ran to her wagging his tail and nudging her with his nose. It was as if he knew something terrible was wrong.

"Good boy Duke," she said, scratching him behind his ears.

Darryl knew it wasn't possible, but he wanted to pour her a shot of bourbon. He sighed and settled for a nice pot of tea. When he brought out the tea, Ron was talking softly to Marian, telling her Joc was strong and he was going to pull through this. Darryl was not so sure.

They were all exhausted, and fell asleep in front of the fireplace. The ringing of the telephone awakened Marian. "Mrs. Fournier? This is Dr. Myers calling. Your husband is awake and asking for you."

"I will be right there. Please tell him, I will be right there," Marian said excitedly.

Darryl and Ron were awake now too." That was the doctor and Joc is awake." They all rushed to the car and arrived at the hospital in less than a half an hour. Marian ran into see Joc first. "Hi sweetheart, Joc said sleepily." What happened?"

"Oh Joc, Vince shot you. You've had surgery to remove the bullets. My poor darling, are you feeling okay?" Marian said.

"I'm sure not feeling any pain," Joc answered.

Darryl and Ron appeared beside Marian, "We really screwed up man," Ron said.

Darryl said, "The good news is you got him. How are you feeling?"

"I remember feeling a sharp burning, and then nothing," Joc said.

The doctor came in and said, "Okay, that's enough now, he needs to rest."

Marian was crying as they reached the waiting room. The doctor joined them in a few minutes. "Joc is going to be fine. We just have to make sure he doesn't get any infection. That is always possible with gunshot wounds. If there are no complications, he will be able to go home by the end of the week.

Marian sighed in relief. "Thank you doctor, thank you so much."

The next few days for Marian were long ones spent going in and out of the hospital. The three of them took turns spending time with Joc as he gradually regained his strength. By Wednesday, he was ready to return home.

Ron and Darryl helped get Joc settled in the new bedroom. "This is not what I had planned for my first nights in this beautiful room." Joc said to Darryl with a laugh and a wink.

Darryl laughed and said, "Plenty of good days ahead, and you won't be in my way as I finish up the rest of the house."

Ron said, "I have a lot of explaining to do to the local police, but right now they are focused on three dead bodies. There are lots of FBI guys milling around, so I'm the least of their worries. I'm headed back to Hollywood tomorrow. Joc, please don't call me about any other strange people you run across. This is getting to be a habit with you," He laughed.

When evening came Darryl had gone to bed and Joc was asleep.

Viewing her image in the mirror once again, Marian remembered the days when a she was a young army wife, a woman who had her whole life ahead of her and dreaming of looking like Lana Turner.

She was a grandmother now. She looked in the mirror reflecting on her life, the good times, and the bad. She thought about Andy, her first love and the father of her two beautiful girls. Then she remembered Robert. She could see now he was what people referred to as love on the rebound.... nothing more. That relationship happened because she wanted to feel desirable again after being rejected by the only man she had ever loved. The years with Pete were due to her addiction. That affair would never have happened if she had not been drinking.

Then she met Joc. He was the real thing, her true sole mate, and she knew he loved her with all his heart as she loved him.

Made in the USA
Charleston, SC
25 August 2013